MOST LIKELY TO DIE

TRUE CRIME JUNKIES
BOOK 8

CHRISTY BARRITT

Copyright © 2024 by Christy Barritt

All rights reserved.

No part of this book may be reproduced in any form or by any electronic or mechanical means, including information storage and retrieval systems, without written permission from the author, except for the use of brief quotations in a book review.

CHAPTER
ONE

DIANE GLASSINE LEANED back in her seat and gripped the armrests on either side of her.

She'd never liked small airplanes. But they were necessary to get around in Alaska. Some places had no roads connecting them to the rest of the world.

A tempting idea.

But she needed to head back to Anchorage from near Prudhoe Bay so she could make her meeting in time. She was thankful to be back at work. Three months ago, she'd been shot and placed in a medically induced coma for nearly a month.

The prognosis hadn't looked good. But miraculously, as the doctors reduced her medication, she'd awoken. Healed. Recovered.

Now she was back on the job, and the man who'd done this to her—Edward Credent—was behind bars.

She should be safe. Yet safety, at times, felt like an illusion.

As she gazed out the window of the Cessna, clouds stretched as far as she could see. The sun was setting, casting beams across the billows of white.

For most, the sight was beautiful.

For her, a knot of anxiety formed in her stomach.

"Can I get you anything?" Charles Sudan asked her.

Charles was in his late fifties with a square face, thick salt-and-pepper hair, and a steady gaze. He'd been her chief of staff—and her righthand man—since she began her political career fifteen years ago.

Really, he was so much more.

He always anticipated what she needed, sometimes even before she did.

She shook her head as she remembered his question. "I'm fine. Just get me off this plane."

He smiled. "I will. In about two hours."

This would be a long two hours. At least there was no one on the small plane she needed to impress. It was a good thing—for so many reasons, really. Besides, this Cessna could only hold four people. There was an empty seat in the cockpit beside Bob Stephens, the pilot.

She hadn't wanted anyone else to accompany her to this meeting, only Charles.

As a senator, she always felt the need to appear cool and in control.

Keeping up appearances could be exhausting.

Only she, Charles, and Bob—whom she'd personally

requested—were on the flight. Bob was the best in the area, and Diane had known him for years.

She closed her eyes.

She would get through with this plane ride, land in Anchorage, and get to her meeting.

She knew what she had to do once she got there. After much soul searching and research, that had become abundantly clear.

Her anxiety mixed with dread.

Her decision would make people unhappy—would probably make the *wrong* people unhappy. But she'd been wrestling with what to do for so long that she'd nearly lost herself in the struggle.

Sometimes she wanted out of this entire line of work. But if she didn't stand up for what was right, then who would? A less stubborn woman would have given in long ago. Would have done what was best for herself instead of her state.

Not just her state.

Her country.

She couldn't live with herself if she compromised her integrity for a paycheck. She was ashamed to say she had been tempted. But the temptation hadn't lasted long before she'd come to her senses.

She wouldn't bow to pressure.

She wouldn't cave to bullies.

No matter the cost.

She'd only told two people her decision. Charles was one of them. He'd faithfully stood by her side so long she knew she could trust him. The other person was—

A loud pop pulled her from her thoughts.

The plane dipped, taking her stomach with it.

She set her glass on the tray and gripped the armrest, her breathing becoming shallower. Faster.

"Charles . . . ?" Her voice—already strained—cracked.

She stole a glance at her chief of staff.

He remained as calm, cool, and collected as ever. "Just some turbulence."

Diane knew his words were true. Little planes like the one they were in could feel the smallest amount of commotion in the air.

The mountains below, so beautiful and rugged, terrified her. They were one of the many reasons people came to Alaska—to see the untouched beauty.

But this vast landscape was also dangerous.

Deadly.

Especially for passengers on small airplanes in cloudy conditions.

Especially in the middle of nowhere—which was exactly what they were flying over right now. Miles and miles of uninhabitable, weathered mountains.

Mountains that had taken out many good people.

Mountains that were a more formidable foe than her toughest political opponent.

Breathe, Diane. In and out. Keep it steady. You can do this.

Just as she got her pulse under control, the plane dipped again.

A dinging noise rang through the cockpit.

Bob's fingers flew over the switches on the control panel, and he began speaking quickly—almost frantically—into the headset.

Diane couldn't make out what he said, though she tried.

"It's probably nothing." Charles's voice remained unwavering. "We've got one of the best pilots in the business. Bob knows this area and how to maneuver an airplane better than anyone."

Charles's words were true. They *should* make her feel better.

But they didn't.

The noise of the plane changed.

Time slowed around her as her thoughts raced.

Then Diane realized what was different.

The engine.

The hum of the motor had gone silent.

Bob's motions upfront became faster. His cheeks flushed.

Something was wrong. No one could convince her otherwise.

Not even Charles.

She jerked her gaze toward him.

He'd gone pale, his peace and reassurance disappearing like a plane in the Bermuda Triangle.

She swallowed hard. Charles knew something was wrong too.

The plane shifted before plunging downward like a roller coaster on a hill.

Only there was no track to keep them secure. This wasn't a thrill ride. The danger was real.

"Mayday! Mayday! Mayday!" Bob yelled into his headset before identifying the aircraft, their present position, heading, and number of souls on board.

"Why did the engine cut off?" Diane shouted, leaning forward in her seat to be heard.

"It shouldn't have!" Bob yelled. "I checked it myself before takeoff."

"Are we out of fuel?" she asked. "Is there a spare tank?"

"We have plenty of fuel." His words sounded grim.

Nausea gurgled inside her.

None of this was her imagination. This wasn't a matter of worst-case scenario panic superseding logic.

This was real. *Dead* real.

The plane drifted downward.

Diane glanced out the window again. The clouds cleared in time for her to see . . . a wall of rock.

A mountain.

Directly in front of them.

"Senator . . ."

Charles's voice reached her ears, but she couldn't pull her gaze away from the window. At any minute,

Bob would pull upward. The mountain would disappear.

They'd all have a good laugh as the engine roared back to life.

Right?

"I just want to let you know that I've really enjoyed working with you," Charles told her. "And I'm honored to have been on your team."

Her throat tightened, and she reached across the aisle to grab his hand. He squeezed it tight.

His words had sounded final. Charles didn't think they would survive either, did he?

"Mayday!" Bob shouted again. "Mayday! Mayday!"

Terror seized her.

Why was this happening? What had caused . . .

The truth hit her.

This wasn't an accident.

Someone had tampered with this plane.

Someone knew about her upcoming vote, knew her plan.

And this person had decided to kill her to stop her.

Still squeezing Charles's hand, she closed her eyes again and began to pray.

She'd known the stakes were high. But she had no idea her enemies would take things this far.

Would this look like an accident? Would the person responsible get away with killing her, Charles, and Bob?

She glanced out the window one more time.

The mountain . . . it still rose in front of them like an undefeatable roadblock.

And the plane wasn't slowing down as it drifted directly toward it.

CHAPTER
TWO

"THANK you both for the ride. I appreciate it." Andi smiled at Ranger Garrett and Simmy Samuels as they sat in the Tahoe.

"Anytime." Ranger reached for the door, about to open it. "Let me help with your bag."

She raised the duffle in the air. "No need. I've got it, and you need to get home to Anastasia. It's way past midnight."

Ranger's daughter, Anastasia, was with a babysitter.

Andi had just returned from Texas, where she'd petitioned the district court to be reinstated to practice law. She'd done her best to prove that doing so was in the best interest of the public, the profession, and justice.

She thought she'd done a good job stating her case.

Now she awaited the decision from the State Bar of Texas.

While she'd been busy with that, Duke McAllister

had gone home for a few days to help his dad recover after hip surgery. Unfortunately, Duke wasn't returning until lunchtime tomorrow.

It was just as well. Andi needed to unwind so she could feel fresh and ready to go in the morning. If Duke had been home, she would have spent entirely too much time with him, catching up on everything they'd missed during the week. Catching up on cuddles and kisses.

Their relationship still felt like a dream, and she often wanted to pinch herself.

She jogged toward her apartment, punched her code into the keypad, and listened as the mechanism unlocked. Pushing the door open, she set her bag inside and gave one last wave to Ranger and Simmy.

As they pulled away, she stepped inside her home-sweet-home, closed the door, and flicked on the light switch.

Nothing happened.

She tried again.

Again nothing.

She wanted to believe the power outage was simply an electrical problem.

But her gut—refined by years of investigating crimes—told her that wasn't true.

Tension crackled in the air.

She turned, knowing she had to flee. Now.

Before she could pull the door open, a deep voice said, "I wouldn't do that if I were you."

A click sounded.

Her breath caught.

Someone had been standing behind the door.

Stood right beside her now.

With a gun.

But the gunman wasn't the one who'd spoken. The voice had come from the other side of the room.

At least two people were in her apartment.

She recognized the man's voice. Knew exactly who it was.

Victor Goodman, the most ruthless man she'd ever met.

Her pulse raced faster.

Andi had no choice but to stay where she was. Her eyes hadn't even adjusted to the darkness so she couldn't see the man beside her or Victor across the room.

But she knew without a doubt a gun was trained on her.

"Victor . . . to what do I owe the pleasure of this visit?" Her voice sounded saccharinely sweet with sarcasm. She couldn't let this man see or hear her fear.

It would give him too much pleasure.

"You and I need to talk," Victor said. "Privately."

"And what better place than in my apartment?"

Victor chuckled. "You've always had guts, Andi Slade. It's part of the reason I like you."

She had to make sure those guts—and her mouth— didn't get her in trouble right now.

"Sit down, Andi," Victor instructed.

She opened her mouth to argue when a red light appeared on her chest.

She realized Victor's henchman had moved, and now the barrel of his gun was aimed directly at her heart. Victor wanted her to know he had the upper hand.

Swallowing hard, she found her couch, knowing her way around her apartment well enough that she could find a seat without hurting herself.

She slowly lowered herself onto the overstuffed cushion. Her mind raced through possibilities of how to protect herself.

She didn't have her gun on her. She couldn't travel with a weapon, so she'd left it locked in a safe in her bedroom.

Victor had known she'd be unarmed.

He'd probably also known Duke was out of town.

His timing was impeccable.

The man was meticulous. Someone didn't get to his position in life by ignoring the details or being careless.

"What are you doing here?" Andi's voice sounded stiff as the words left her lips.

The light on her end table flickered on at the lowest setting, casting a yellowy-dim glow to the room. Shadows fell across Victor's face, making the sixty-three-year-old appear even more dangerous than usual with his dark hair and heavy brows.

He smirked as Andi stared at him. "Like I said, you and I need to talk privately."

"You could have just texted, you know." She wasn't sure where her sarcasm came from.

Probably months of pent-up frustration. Months of trying to bring down Victor but hitting walls. Months of fighting for what she believed in without seeing progress.

"I've been trying to nicely warn you to mind your own business." Victor remained shadowed as he spoke.

Andi glanced down and confirmed the red dot was still on her chest. If she got out of line, it would all be over. Victor probably already had a plan to cover his tracks.

She looked back at Victor. "Trying to harm me and my friends is your way of nicely warning me?"

She knew he was the one behind those attempts on their lives. Not all of them, but some of them, at least. Andi had been pursuing the man for almost a year, trying to find evidence against him.

She'd been on his defense team in Texas, but the man wasn't as innocent as he claimed. When she'd confronted him, Victor set her up, making it look like she'd falsified some documents for elderly clients, which resulted in them leaving all their money to her upon their deaths.

When the state board found out about it, Andi had been disbarred.

Then her colleague Stockton had been killed in what appeared to be a convenience store robbery. Andi had known the crime was anything but a simple robbery. It had been a setup.

Afterward, her vigilantism had kicked in. She couldn't let Victor get away with the evil deeds he'd done, deeds that went far deeper than she'd ever realized.

Now she was in the middle of a dangerous game with far-reaching consequences.

The closer she got to finding answers, the deeper she sank into a pit of danger that was becoming impossible to escape.

"Aggressive people require aggressive measures," Victor crooned. "You weren't taking the hint."

Andi said nothing. There was nothing she could say to that.

Everyone else had turned a blind eye to the man.

Everyone but Andi.

"This is your last warning to stay away from me and my business associates," Victor said.

Her throat tightened. "And if I don't?"

"Then people on your team will die one by one."

A chill rippled through her at the definitiveness of his words.

"Leave my friends out of this." The words slithered through her gritted teeth and hardened jaw. "They don't have anything to do with what's going on."

"I know."

Andi heard the smile in his voice, and her blood moved from a steady simmer to an outright boil.

"Which is why it's a shame you pulled them into your circle," Victor continued. "Unfortunately, bad character corrupts good company. Now they're all on my list. Duke, Ranger, Simmy, Mariella, Matthew . . . such a shame that good people may have to die."

Andi's hands fisted at her side.

He shouldn't mess with her friends.

This exact scenario had been Andi's worry all along. She'd wanted her friends to keep their distance. But they'd insisted they wanted to help.

She should have been firmer as she tried to keep them away. It was too late for that now.

"I'm the only one you need to worry about," she insisted.

"We both know the best way to slow you down is by going after your friends."

She swallowed, her saliva burning her throat. Victor knew entirely too much about her. Knew how to get to her. How to mess with her mind.

Andi didn't like anyone having that power over her.

"What do you want from me?" she finally asked. "I know there's something. Otherwise, you wouldn't be here right now."

"I want you to mind your own business. I want you to tell your friends you were off base with all your theories. That you became obsessive after losing your license to practice law. That your anger was misplaced."

The thought of saying that—of letting Victor get

away with multiple murders, among other vicious crimes—made nausea swirl in her stomach.

This was a game to him, and Andi needed to play by his rules—on the surface, at least. She had to do whatever she could to protect the people she cared about.

She kept her voice even as she asked, "You really think my friends are going to believe that?"

"I want you to walk away," Victor continued, almost as if he didn't hear her. "Leave Alaska. Go someplace where I won't hear from you or see you ever again."

His words floated in her mind a moment. "You're saying that if I do that, you'll leave them alone?"

"That's right. I'm not the monster you think I am."

That was *exactly* what Victor Goodman was. "I know you had Stockton killed."

"Collateral damage."

Ice filled her veins. Andi knew with absolute certainty that Victor could kill each of her friends and get away with it.

Andi considered his demand. Thought about what it would look like for her to make that confession to her friends and then leave.

Her thoughts raced. She wasn't sure she could be convincing enough to make that happen. Her friends would know something was up.

Especially Duke.

"Did I make myself clear?" Victor's voice hardened.

"Crystal," Andi muttered.

"Good. Don't make me have to come back and visit you again."

Footsteps drew closer.

The shadowy figure of the gunman moved in front of her.

She squinted, trying to make out his features. No doubt, the man was one of Victor's many hired thugs.

The man shifted. Raised his arm.

His gun appeared in front of her face.

Andi bristled.

Then the butt of the weapon collided with her head, and everything around her went black.

AS SOON AS Duke McAllister stepped off the plane, he pulled out his cell phone and dialed Andi's number.

He couldn't wait to see her.

Maybe it was sappy. But being away from her this long after officially beginning their relationship only five weeks ago was harder than he'd thought it would be.

Now the waiting was about to be over.

Andi was picking him up. He just needed to let her know his flight had landed.

The phone rang and rang before going to voicemail.

Duke squinted as surprise filled him. He'd figured Andi would be waiting for his call. They'd talked every day since they'd been apart and had both mentioned how they couldn't wait to see each other.

He'd also talked to Andi before his last flight, and

she'd sounded fine, like nothing was wrong. She'd even sent a text a few minutes after they ended the call.

Maybe the call not going through was a glitch.

Duke dialed her number again.

Again, there was no answer.

He grunted and shoved the phone back into his pocket. Maybe Andi would call him back in a second. Or maybe she was waiting in the pick-up area outside and couldn't talk right now. Or maybe she hadn't heard her phone ring.

He hiked his backpack on his shoulder and continued down the concourse at the Fairbanks airport, through the exit, past the luggage claim area, and outside.

As he stepped into the chilly September afternoon air, he scanned the crowd. Still no Andi.

He looked for her gray 1988 Dodge Ram to no avail.

Duke's gut tightened. He didn't want to be an alarmist, but something didn't feel right.

He scanned the airport pickup area one more time before looking at his phone again.

No missed calls.

He tried not to let his thoughts get ahead of him.

Instead, he dialed Andi one more time.

This time when she didn't answer, Duke left a voice-mail. "Hey. It's me. I'm here at the airport. You still able to give me a ride? Let me know. Maybe we got our times mixed up or something."

He shoved the phone back in his pocket.

When he still hadn't heard from her after a few more minutes passed, Duke considered calling another friend. But he didn't want to complicate things. Instead, he decided to get an Uber. That would make everything easier for now. He'd find out more information before raising concerns.

According to the app, his ride was only five minutes away.

While he waited, he sent Andi a text telling her his updated plans. Maybe she'd gotten caught up in something—hopefully, something simple and not life-threatening. Though life-threatening was the way it seemed to work for them lately.

His gaze wandered to a TV in the corner as a news story played across the screen.

As he watched, all other sounds disappeared from around him.

Diane Glassine was missing.

His heart thumped harder against his chest.

The senator had gotten on a plane last night near Prudhoe Bay with plans to fly to Anchorage and then on to Washington D.C. Tomorrow, the senate subcommittee she was a part of would vote on the new proposal to drill for more oil near Prudhoe Bay.

Many were angered at the prospect. Petitions had been started. People had picketed outside of her office. She'd gotten hate mail. Death threats.

Both sides reacted strongly about the possibility of drilling.

Everything hinged on her vote.

But now her plane had disappeared. A mayday call had gone out before the radar lost them.

Duke's thoughts raced.

Andi had been investigating the senator and thought the woman had ties with Victor Goodman. In fact, Andi had even broken into the woman's office to look for evidence.

Not Andi's wisest move.

But she'd discovered Victor Goodman had made campaign contributions to the woman.

Then the senator had been shot. After nearly four weeks, Glassine had been released from the hospital, and a big deal had been made over the fact she'd returned to work so quickly, despite what had happened. She'd been deemed a hero.

Now the senator had disappeared, and Andi wasn't answering her phone.

Coincidence?

Duke wanted to believe more than anything that the incidents were a fluke.

But he knew they weren't.

Something was majorly wrong.

———

Andi hadn't been sure what to do after her encounter with Victor.

She'd woken up on her couch with a splitting

headache and the undeniable reality that she had to make a choice.

Listen to Victor and leave this alone.

Or continue working to bring him down.

As darkness stretched outside and her temples throbbed, she'd taken a minute to collect her thoughts. She'd known what she had to do.

Now, she was alone in a bland motel room.

Away from everyone she cared about.

Keeping them all safe—she hoped.

She sat on the bed, one with an ugly dark green and burgundy comforter that had been popular back when *The Golden Girls* was still a hit TV show.

Papers were spread out in front of her.

Everything she'd ever collected on Victor.

Most of the information had also been scanned onto a jump drive just in case anything happened to these hard copies.

Andi had pictures of people with whom Victor had met. Logs of when he'd had these meetings and how long they lasted. Copies of his financial transactions and business proposals. Printouts of news articles featuring him.

Then there was the upcoming legislation scheduled to be voted on by the senate subcommittee today. Andi had also printed everything she could on it, all the fine details.

That legislation could mean Victor would get his way. If he won, more drilling would take place near

Prudhoe Bay.

From an environmental standpoint, Andi wasn't sure where she stood on more drilling. She could see both sides of the argument.

The environment wasn't her main concern at this very moment.

Her biggest concern was with the bigger picture. Victor Goodman wanted that oil drilling for a reason. He'd invested heavily in the project.

Control the oil, control the people.

She'd seen that written in one of Victor's documents.

Withhold oil, and people—as well as governments—became desperate. They would do whatever Victor wanted to get what they needed to survive. Oil was the ecosystem of society, allowing transportation, heat, even cooking.

Then there was the environmental impact on the land and water, on the animals in the area, and on the indigenous people living near the new oil fields. Each of those things would also be impacted.

One of the purest areas of the earth could be irrevocably harmed.

If the legislation passed, Prometheus could be enacted.

Prometheus was what Victor called his plan. Andi didn't know everything that it entailed, but she suspected that he stood to profit in big ways if the drilling was approved. More money meant more power, which would ultimately make Victor unstoppable.

Nothing made Andi more furious than the rich and powerful thinking they could get away with doing whatever they wanted just because they had the resources to do so.

She would fight with everything inside her to ensure that didn't happen.

Right now, her investigation would look different. She would need to hide in the shadows a while. Pretend as if she'd given up. Disappear from everyone's radar.

Giving up was the last thing on her mind. However, Andi had to protect those she loved.

Duke's image flashed through her mind, and her throat went dry.

She glanced at the time on her watch. By now, he should have landed at the airport. No doubt he'd tried to call her. Had discovered that she wasn't answering. That she wasn't there to pick him up.

She hated to put him through this—especially after what had happened with Celeste, his ex-fiancée who'd disappeared.

More than anything, Andi had wanted to be there to greet him. To throw her arms around him. To tell him how much she'd missed him.

Instead, she'd left him some breadcrumbs. She hoped Duke knew her well enough to follow them.

That was yet to be determined.

She had to think of the bigger picture, even if her sudden departure might leave her friends feeling hurt.

Andi stared at the papers again, wondering what she

was missing. She needed some solid evidence before she presented her case to someone who actually had the power to stop Victor. She couldn't leave any room for doubt.

She was close but not quite there yet.

Footsteps sounded on the walkway outside of her room.

Her muscles tightened.

She'd chosen a motel in the middle of nowhere. She'd seen a few other guests. Mostly long-haul truckers, it seemed.

Maybe what she'd heard was simply someone headed to their room.

But the footsteps had stopped.

Outside of *her* room.

Was it one of Victor's men? How could they have followed her here? Andi had made sure to cover all her tracks.

She should be safe.

But something was wrong. She was certain of it.

As if to confirm, a shadow moved outside her window.

Andi bristled as she figured out her next move.

HECTOR LOOKED BACK at his home as tears rolled down his cheeks.

"Mama." His voice cracked. "I don't want to go."

His mom gripped his shoulder hard enough that he flinched. Then she continued leading him down the sidewalk toward the street. "We have no choice. This place is no longer ours. It was a dump anyway."

"But . . ." He couldn't take his eyes off his house.

It wasn't big or fancy like some of the ones he'd seen on TV. But it was home, his favorite place in the whole world.

Behind the house was the small creek he liked to explore. His hideout was in the trees on the side of the property. He loved playing hide-and-seek there. He'd played that game all the time with his friend, Johnny. Until Johnny had moved two months ago.

His bedroom contained all his favorite things—

comic books, a Batman poster, and some matchbox cars his dad had given Hector before he left. There was also Risk, the board game. Everyone thought Hector was too young to play. But he wasn't.

Adults just didn't like it when he beat them.

But Mama wouldn't let him bring those things with him. She said there was no room where they were going now.

Maybe if Mama could just see how much this place meant to him, she'd change her mind. It was worth a try.

Hector looked up at her, tears still streaming from his eyes.

But her expression remained unchanged. She never listened to him. Had told him children didn't have voices in these kinds of things.

Sometimes he wondered what it would be like to have a mom who liked to hug him, to do things with him, who . . . who loved him.

"Sometimes in life you just have to say goodbye to things." She continued to hurry down the sidewalk with a single bag in her other hand. "Crying and feeling sorry for yourself will do no good. This is life. These are the lessons you need to learn."

Despite her words, more tears flowed. He wished Dad was here. Maybe things would be different.

Maybe *everything* would be different.

But Hector was only nine. It was like Mama had

said, he had no power or voice. He could only do as he was told.

They paused on the cracked sidewalk near the mailbox.

"You know those games you like to play?" Mama let go of his arm and leaned down to meet his gaze instead. "Think of this like a game."

"How?"

"You've just rolled the dice, and you don't like what you see," she explained. "But you have to make the best of it. That's what you're doing right now. You're rethinking your strategy."

Sometimes, Hector thought Mama was smart, especially when she said things like that. He'd overheard a conversation once between Mama and Dad. Apparently, Mama had gone to college on a scholarship. Then she'd gotten pregnant and had to drop out.

A few years later, Dad had left. Hector hadn't seen him since.

Mama had most likely driven him away.

Then they had no money. They ate rice almost every night for dinner.

But Mama promised that things would get better.

They hadn't. In fact, they were getting worse.

Where would he sleep at night? What would he do when he was bored? Would he have any safe places to hide when Mama got in one of her moods?

A car pulled to a stop in front of the house, dust

flying behind the wheels. A moment later, the driver flung the passenger door open.

"Put your stuff in the back and get in," he said, his voice gruff.

Hector's stomach clenched.

Robert. Hector had never liked this man.

He was one of the reasons Hector and his mother were leaving. Robert had convinced Mama this was a good idea. Hector had overheard it.

The man made himself seem like he was so smart. But he wasn't.

Plus, he was meaner than Scar, the stray cat that hung around Johnny's old place. Scar didn't have that nickname because of his own scars. He had the nickname because he gave other people scars.

"Come on." Mama scowled, her face all hard lines and irritation. "There's no need to just stand there."

She nudged him, and Hector put his bag into the back of the beat-up gold Datsun. He climbed into the back seat and stared at Robert in the front.

Robert with his thick, bushy mustache. His bald head. The hula girl on his dash.

Hector thought a moment about what it would be like to destroy something Robert cared about, to give the man a taste of his own medicine.

Robert had destroyed so many things Hector cared about. It only seemed fair.

He pictured himself grabbing that hula girl and

throwing her out the window. Then he imagined another car running it over.

He smiled.

But the smile faded.

Mama would never forgive him if he did that. She'd be so mad, and he didn't want to know what kind of punishment he might face. Sometimes, she locked him in his room. Sometimes she used an old dog kennel with a lock on it.

Once, Hector hadn't eaten for three days. His stomach had hurt so bad. But Mama didn't care.

That punishment had been Robert's idea. The man had smirked at him while eating pizza at the kitchen table.

Hector didn't grab the hula girl. He restrained himself.

But he couldn't stop fantasizing about how good it would feel to hurt Robert like Robert had hurt him.

Mama should never have sold this house. Even though she said they didn't have a choice, Hector didn't believe her.

One day when he was old enough to do something about it, he would.

He glanced at the place one more time as it disappeared out of sight.

DUKE HAD his Uber driver drop him off at Andi's place.

On the way there, he'd changed his mind about keeping quiet. He'd called everyone in the Arctic Circle Murder Club to check in with them and ask a few questions.

No one had heard from Andi since last night when Ranger and Simmy had dropped her off at her apartment after her flight arrived. Ranger told Duke that Andi was in good spirits when she said goodbye and that nothing seemed wrong.

As Duke stood on the sidewalk where the driver had left him, he scanned the parking lot at Andi's apartment complex.

Andi's truck wasn't in its normal spot, nor did he see it parked anywhere else. He stored that fact away before heading to her apartment.

He pounded on the door, trying to keep his thoughts positive. "Andi?"

No answer.

He hesitated a moment before typing in her code. Barging into her place seemed like an invasion of privacy. But his gut told him something was wrong. Andi *had* given him the code, however, and this seemed a good time to use it.

The mechanical lock turned, and he opened the door. "Andi? It's me. Duke. Are you here?"

Only silence answered.

Duke reached for the light switch, and illumination filled the room.

He held his breath as he looked around, preparing himself for the worst.

Andi's living room stared back at him.

She wasn't exactly a neat freak, so her apartment wasn't perfect. No, it was lived in and cozy. Everything looked normal.

So where was Andi?

Ranger had said he dropped her off almost twelve hours ago.

Duke wished he had his gun with him, but he couldn't fly with it. If he encountered trouble, he'd have to handle it the old-fashioned way.

He paced the living room, looking for any signs that something had happened. He checked each room. No one was in Andi's apartment.

He wasn't sure if that made him feel better or worse.

After all, Andi hadn't just disappeared into thin air.

His heart lurched into his throat.

Images of Celeste filled his thoughts.

Because that was precisely what his ex-fiancée had done.

Disappeared into thin air.

For two years, Duke had turned his life upside down as he'd tried to find her.

He couldn't bear the thought of going through that again.

Please, Lord . . . no. My soul can't handle that.

He wandered back into the living room and glanced around.

Something on the cushion of the pale blue couch filled him with trepidation.

He slowly walked toward it, not wanting to admit to himself what he was seeing.

His lungs tightened.

Two small, red smears stained the cushion.

Blood.

And it was fresh.

———

Andi crept toward the motel door.

Had Victor or one of his men found her here?

How was that even possible? She had been careful. Had taken precautions.

"I know you're in there."

The man's deep, nasal voice sounded vaguely familiar, but Andi couldn't place it. One of Victor's hitmen? She didn't think any of them had actually spoken to her. They'd terrorized her in other ways instead.

Shivers raced down her spine—and not the good kind.

She held her gun which she'd grabbed from her apartment before she left, and approached the door, pressing her back against it. Drawing in a deep breath, she turned to peer through the peep hole.

Her eyes widened.

A scrawny man with a pointy nose, crooked teeth, and mangy hair stood outside staring at her door.

Skeeter Pitts.

She never thought she'd see him again.

Andi had pressed charges against the man earlier this year. He should be locked up, but maybe he'd gotten out on bail. Or maybe he'd escaped.

No, the idiot wasn't smart enough to pull off something like that.

How in the world had the first-class creep found her here?

As if he could read her thoughts, he called, "I was passing by when I thought I saw you check in, Andi. Just wanted to pay my respects and catch up for a minute."

Pay his respects? Catch up? She resisted a snort. The idea was ludicrous.

Andi had seen the way the man looked at her when

they'd worked for the same trucking company. He was trouble, and he'd stop at nothing to get what he wanted.

What he'd wanted back then was Andi.

She shivered as she stared at the door.

The last time they'd come face-to-face he'd attacked her.

If he managed to get into this room, Andi might be forced to use her gun.

That would ruin her plan to hideout.

She had to quickly figure out what to do.

First option: Pretend not to be here. But Skeeter had probably seen the car she'd pulled up in. Knowing Skeeter, he may have even been watching her since she checked in.

Second option: Open the door and let him come inside—under gunpoint. Then they could calmly talk, and Andi could instruct him to forget he'd ever seen her.

But could she trust him to stay quiet?

Definitely not. Liars were liars. Trusting him even the slightest could be a fatal mistake.

She didn't think the man was working for Victor. But . . . she couldn't rule out the possibility. Slimeball Victor had innumerable people under his thumb.

Her nerves tightened as the door rattled.

Skeeter was trying to force his way inside.

A click sounded. Then another.

What was that? Was the man trying to pick her lock?

The muscles across her chest tightened.

Then something slammed into the door.

Apparently, picking the lock hadn't worked. Now Skeeter was trying to ram his way inside.

If he broke into this room, then he'd have the upper hand.

Andi couldn't let that happen.

Instead, she lifted a quick prayer that her impulsive decision wouldn't be the death of her. But this appeared to be the only option.

Quickly, she twisted the lock before scurrying backward. She raised her gun toward the door.

Just as she did, Skeeter burst inside the room. It happened so quickly that he nearly toppled onto the nasty carpeted floor.

He straightened and saw Andi.

His eyes lit with that sickening hunger, a look she'd seen too many times before.

"What are you doing here?" Andi refused to let a trace of fear slip into her voice.

He rose to full height. "You're about to find out."

"No, you're about to find out."

"Find out what?"

She raised her gun higher to get his attention.

As his gaze sank to her Glock, his smugness disappeared.

CHAPTER
SIX

"SOMEONE MUST HAVE BEEN WAITING for her when she returned." State Police Trooper Logan Gibson stood near the door of Andi's apartment and surveyed the space.

Duke had asked his friend if he would come. Gibson showed up ten minutes later, dressed casually and not in uniform. He'd explained it was his day off.

Usually, his uniform covered the tattoos on his arms. Not today.

At first glance, no one would suspect him of being a cop.

"Look at this." Duke pointed to the blood on the couch.

Gibson crouched and examined the spots before shaking his head. "I don't like seeing that. We should check her security camera footage. Maybe something's there."

"I already tried. Someone painted over the lenses."

Gibson's jaw flexed. "Of course they did. Who do you think did this? You guys have made a lot of enemies, so I'm sure you have your choice."

Duke didn't have to think about his answer. "Victor Goodman."

Realization spread through Gibson's eyes. "It's easier to have a one-on-one with the president of the United States than it is to talk to that man. He has more lawyers than anyone I've ever met."

"Believe me, I know." Duke's eyes slid to the side in an exasperated eyeroll. "He covers his tracks carefully."

"And he's the last person you want as an enemy." Gibson's words hung in the air.

Duke already knew that, but the reminder made the hollow pit in his stomach feel even larger and deeper.

Thinking about what Victor was capable of would do him no good. He needed to think of solutions instead.

"Too bad we don't have a way of tracking her," Gibson murmured.

Duke's breath caught.

Andi had just added him to the Find Friends app on her phone. Why didn't Duke think about that earlier?

"You're brilliant," he told Gibson.

"Can't wait to hear why."

Duke opened the app and waited as it refreshed.

He tried to be patient, but the last thing he wanted was to stand idle.

Finally, the screen changed.

His throat tightened. "I have a location. It looks like her phone is . . . at the airport."

Gibson squinted. "The airport?"

Could this all be a misunderstanding? Could Andi have gone to pick up Duke? Had something happened while she was there?

That wouldn't explain the blood on her couch. Or her cameras being painted over.

Something was *definitely* going on. He wasn't crazy.

Duke needed to head to the airport. Now.

Maybe the answers waited there.

———

"You're not going to use that gun on me." Skeeter stared at Andi from the doorway, a challenging look in his gaze.

He liked danger, didn't he? Liked being told no. Liked seeing fear in women's eyes.

"Don't test me." Andi narrowed her eyes and made sure her voice didn't waver. She refused to show any weakness around him.

Skeeter didn't deserve any kind of power over her.

His eyes widened as if her words scared him.

Good.

Then the cocky amusement returned to his gaze. "The moment I saw you walking into this motel, I couldn't help but think to myself how fortuitous it was that we ran into each other again."

"Fortuitous isn't exactly the word that I would use." Andi paused, trying to control her contempt for the man so she wouldn't do anything rash. "What are you doing here, Skeeter? Why did you stop to see if it was really me? Don't you have a reservation at Hotel de la Prison?"

"You think you're so funny, don't you?" Skeeter shook his head back and forth. "As a matter of fact, I'm out on bail. When I saw you, I just thought we could catch up. As one colleague to another."

Skeeter was an ice road trucker. Andi had gotten her certification when she'd moved to Alaska, primarily because it was a means of going to Prudhoe Bay, where she could try to find more about what Victor Goodman might be up to. It had all been part of her plan to bring Victor down.

When those leads fizzled and the Arctic Circle Murder Club had formed, bringing with it the *Round Table Podcast*, Andi had moved on to other ventures that might also bring in some cash, freedom, and possible answers.

"I didn't invite you into my room." Andi pointed at the door with her gun. "You need to leave."

"What if I don't want to?" He stepped closer, still appearing to enjoy this confrontation.

Her shoulders tightened. Skeeter would push this as far as he could, wouldn't he?

Andi shouldn't be surprised, but she'd hoped the man might have some sense slapped into him in jail.

She had to get Skeeter out of here. There was no scenario where Andi could trust him. No scenario where he could know where she was and have her be okay with that.

"I said you need to get out of here, and I didn't give you a choice." Her Texas twang came out as she slowly said the words. "Am I right?"

"You've always been so sassy. I like that." Skeeter stepped even closer, smiling as he looked her over. "I *really* like that."

Andi raised her gun higher. Nausea swirled in her gut at his insinuations.

"Don't even think about touching me," she warned him.

"Oh, come on, Andi." He lowered his voice to an intimate, gross murmur. "I've always known you liked me. I can see it in your eyes. Stop denying it, and let's give the two of us a whirl."

"I like that idea about as much as I like having a cavity."

He laughed as if she was flirting with him.

She wasn't.

The next instant, he lunged at her. Grabbed her wrist. Tried to wrestle the gun from her hands.

Oh no . . . he was *not* going to do this.

Andi braced herself for the fight, determined not to let Skeeter win.

He bent her wrist back, and Andi yelped as pain shot through her.

But she didn't let go of the gun.

"Give it up." His halitosis hit her nostrils.

Her stomach revolted. "Over my dead body!"

"Have it your way!" He released her wrist, drew his fist back, and rammed it into her jaw.

She staggered backward as she lost her balance. She fell on the floor next to the bed, the threadbare carpet doing nothing to ease the impact.

Pain—and shock—ripped through her, causing her grip to loosen.

The gun fell from her hands and skittered across the floor just out of reach.

Panic raced through her as she stared at the weapon.

Skeeter twisted his neck also in the same direction.

Then he dove for it.

Before he grabbed it, Andi pounced on Skeeter's back.

He threw her off. Somehow, she managed to land on her feet.

As he reached for the gun, his fingers mere centimeters away, Andi rushed forward and stomped on his hand.

A sickening crunch filled the air.

Skeeter cried out.

The next instant, he ripped his hand from beneath her foot and popped to his feet, turning toward her in a crouched position.

The amusement in his gaze turned to a dark animosity.

"You little . . ." He muttered some choice words.

Then he growled and lunged at her again.

As Andi dove out of his way, Skeeter collided with the wall.

His forehead slammed into the plaster with a sickening thud, his head snapped back, and he let out a guttural moan before collapsing into a heap on the floor.

Andi straightened, heaving in deep breaths as her limbs quivered.

Wasting no time, she grabbed her gun—just in case Skeeter had a sudden burst of energy.

Then she observed the man.

He wasn't moving.

Her heart pounded harder. Was he dead?

How was she going to explain this? She'd been an attorney, so she knew how this worked.

She'd unlocked her door, leaving no obvious signs of forced entry.

Sure, she had some bruises. But her injuries were minor compared to Skeeter's.

But she *had* warned him.

She let a few seconds pass to see if he stirred. Then she felt for his pulse.

A soft thump hit her fingertip.

He had a pulse, and he was breathing.

He wasn't dead.

That was good . . . she supposed.

But Andi had to get out of here before he woke up.

CHAPTER
SEVEN

DUKE AND GIBSON parked at the airport and rushed inside.

Following the tracker on his phone, Duke paused near the check-in counter. "If this app is correct, Andi is still here."

Duke scanned the airport patrons around him as they walked with their rolling suitcases and backpacks, oblivious to his rising panic. The place wasn't especially busy right now, which made it easy to scan everyone in sight.

Gibson paused beside him and frowned. "I don't see her."

"Me neither." He attempted to hold his panic at bay. Overreacting would do him no good.

As Duke continued to scan his surroundings, he tried to think like Andi.

Why did the tracker indicate her phone was in this area?

On a whim, Duke dialed Andi's number.

As the phone rang on his end, he pulled the device away from his ear and listened to the sounds around him instead.

"Do you hear that?" A muffled ringtone sounded nearby.

Gibson paused then nodded. "It's a phone."

They moved closer to the sound before stopping at a trashcan near the security check area.

Gibson took the top off and snapped on a latex glove before beginning to search the trash. A moment later, he withdrew his arm, a cell phone grasped between his fingers.

The device was still ringing.

It was Andi's.

Duke knew by the small crack on the upper lefthand corner. The faded blue case. The picture on the screen of Resurrection Bay she'd taken while in Salmon-by-the-Sea.

His gut clenched even tighter.

Why would her cell phone be in a trashcan?

Unless someone else had put it there. But if someone had done something to her, wouldn't they have destroyed the cell phone and not left it still in operation in a public place?

"May I see it?" Duke asked.

Gibson handed him a glove and waited for Duke to

slip it on before handing him the phone. They needed to preserve any fingerprints, just in case.

Andi had never told him her passcode, but he had a few guesses based on what he knew about her.

Most likely? The date she'd passed the bar exam.

She'd talked about the monumental feeling of accomplishment she'd felt that day. Her dad had been a truck driver and her mom a homemaker. Being the first to get an advanced college degree had been pivotal, especially for her father.

Duke typed the digits and waited.

A second later, the phone screen changed.

It worked! He'd unlocked it.

Duke scrolled through Andi's phone call history. He saw missed calls from him, as well as Mariella and Simmy.

Scrolling back further, he saw calls between the two of them from when she'd been in Texas.

He searched her emails. Again, nothing surprising or unusual showed up.

"Anything?" Gibson asked.

Duke stared at the screen, wondering if he'd missed anything. "Unfortunately, no. Nothing obvious, at least."

He tried to force things to make sense. But they didn't. He needed more information.

Duke turned to Gibson, his thoughts still racing. "Do you think we could see the airport security footage?"

Gibson didn't have to think about the request for long. "Let me see what I can do."

———

Andi needed to tie up Skeeter. She couldn't take any chances that he'd regain consciousness and come after her again.

She searched the motel room for something she could use as a restraint.

The landline phone on the motel room's nightstand caught her eye.

That would work.

She jerked the cord from the phone, then the wall. Scrambling back toward Skeeter—who still lay passed out and slumped against the wall—she jerked his hands in front of him.

Working quickly, she wrapped the cord around his wrists and pulled tight before knotting the makeshift restraint.

She needed to make sure he couldn't follow her, and this was the only solution she could think of. Unfortunately, she couldn't call the police.

Victor would confirm she'd left town. If her name showed up in a police report, he might see it. He seemed to have eyes and ears everywhere.

She shoved everything she'd brought with her into her backpack before hiking it on her shoulders.

She scanned the room once more and didn't see

anything she'd left behind. Her gun was safely stashed in her waistband. She'd checked in using an assumed identity, and she'd paid cash—something she'd need to do for a while since her cards might be tracked.

Security cameras had probably recorded her features. Even though she wore a baseball cap with her hair secured beneath it, she knew if the cameras were decent enough they'd pick up on some details. Besides, Skeeter had somehow recognized her.

Maybe everything she'd done was overkill, but she *had* to remain off grid—just in case. Just in case Victor came. Just in case the police came. Just in case *anyone* came.

She stepped toward the door and took one last glance at Skeeter as he slouched against the wall, mouth open and hands bound in front of him.

He should have never come here looking for her. Should have never attacked her.

This wasn't her fault.

But that didn't mean this was over.

Skeeter's ego would be bruised when he woke up, and he wasn't the type to let this go.

What would he do next?

She didn't want to find out.

Andi stepped outside, closed the door, and glanced around.

No one suspicious lingered nearby.

She hurried toward the car she'd borrowed, wishing it was more inconspicuous.

But borrowing it hadn't been part of her plan.

Neither had coming to this motel. But she'd thrown it together at the last moment. Now she needed to come up with yet another plan. There weren't many options in this area.

She could head back north to Fairbanks. But Victor had his men all over that city.

She could head south to Anchorage. But she wasn't sure how that would help either.

Her best option was to go somewhere off the beaten path where no one would find her.

But then those breadcrumbs she'd laid for Duke would be meaningless.

Maybe it was better that way. Leaving clues had been a risky move. But she could really use Duke's help right now.

No matter what she did, things continued to grow more complicated.

But she *would* get through this.

As Andi slammed the car door, she glanced up at her motel room one more time.

No movement or signs of life.

Hopefully, Skeeter would remain unconscious long enough for her to get away.

Still, a bad feeling brewed inside her.

Andi had known she couldn't make any mistakes if she wanted her plan to work.

And Skeeter finding her was *definitely* a mistake.

THANKS TO GIBSON'S position with the state police, he and Duke were able to see the airport security footage.

They'd been led to a secure office where a TSA agent waited, numerous screens in front of him. Apparently, this was the smaller security room. A larger one had other TSA agents surveying all aspects of the airport.

Agent Steerman was in his forties and looked bored to tears as he sat behind the desk in his uniform. Duke prayed the man could help them.

Ranger had told Duke that he'd picked Andi up from the airport last night at one a.m. and dropped her off at her apartment shortly after.

With that timeline in mind, they began looking at footage from the airport beginning at three a.m.

Even at the early hour, the airport was busy. They

watched streams of people come and go. Some were tourists with suitcases about to head home from the Last Frontier. Others were locals heading out on trips. There were families and businessmen and women and couples of all ages.

Duke mostly kept his eye on the trashcan. He wanted to see the moment someone dropped that phone inside.

On his second cup of coffee—Steerman had offered them some from the small pot behind them—someone caught his eye.

"Right there." Duke pointed to the screen.

Agent Steerman hit Pause.

It was Andi. Her almost-white, blonde hair could be spotted a mile away.

At 7:05 a.m. this morning, she'd strolled past the trashcan. If Duke hadn't been watching, he would have never seen her hand slide back and drop her phone in the receptacle.

It almost appeared as if she'd rehearsed the move. As if she wanted to be as subtle as possible in order to not draw attention.

Duke studied the people around her.

She didn't appear to dump the phone under duress. No one lingered close as if threatening her. In fact, she appeared to be alone.

"Can you keep following her through the airport?" Duke asked.

"Sure." Agent Steerman sat up straight, his fingers

hitting the control in front of him. "Let me see what I can do."

Steerman trailed Andi to the ticket counter. She spoke to the agent several moments before pulling out what appeared to be her driver's license and credit card.

Then she started toward the escalator leading to the security check.

By eight a.m., just four hours before Duke landed at the airport, she reached her gate.

Duke had a lot of questions. But the main one running through his mind was: why had she decided to leave without telling anyone?

It wasn't like Andi to just take off. Even if this had something to do with their relationship—which Duke didn't believe it did—she would have said something first. Besides, she'd promised to pick him up.

Something wasn't right.

Duke's pulse quickened as his adrenaline surged.

He turned toward Steerman. "Do you know where that plane was going?"

"I can find out." Steerman typed something into his desktop computer.

As he did, Duke continued to watch the security footage. He observed Andi as she took a seat at the gate, positioning herself to face the camera.

Whether she knew the device was there or not, Duke didn't know. But Andi was usually perceptive and undeniably smart.

As she sat there, nothing unusual happened. There

were no sudden movements or strange meetings. Andi only waited and watched people.

When it was time for the plane to board, Andi rose. Stood in line behind her boarding group. Then she disappeared down the bridge.

She left.

Duke tried to take a deep breath, but his lungs were tight. Actually, his entire chest was.

"Alabama." Steerman twirled away from the computer and turned back toward Duke.

Duke turned his gaze away from the security monitor and glanced at the agent, certain he hadn't heard correctly. "Come again?"

"The flight your friend got on was to Alabama. It appears she boarded this morning, and she should be landing"—he glanced at his watch—"in two hours."

———

Should Duke get a ticket to Alabama? That was the question he asked himself as he sat in the small office with Gibson and Steerman.

What reason would Andi have to go to Alabama?

It didn't make sense.

He was missing something. He was certain of it. He just had to figure out what.

Duke shifted in the uncomfortable metal chair and turned toward Gibson and Steerman. "I have an idea."

"What are you thinking?" Gibson leaned back in his seat and took a sip of his coffee.

"Can we keep watching the security footage at this gate?" Duke asked.

Steerman's eyebrows flickered as if he thought the idea was a waste of time. But he obliged him. "Why not?"

Duke kept his gaze focused on the gate as he waited for the agents to close the doors on the flight.

As he continued studying everyone boarding, something caught his eye. "Can you rewind that?"

Steerman did as he asked, suddenly appearing more interested.

"Stop right there," Duke said.

Steerman paused the video.

Duke leaned closer, trying to get a better look. "Can you blow up that frame?"

The agent hit a few buttons until the picture enlarged.

"What are you thinking, Duke?" Gibson's gaze volleyed back and forth from Duke to the monitor.

"Look right there." Duke pointed to the screen. "Someone went through as if boarding the plane, then slipped out a moment later and walked behind the gate agents. The area was so busy with people boarding that no one noticed."

"But the flight crew would get a final count when everyone got on the plane." Steerman narrowed his eyes as if trying to figure out what was going on.

"Usually," Gibson said. "But sometimes things can get overlooked. Right?"

Steerman shrugged, appearing unconvinced. "I suppose."

"Can you switch to the camera that shows where this person went?" Duke's gaze remained fastened on the screen. "There were so many other people in the frame that it was hard to make out if it was even a man or a woman."

The agent did as he asked.

When the screen switched to a different feed, Duke saw that the person who'd left the flight was a woman wearing a black hat with her hair tucked underneath it.

Duke knew by the way the woman walked that it was Andi.

She had exited the plane after boarding.

The feed followed her path as she slipped into a bathroom.

Duke waited for her to emerge again.

When she finally did, he hardly recognized her. Her hair was now long and dark. She wore a white sweatshirt and had a different backpack on her shoulders.

The casual observer wouldn't have thought she was the same person.

Which had probably been Andi's intention.

"You really think that's Andi?" Gibson leaned closer to the screen, his eyes narrowed.

Duke's gut tightened. "I'm positive. She switched up how she looked in case anyone was watching."

"Why would she do that?" Steerman scratched his head as if earnestly confused.

Duke squeezed his eyes shut, unable to deny the truth as it screamed at him. "Because she's in trouble."

CHAPTER
NINE

ANDI GRIPPED the steering wheel as she headed away from the motel, her thoughts racing at a frantic pace.

She didn't do frantic. That was what she'd always told herself.

Funny how life had a way of showing her differently.

What would she do now? There weren't that many places to stay out here.

When Skeeter woke up, finding her and getting revenge would become his goal. He might even recruit some of his friends to help or maybe even his father, a man who went by the nickname Lockjaw.

The man was as scary as his name sounded.

Lockjaw had been Andi's boss at the trucking company. He operated from intimidation, and when people didn't live up to his expectations, he punished them with his fists.

He was scary in a different way than Victor. Lockjaw was all brute strength, street smarts, and fearless testosterone.

Victor, on the other hand, was calculated and smart with more resources than anyone else she knew.

Both were dangerous.

And both might have her marked as a target.

Andi swallowed hard as anxiety tried to consume her.

She continued down the highway, her thoughts still swirling. She needed somewhere off the traveled path.

She drove another hour before she found what she was looking for.

A campground.

The location wouldn't be ideal, but it would work for now. At least for a night.

The good news was that it wasn't so cold outside that Andi would be miserable, and there weren't many people who used these areas this time of the year. The summer tourist season was over.

She pulled off the highway and traveled several miles up another road. Finally, she arrived at the campground.

Andi paid at the office, got her site number, and drove inside. She'd picked a site on the backside of the campground. Reaching it, she tucked her vehicle near the trees, as far out of sight as she could manage. She didn't have a tent, so she would sleep in the car tonight.

She stepped out, desperate to gain control of her panic. She stretched, breathing in the refreshing, clean scent of birch and aspen.

But when she moved, aches hit her from all angles.

Her head still pounded from the gunman hitting her. Her jaw hurt from Skeeter's punch to the face. Her shoulder and elbow throbbed from diving away from Skeeter.

All injuries that would heal. But they reminded Andi of what she'd been through so far.

She pressed her eyes closed.

She knew for a fact that she wouldn't get through this unscathed.

But she would never give up.

As soon as she had all the information she needed, she'd call Attorney General Dabney Eldridge. The man had said he owed them a favor after Duke had saved his daughter from a house fire.

Andi had been waiting a few months to cash in on that favor.

When she did, it would be a doozy. That was why she needed to have everything in place before she presented Dabney with what she knew. If she got one detail wrong, he might dismiss her claims.

She couldn't let that happen.

She opened her eyes and glanced around.

Her breath caught at the landscape around her.

Denali stood in the background. The clouds had cleared long enough for the looming mountain to appear like a giant overlooking the land.

The sight of it was mesmerizing.

Yet the mountain she faced with Victor Goodman seemed bigger and more formidable.

———

"What do you want to do now?" Gibson asked as he and Duke sat in Gibson's Suburban at the airport.

They knew Andi had come here. Had bought a ticket to Alabama. Had walked off the flight. Had changed her appearance.

Her truck was still in the lot. They'd found it a few minutes ago.

Gibson had managed to unlock the door with a Slim Jim tool he kept on hand, and Duke had searched the vehicle. There was nothing helpful inside.

Thanks to Steerman, they knew Andi had left the airport, walking down the sidewalk away from the building instead of toward the parking garage.

That was when they'd lost her trail. Security camera footage had ended, so they had no idea where she'd gone.

Duke imagined someone had picked her up.

But he'd already talked to the members of the murder club. None of them knew anything about it, and

Duke believed them. He didn't think they'd helped Andi run.

In fact, they were all worried and made him promise to update them as soon as he could and were eager to help in any way they could.

What do you want to do now? That was what Gibson had asked him.

Duke had been thinking about the question for entirely too long.

"I don't know," Duke finally admitted. "And I don't like not knowing. Something must have spooked her."

"Something with Victor?" Gibson tapped his thumbs on the steering wheel.

"There's a good chance that's true. He makes the most sense. But it's not as if he would ever admit it, even if we were able to talk to him. Still, I'd like to try. Is there any way we could find out where he is right now?"

"I can tell you exactly where he is today. He's in D.C. The senate subcommittee is supposed to vote on some legislation."

Realization rocketed through Duke.

Was *that* what this was about? The legislation?

"Give me a minute." Duke pulled out Andi's cell phone, not bothering to pull on gloves this time, and began to play around on it. He knew it was a longshot, but he wanted to see if he'd missed any clues.

He went back through the same routine as earlier.

Checking her call log. Her text messages. Her emails. Her social media.

But he still found nothing.

He flipped through the rest of the apps, looking for anything he might have missed.

His gaze stopped on a calculator app.

Andi had two of them on her phone.

Which was curious.

One was the app that came with her phone, but the other was one she'd downloaded.

He clicked on that one.

Gibson peered over his shoulder. "I've seen those apps before. They were created to hide information—usually used by kids to conceal things from their parents or cheating spouses who don't want to be caught. You just have to use the calculator pad to type in a code, and it unlocks a hidden screen behind the calculator set up."

"I just need to figure out what her code would be." Duke stared at the numbers.

"Maybe the same as the one for her phone?" Gibson suggested. "I guess it depends on how easily Andi wanted someone to be able to get into the app."

That was Duke's thought exactly.

What if Andi had downloaded this hidden app for a specific purpose? Andi had to know Duke would look for her. Maybe she'd even guessed he'd find her phone. Maybe she'd guessed he'd see the app and try to figure out what was on it.

It seemed like something Andi might do.

After all, if Andi wanted to run, why would she bring her phone at all? She had to know the device could be traced. Why leave it on when she threw it in the trashcan? Why not wipe it completely?

Duke tried the code and waited.

As the app opened, relief washed through him.

Just as Gibson said, the screen changed, revealing what was on the other side.

But there were no photos or maps or files concealed there.

It was only an address that Andi had typed.

Duke read the location aloud to Gibson, who typed it on his laptop.

A moment later, Gibson said, "That appears to be a motel on the way down to Anchorage, just north of Denali."

Duke narrowed his eyes with thought. "Was she trying to let me know that she's staying there?"

Instead of responding, Gibson's gaze remained fixated on his screen, almost as if he wasn't listening.

"Gibson?" What had captured his friend's attention?

Gibson looked up, his expression suddenly tight. "When I typed in that address, an alert popped up."

"What kind of alert?"

"A man was found dead at that very motel less than an hour ago. A person of interest in his death is on the run."

Duke's heart thudded in his ears. "Are any names listed?"

"It appears the victim is a man named Billy Pitts . . . but he goes by the nickname Skeeter. No name for the suspect."

Duke's head began to spin.

Skeeter? Duke hadn't heard that name in a long time. The man was supposed to be behind bars.

Duke had witnessed the man attack Andi. Even though Duke believed women could defend themselves, Duke knew if he hadn't been there, something terrible would have happened to Andi that night.

She was strong, but she was small and no match for Skeeter. Even if the man was scrawny, he had muscles and wiry strength.

How did *Skeeter* tie into all this? The possibility that he was a part of this hadn't even been on Duke's radar.

What exactly had Andi gotten herself into?

CHAPTER
TEN

AFTER STRETCHING and getting some fresh air, Andi climbed back into the car and opened her bag.

She began to study her notes again, hoping to find something she'd missed earlier. What she really prayed for was some kind of divine intervention that would lead her to some answers.

The events of the past twenty-four hours had changed things. Andi knew without a doubt nothing would be the same. But would it be for better or for worse?

Duke's face filled her mind, as well as the faces of everyone in the murder club. The group had become like family to her. She hated to think about how Victor's threat might affect them.

But they were strong. They would bounce back from any scandals her name—and by default their names—might be tied to. They'd be okay with time.

If Victor didn't go after them.

The more obstacles they faced in the important work they were doing, the closer they came to finding answers.

Was the risk worth the reward?

Duke's image filled Andi's mind again.

She was in love with the man, even though she hadn't told him yet. Now that everything with Celeste had cleared up, she couldn't deny the truth anymore.

Why hadn't she told him? What had been stopping her? She wasn't sure.

Maybe the fact that Duke seemed too good to be true. Maybe her fear of blowing it. Maybe . . . a million things, she supposed.

As her head continued to pound, she realized she could use more fresh air.

She climbed from the car again and glanced at the gravel road looping around the campground. As she did, she spotted another vehicle slowly heading down the lane—a black F-350 with a ten-inch lift, cab lights, and an oversized grille with deer antlers attached.

Her heart caught in her throat.

She recognized the vehicle from when she'd been a truck driver.

It belonged to Lockjaw.

Andi's pulse pounded faster.

He must have heard what had happened to his son. Skeeter must have called him and ratted her out. Now Lockjaw was coming after Andi for revenge.

She stepped back, her legs hitting the car.

She couldn't stay here.

If that man found her, he'd kill her.

She glanced at the vast wilderness surrounding her.

Running into the mountainous woods would mean leaving one danger to plunge into another.

But Andi would have to take her chances. She had no other choice right now.

———

Duke and Gibson pulled up to Big Bear Lodge, which looked nothing like the cozy lodge Duke had envisioned. No, it was a cheap motel located on the George Parks Highway.

Two state trooper vehicles were already there.

Duke stayed with Gibson as the officer strode toward the crime scene tape stretched across the front of the building.

Another officer recognized him and nodded. "Officer Gibson. Didn't know you were working out this way."

"I'm not officially. Just happened to be nearby. This is my friend Duke, by the way. Duke, Officer Sonata." Gibson paused and glanced at the motel. "What's going on?"

"Apparently, the cleaning lady went into room 209." Officer Sonata nodded to the second floor. "She found a dead man inside. Goes by the name Skeeter. I ran a background check on him, and up until a week ago, he was in jail awaiting a trial. Got out on a forty-thousand-dollar bond."

Gibson's eyebrows shot up. "That's a lot of money."

"Yes, it is."

"Cause of death?"

"Gunshot wound to the chest."

Duke's thoughts raced as he listened to the conversation. Would Andi really shoot someone? Only if her life or the life of someone she cared about was threatened.

Skeeter must have found her. It was the only thing that made sense.

Duke didn't want to imagine what the man might have tried to do to her. The thought caused a visceral reaction, and testosterone pumped through his blood.

"What else can you tell me?" Gibson asked. "Any idea who did this?"

Officer Sonata glanced at the notepad in his hands. "The woman who checked into the room used an alias. I tried to run her name through the system, but she's not there. Paid cash."

Gibson glanced around. "What about cameras? Did they pick up on anything?"

"The ones outside the building aren't working. But there was one in the office when she checked in. We can't tell much about her by looking at the video. She was wearing a baseball cap, plus she had on a coat. We're estimating she was maybe five foot two at the most. That's about all we have at this point."

Gibson grunted. "Anything else?"

"A witness saw a car leaving the motel about fifteen minutes before the body was discovered," Sonata said. "It was a 1980s burgundy El Camino."

An El Camino? Was that what Andi was driving?

Duke couldn't even picture Andi behind the wheel of one of those. It wasn't her style. She usually liked trucks—*real* trucks, not car/truck hybrids. Plus, a car/truck like that would have garnered attention.

He tried to make sense of the details but couldn't.

Gibson's gaze slid to Duke, a questioning look in his eyes, before he looked back at Sonata. "That's it?"

"Other than that, we know our victim was a truck driver up on the Dalton Highway. Sometimes those guys will do runs down this way in the off-season. We think maybe our victim stopped here for a rest, and then . . . well, that's what we're trying to figure out." Officer Sonata shrugged.

Duke continued to listen. Had it been a coincidence that Skeeter showed up here? Duke couldn't think of any reason Andi would have asked the creep to come.

Unless Skeeter had somehow followed Andi.

Now he was dead.

Andi was on the run.

And in danger. In even *more* danger than she had been before.

What if Skeeter had gotten out of jail and gone after Andi? If he'd forced her to come to this motel and then . . .

Duke's throat tightened with enough intensity that he could hardly breathe.

His phone rang, pulling him from his thoughts.

He paced away from the police line and put the device to his ear. "Ranger. What's going on?"

"Any updates on your end?" Ranger asked.

Duke stared at the motel, contemplating what to say. "A couple of things. A dead man has been found in the motel where Andi was staying. I'm afraid his death will be blamed on her."

"What?" Ranger's voice rose with shock.

"We're still gathering all the details. I'll share more as soon as I know more." Duke didn't feel like getting into everything right then. "Any reason why you're calling?"

"As a matter of fact, yes. Alfonso called Mariella. He said the police just contacted him and said his vehicle may have been used in a crime."

Alfonso owned the Grayling Lodge, a quirky motel where the gang often stayed when they got together. The man was just as eccentric as his lodge, and he was generous to a fault—not to mention obsessed with their podcast.

Duke tried to figure out why Ranger was telling him this, especially considering everything else going on. "Okay . . . what does this have to do with anything?"

"Alfonso told the cops the car had been stolen. The truth is, Andi called Alfonso this morning and asked him to pick her up at the airport in a car she could borrow. He agreed, and Andi swore him to secrecy. The only reason Alfonso let us know is because he's concerned about her. Of course, he hasn't told the police any of this."

Realization filled Duke. So *that* was how Andi had left the airport.

Alfonso was willing to help them out when he could, so it didn't surprise him that the man had loaned Andi a car.

Another puzzle piece snapped in place.

Duke turned his attention back to the phone conversation with Ranger. "Tell Alfonso thank you. We're doing our best to help Andi right now. If he could stay quiet about this for a little longer . . ."

"I'll let him know," Ranger said. "You tell us what you need, and we're there for you."

"I know and thank you." Duke looked back at the motel with the crime scene tape stretched around. He remembered Andi had been here. Remembered Skeeter's dead body. "Right now, things aren't looking good. We need a lot of prayers."

That felt like the understatement of the year.

ELEVEN

ANDI OPENED the driver's side door and leaned into the car.

Quickly, she stuffed everything into her backpack and pulled it on her shoulders. Then she slowly—quietly—shut the car door, careful not to draw any attention to herself.

She glanced around again. There was no way she could flee using the road that twisted through the campground. She'd be too obvious, like a deer in a field during hunting season.

She would have to run toward the woods.

Acres and acres of the highest mountains in the United States surrounded her. Snow still covered many of them, despite the fact that summer had just ended.

Not only that, but the ground was soft and muddy. She'd need to be especially careful not to leave tracks.

But she couldn't stay at this site. Her best bet was to hide until Lockjaw left.

Wasting no more time, she rushed between the trees. She had to run far enough away to find cover. But she needed to stay close enough to see what was going on—and to not get lost.

Just as she ducked behind a tree, she saw the truck stop by the El Camino.

Dread pooled in her stomach.

Lockjaw and a man Andi had never seen before climbed out. The new guy was younger than Lockjaw but equally scary. His head was shaved, and he wore a flannel shirt with the sleeves ripped off, dirty jeans, and thick boots.

The truck's engine still hummed as they checked out the El Camino.

Lockjaw must have somehow heard Andi was driving that car. Now these men were trying to track her down. Maybe Skeeter had told them. Maybe Skeeter was with them, for that matter.

Fear shimmied through her.

Andi remained where she was, desperate not to make a sound. Thankfully, her backpack was a boring beige that mostly blended in with nature.

Lockjaw pulled out a gun as he crept closer to the El Camino. He circled the car, looking through each of the windows.

Then he paused, cocked his head, and scowled. "She's not here."

"Then where is she?" the other man asked.

"Good question." Lockjaw looked up before calling out, "Frostbite . . . I know you're out there."

Frostbite had been Andi's handle when she was a truck driver.

Hearing the man say it now caused acid to bubble in her stomach.

If Lockjaw had found her inside that car, he would have shot her on the spot.

If he found her out here, he would still shoot.

The men circled the vehicle, studying it.

Lockjaw tried the door handles, but Andi had locked them both.

The other man placed a hand on the hood of the El Camino. "It's already cold. She's been here a while. What do you want to do?"

Lockjaw growled as he surveyed the woods around him. Then he crossed his arms, planting himself by the car. Danger seemed to surround the man.

"We're going to wait for her to come back," he announced. "She can't be that far away. Skeeter's body hasn't even grown cold."

Grown cold? Did that mean Skeeter was . . . dead?

Andi's heart thumped harder as shock washed over her.

She couldn't have heard Lockjaw right.

Skeeter had been alive when she left.

Had the man hit his head hard enough to kill him?

Probably not.

But, if not a head injury, then who would have killed Skeeter? And why?

Were the cops now after Andi for his death?

This day had just gone from bad to worse.

Now she was stuck in the woods. Alone. No one knew where she was. She doubted her burner phone worked. She wasn't sure if Duke had followed the clues she'd left for him. Even if he had, those clues wouldn't lead to this campground.

How would she get out of this situation?

She glanced around. The sun was beginning to set. As soon as it disappeared behind that mountain, the temperature would drop another ten or fifteen degrees.

If she had thought ahead, she would have brought a heavier coat. Maybe some water and food. A blanket.

But all she had were some semi-incriminating documents against Victor Goodman. They wouldn't do her much good in a physical struggle.

As Lockjaw stepped toward the woods, Andi closed her eyes and prayed for wisdom.

———

Duke climbed back into Gibson's Suburban after his friend had wrapped up his conversation with the officers.

"Thanks for letting me come with you," Duke murmured.

He knew his friend was going above and beyond.

"Of course." Gibson cranked the engine, turning his police radio down. He'd brought it with him, just like many cops did even when off-duty. "If my colleagues figure out Andi could be behind this, the police will search for her. It's going to look bad, especially considering she used an alias, paid in cash, and fled the scene of the crime."

Duke's jaw hardened, even though he couldn't deny the words. This situation *did* look bad. Really bad.

"The only reason Andi would have shot Skeeter was in self-defense." Nothing anyone said would change Duke's mind on that. He knew Andi. Knew what kind of person she was.

"I believe you," Gibson said. "The trick is getting everyone else to believe you."

Duke ran a hand over his jaw.

He wanted to believe this would all have a happy ending. To believe Andi would be found safe—and cleared. That Victor would be brought down. That life could resume normally and peacefully.

That he and Andi could continue to explore what their future together might look like.

Unfortunately, Duke had never been much of an optimist. He knew a struggle waited ahead and that things might not turn out the way he wanted.

He lifted a prayer anyway.

"Where to next?" Gibson's voice pulled Duke from his prayer.

He whispered a silent amen before turning toward Gibson. "I figured you'd take me back to Fairbanks."

"I'm in this now. I need to know Andi is okay." His words sounded firm and unwavering.

Duke wanted to feel gratitude at his friend's statement, but he couldn't. Not yet.

He had more questions first.

He studied Gibson's face. "Are you in this as a cop who wants to arrest her? Or are you in this as a friend?"

Gibson's gaze remained clear without a hint of guilt. "A little bit of both. I don't plan on arresting her, but I *would* like to talk to her and hear what happened. Plus, I'm worried."

Duke tilted his head. He didn't know if that was good enough.

He knew that Gibson, as a sworn officer of the law, was obligated to tell the truth. If he didn't . . . he could lose his job. His reputation. Maybe even go to prison.

Gibson seemed to read his expression. "Look, I'll do whatever I can to protect Andi. But right now, you and I both know she needs help. I think you can admit you'll be better off if I was with you than if I wasn't."

Duke couldn't argue. Doing this alone would have its challenges. Plus, they had no time to waste—and going back to Fairbanks would be wasting time.

"You're right," Duke finally said. "You haven't let me down yet."

Gibson nodded as if satisfied with that response. "So where do we go now?"

Duke tried to think. Where would Andi go from here?

"She wouldn't head back to Fairbanks. It's too risky." He pointed down the road. "She would keep going south."

Gibson jerked the wheel to the left. "Then that's where we'll go too."

HECTOR OFTEN HUNG out with one of his classmates, a guy named Tito Sanchez. He hung out with him even more when Tito got his driver's license. He personally found the guy to be annoying, but at least he could drive.

And he had a nice-looking sister. Hector would put up with dumb-as-a-brick Tito if it meant getting to talk to Donna.

There wasn't much to do in this area. It was mostly red dirt and desert. There were two restaurants, neither very good. No movie theaters. No lakes to swim in.

Some people called this town godforsaken.

They had to get creative in order to entertain themselves.

"Where you want to go?" Tito tapped his fingers on the steering wheel of his sky-blue Falcon. His friend practically worshipped this car.

Hector's mind raced through the possibilities. Maybe he could go visit Donna. But he knew she was working at the local laundromat.

She kept telling him she wasn't interested in dating, but Hector didn't believe her. She was just playing hard to get.

So what could they do out here in the middle of nowhere?

"You want to see my old place?" Hector finally asked.

Tito raised his eyebrows. "You have an old place?"

Hector didn't like to talk about his past too much. Instead, he'd let his studies consume him. He'd begun to play football at the high school. He'd even talked about interning at a place in San Angeles next summer.

"That's right." Hector's mind drifted back in time. "It was a great little house . . . until my mom sold it." His voice hardened at his last statement.

"Let's go see it." Tito pressed the accelerator harder. "I want to hear more about my pal Hector's former life."

Seeing the house would confirm what he already knew—that his mama had been taken advantage of. As a result, the course of his life had been altered for the worst.

They headed out of town, signs of life becoming more sparse as they did.

Finally, twenty minutes later, Tito pulled to a stop beside a new metal fence that was starkly out of place in the barren desert.

Still in the car, Hector pointed to an empty area in an empty field beyond it. "My house was right there."

Tito glanced at him in confusion. "Your house was on the oil fields?"

"We didn't know it was an oil field at the time. In order for rich men to become richer and build their empire, as well as access the pumps for the oil drilling, they needed the infrastructure to reach their equipment. That's when C.W. Wells stole this land from us."

Tito grunted. "They couldn't force you to give it up, right?"

"They made a very compelling offer, and my mother, under the influence of her then boyfriend, agreed to it."

Robert was now long gone, taking any of the money Hector's mother had made from the sale of the home.

They'd been poor before. However, Robert leaving with everything they owned only compounded their problems—and only made his mother drink more, as well as make other questionable choices.

Since selling their home, he and his mother had moved at least once every year. They'd stayed in the same basic area, just with new housing.

Sometimes Mama found a job as a live-in house-keeper. In those cases, Hector would sleep on the floor. Once she hadn't even told the homeowner she had a son. Hector had been forced to sneak into the house at night and leave early in the morning so the homeowners wouldn't know. When the homeowner found out, Mama lost that job.

They had also lived with some of his mother's friends. They'd spent some time in a homeless shelter. They'd lived with other boyfriends.

His dad would never have approved.

Mama said Dad was in prison for killing a man. But she was full of lies. Dad would never kill someone.

Now that Hector was old enough, he'd done his research. He knew his mom should have gotten more money than she had for that property. C.W. Wells had exploited her.

The cutthroat businessman had known Mama wouldn't know better. He was a predator who'd preyed on the weak and vulnerable, all so he could profit off their losses.

Fire shot through Hector's veins at the thought.

Tito looked away from the oil fields and back at Hector. "Cool story, bro. Where do you want to go now?"

Hector thought about the sprawling estate where C.W. Wells lived. No one person needed that much house. Of course, C.W. Wells would have known that. It was more of a trophy to him.

Hector had gone past the house many, many times.

He liked to visualize what he'd say to the man if they ever met face-to-face. All kinds of scenarios had run through his mind. Scenarios where Hector was nice. Scenarios where he was mean.

Scenarios where he taught the man a lesson for what he'd done—and what he was continuing to do.

Hector had talked to others. He knew he and his mother weren't the only ones the man had taken advantage of. Johnny and his family had been used also.

They'd moved into another house that had burned to the ground. The whole family had died.

That wouldn't have happened if greedy people hadn't cheated Johnny's family out of their home.

His jaw hardened. "There *is* something else I'd like to see."

He rattled off directions to C.W. Wells's house.

One day, Hector would work up the nerve to walk up to the door and confront the man.

In fact, maybe today would be that day.

A grin spread across his lips at the thought.

AN HOUR LATER, a sign on the side of the road caught Duke's eye. "Turn there."

Gibson eased off the highway toward a local campground.

"Do you think Andi is the type to hide out in the woods?" Gibson glanced at him before looking back at the narrow road.

Duke pressed his lips together in thought. "I think in this situation, it's a possibility. She'll know the police are looking for her. She won't want to stop at another motel tonight. This place is worth checking out while we're out this way. It's better than backtracking later."

They continued down the gravel road, aspen and birch trees stretching to the sky on either side of them. Mountains loomed above them and parts of the road had drop-offs on either side.

This was Alaska at its finest—beautiful, wild, and untamed.

In the summer, this was a popular area for tourists. But as the weather got colder, mostly adventure seekers frequented these areas until finally the campgrounds closed for the season in October.

Duke had always told himself he wanted to explore more of this area. But when Celeste had disappeared, he'd dedicated his life to finding her.

Finally, six weeks ago, he had.

Now he had the closure he needed.

As he'd put that part of his life behind him, he hoped to make some changes.

A lot of those changes involved Andi. He'd enjoyed finally being free to date her.

He couldn't let anything happen to her now.

They had too many plans and memories to make together.

A few miles down the road, Duke saw another sign for the campground. They turned toward it, pulling near the gate. Gibson paid for a site for the night—even though they didn't plan on staying.

Gibson and Duke had discussed explaining what was going on to the woman at the gate. Telling her Gibson was a cop. Showing her Andi's picture.

But they didn't want to bring any more attention to Andi than necessary—just in case.

Once through the gate, they slowly drove through

the campground, keeping their eyes open for the El Camino.

Instead, Duke spotted another vehicle that caught his eye. An oversized truck had pulled to the side of the lane. The way it had been parked seemed haphazard, like it had been left there in a hurry.

"You thinking what I'm thinking?" Gibson glanced at the truck then at Duke.

"Let's check it out."

They found an empty campsite near the truck and stowed Gibson's SUV there. Then they used a patch of woods for cover as they inched closer to the vehicle.

As they reached the edge of the woods, Duke studied the Ford F-350.

There was nothing remarkable about it—other than the antlers on the front grille. He may not have even noticed the truck if not for the way it was parked.

He peered at the campsite near the truck.

His breath caught. A 1980's Chevy El Camino was parked in the shadows.

How many vehicles like that could there be out here? Especially in Alaska.

That was Alfonso's. It had to be.

That meant Andi was here.

Or she *had* been here.

Trepidation immediately replaced any hope Duke had begun to feel.

Two men stalked near the edge of the woods. They looked rough with their big builds and sneering expressions. One had tattoos slithering up his neck and onto his face. The other kept fisting and unfisting his hands as if he wanted to punch someone.

Duke didn't know who the men were, but it was clear they were looking for Andi.

He had to find her before they did.

———

Andi ventured farther into the woods—which was the last thing she wanted.

But fifteen minutes had passed, and those men were *still* tracking her.

The air had turned colder. Despite her light jacket and jeans, she found it hard to stay warm. Her body wouldn't stop shivering.

How long could she keep this up?

Based on the vengeance she'd seen in Lockjaw's eyes, he was willing to stay all night if that was what it took to find her.

Andi couldn't hike too far up the mountain because the trees and vegetation became too thin and sparse at the higher altitude. Instead, she tried to stay in the gorge. The ground was wet from the snow melt earlier in the season, however. A wet ground meant more chances to leave footprints.

She'd do the best she could with what she had right now.

She paused behind a tree to gather her bearings.

When she'd fled, Andi had headed east, closer to the highway. She figured her odds were better near the road. If worse came to worse, maybe she could flag someone down.

She really hoped it didn't come down to that.

Taking a deep breath, she began walking again.

All her senses remained on high alert.

At first, she heard nothing.

She wanted to feel relief at the near silence, but she couldn't. Not with so much on the line.

In some ways, not hearing anything was even more unnerving. She had no idea where the men were.

She continued to listen, taking a moment to catch her breath.

Voices drifted her way.

One was Lockjaw's. She was certain of it.

If she moved now, she'd only make her presence more obvious. Her best bet was to find a place to hide and to lie low until the men passed.

She glanced around. Mostly, there were trees.

Then she spotted a huge beaver dam by the stream flowing through the gorge. It was big enough that she might be able to hide on the other side. The gurgle of the stream might conceal any noises she made.

She stayed low, praying Lockjaw and the other man wouldn't see her as she darted toward it.

If those guys killed her out here, the chances were good that no one would ever find her body.

She couldn't do that to Duke.

She'd seen him struggle while searching for his missing fiancée. It had been torture.

If Andi also just disappeared . . . he would be devastated.

Which was just one more reason why Andi had to figure out how to stay alive.

AS THE MEN disappeared into the trees, Gibson took off after them, taking the most direct route so he wouldn't lose them.

While he kept an eye on the men, Duke searched the ground for Andi's footprints. He felt certain she'd come this way. He just needed to track her.

Ten minutes later, he found what he was looking for.

A footprint that matched Andi's approximate size. And it was fresh.

Duke began tracking her through the forest. The prints traveled slightly up the mountain and then down again, headed toward the highway.

Based on the distance apart of each step, Andi wasn't running but walking, which probably meant she was keeping a cool head about this situation.

That made Duke feel a little better.

However, those men had also headed this direction.

He needed to catch up to them, circle around, and then get ahead of them.

Thankfully, Gibson had come along, but there was no cell phone service out here, so communicating with his friend would be a challenge.

For the next twenty minutes, Duke continued following the tracks as they laced their way between the trees.

But there was still no sign of Andi.

How far had she gone? Had the men found her? Was he getting close?

Movement up ahead caught his eye, and he paused, ducking behind a cluster of trees.

He shifted to get a better look, which confirmed his theory.

He had caught up with the men.

They'd stopped beside a small stream and studied something in the mud nearby.

Duke's heart pounded in his ears as he watched.

Had they found Andi? Or had she simply passed by the area and kept going?

He couldn't understand what the men said to each other as they stood there.

As they started to head in a different direction, something stopped them.

They paused and turned toward a beaver dam in the small stream that trickled through the landscape.

Duke shifted around the tree for a better view.

A beige backpack peeked out from behind the dam.

His breath caught.

That was Andi's, wasn't it?

Somehow, those guys had spotted her backpack. In turn, they'd found Andi.

Adrenaline pumped through him as he sorted out his options.

Duke glanced around. Where was Gibson?

He should be close. After all, he'd been following these men. But Duke didn't see him.

He prayed nothing had happened to his friend.

Duke might have to take these guys down on his own.

His gaze turned back to the two men in the distance—men who were entirely too close to Andi.

Did she even realize she'd been discovered? Did Andi know they were this close? Could she hear them over the sound of the trickling water?

He didn't know.

Duke braced himself to act.

———

Andi sucked in a breath.

As she'd crouched behind the dam, her bag had caught on a stick.

The movement had sent several pieces of wood tumbling into the water.

The men had paused from their conversation. Even

though Andi couldn't see them, she felt their eyes on her.

They were coming her way. She was certain of it.

If she didn't get out of there, she was as good as dead.

She sprang from her hiding space and took off in a run.

"Hey!" Lockjaw shouted.

She didn't slow down. Those guys might be bigger than her, but she should be faster.

She scrambled up the embankment, desperation seizing her.

She had to gain more space.

Her foot hit mud, and a cry escaped from her lips.

She began sliding down the slope, losing valuable time.

No!

She grabbed a rock and pulled herself upright. Then she climbed up the small slope along the stream.

Her misstep gave Lockjaw time to grab her arm. She nearly flew off her feet as he swirled her around. Then just as suddenly, he released her, and she fell back onto the rocky ground.

Pain shot through her shoulder.

The discomfort fled her mind when she saw Lockjaw leering over her.

"You killed my son!" His nostrils flared as rage filled his eyes. "I *knew* you were trouble. I should have never hired you!"

Andi turned, trying to dash away.

Before she could, Lockjaw grabbed her injured shoulder.

More pain ripped through her.

He flipped her over and raised his fist.

She closed her eyes and tried to shield her face. At any minute, she would feel the pain of having her face smashed in.

Instead, Lockjaw flew off her and grunted.

Andi didn't have time to figure out what had just happened.

Instead, she turned, and on all fours, she crawled as fast as she could up the embankment.

Only when she reached flat ground did she turn back.

Lockjaw and another man wrestled on the ground.

What . . . ?

The man's face came into view.

She sucked in a breath before whispering, "Duke?"

Was she seeing things?

She had to be.

How had he found her?

She didn't have time to figure it out. Those details weren't important. She only cared that he was here.

She wanted to help. To do something to ensure Duke wasn't hurt.

Before she could act, the man who'd been with Lockjaw stepped from the woods and charged straight toward her.

She scrambled back even farther. The slippery mud made it nearly impossible to find traction.

"You ain't getting away with taking Skeeter out." The man sneered at her, hatred filling his face. "We look out for our own."

As he reached for her, Andi kicked her leg. Her foot hit the man in the nose, and blood began pouring down his face.

He let out a few choice words as vengeance dripped from his gaze.

She spared a glance at Duke just as Lockjaw slammed his fist down. Duke turned before the man's hand collided with his face.

Andi wasn't sure she and Duke would get out of this situation alive.

Then gunfire split the air.

Everyone froze.

"Police!"

The police?

Andi should be relieved backup was here. Instead, panic raced through her.

Were the cops coming for her? Or for Lockjaw?

Lockjaw and the other man glanced at each other.

Then, without a word, they turned and scampered away.

DUKE ROSE and rushed across the slippery landscape toward Andi. The mud made every step twice as hard. But he didn't let that slow him down.

He had to get to her.

Finally, he reached her and fell to his knees. He cupped her face, needing to make sure his eyes weren't tricking him.

This was really Andi. She was really here. She was really okay.

"Am I glad to see you . . ." he murmured, his shoulders softening with relief.

"You found me . . ." Her voice cracked as she said the words.

They threw their arms around each other.

If Duke had the choice, he would never let Andi go. But this wasn't the time for a never-ending hug.

He pulled away just enough to study her face.

His smile turned into a frown when he saw the cuts and bruises there.

"Who did this to you?" His voice hardened as he asked the question. "Was it all Lockjaw?"

"It's a long story." Andi sounded throaty and emotion clouded her gaze.

Duke's mood darkened as scenarios ran through his mind, scenarios where he sought vengeance ten-fold in return for what had been done to the woman he loved.

Then he swallowed hard, thinking better of his reaction.

There were better ways to seek justice.

Instead, he helped her to her feet. "Let's get you out of here. You can tell me more about it later."

She flinched as she rose. Her body clearly hurt, but she was trying to hide it in typical Andi style.

Duke held onto her arm, making sure she was steady on her feet.

As he looked across the stream, someone else emerged from the woods.

He tensed—but only for a moment.

Gibson.

The officer rushed toward them, his gaze stopping on Andi. His eyes widened as he soaked her in. "Andi . . . what happened to you?"

"Long story." Her attempted smile quickly turned into a frown.

Familiar rage stirred inside Duke again, but he held it at bay.

Gibson's expression hardened as he turned back to Duke. "I was following those guys, but a moose stopped me in my tracks. I couldn't get past him, so I had to go around the long way."

Duke looked in the opposite direction. "They took off that way."

"We can't afford to go after them now." The lines around Gibson's eyes tightened. "We need to get you out of here before it gets dark."

"Did you tell your colleagues I was here?" Andi sounded high-strung as the question rushed from her lips.

Gibson's expression softened as he shook his head. "No, I thought it was better not to—at least until I figured out what was going on. Do you think you can make it back to my SUV? We can't take the El Camino. There's a BOLO out for it."

"I can make it back." Andi paused. "Does that mean you're coming with us?"

"I'm not staying here." Gibson shrugged nonchalantly.

"But won't you get in trouble?" Andi narrowed her eyes, concern in her voice.

"Let me worry about that," Gibson told her. "You just worry about getting yourself out of this situation."

———

There was no time to talk as Andi and Duke hurried through the woods toward Gibson's Suburban.

Andi's thoughts raced with every step. She was so thankful Duke had found her, and that she was mostly okay.

But they couldn't afford to let down their guard. There was more going on than met the eye.

When they reached the SUV, Duke ushered her into the back seat and then climbed in beside her.

She stayed low and out of sight as they left the campground.

She was grateful no one had asked too many questions yet. She was exhausted.

But she knew those questions were coming.

When they reached the highway, Gibson asked, "Which direction? Anchorage or Fairbanks?"

Andi considered it before nodding to the north. "Back to Fairbanks."

Gibson turned in that direction.

When they were finally on the highway, Duke pulled away from their side embrace enough to ask, "Why did you run? Why set up that farce at the airport?"

She winced at his inquiry. In some ways, that felt like a million years ago. "I need people to think I left Alaska."

"I saw the video of you at the airport," Duke said. "Everyone *should* think you left. But why?"

She rubbed her throat, her voice raw as she said,

"Victor was waiting for me in my apartment when I got home from the airport. Told me if I didn't stay away that people on my team would die one by one."

"You need to press charges." Gibson's voice hardened.

"Why bother? Nothing will happen." Andi crossed her arms but cringed. Every movement hurt. She dropped her arms to her sides instead.

"Not necessarily," Gibson said.

"People like Victor *always* get off. The evidence I have right now will be dismissed or Victor will claim someone else is guilty and he knew nothing. I need something solid and irrefutable."

"Or maybe there *will* be enough evidence collected to charge him soon," Gibson said.

Her breath caught as his words swirled around in her mind. She'd missed something. But what?

She swerved her gaze toward Duke. "What does that mean?"

"With everything that happened with Glassine, maybe Victor will be scrutinized a little more deeply." A wrinkle formed between Duke's eyes as if he was confused about her reaction.

Everything froze around Andi as she tried to comprehend his words. "What happened to Glassine?"

Duke did a double-take as realization washed over his features. "You didn't hear?"

"Hear what?"

"The plane Glassine chartered to return to Anchorage . . . it disappeared," Duke told her. "People think the plane crashed, and it all happened the day before the vote was supposed to be cast."

DUKE TIGHTENED his arm around Andi. She was quiet, no doubt mulling over the implications of Senator Glassine disappearing—as well as other things.

He wanted to ask more questions, and he would. Later.

She needed to recover more first.

He wished he never had to let Andi go.

The situation back in those woods . . . it could have ended badly.

If he hadn't gotten there when he did . . . well, he didn't even want to think about what Lockjaw might have done to her.

Though they had one victory, none of them were in a position to relax or let down their guard. They still had to figure out their next move. The problems they faced felt insurmountable.

"I know where we can go," Gibson said as if reading

Duke's mind. "A place where we can lie low for a while."

Duke's throat tightened. He knew what a precarious position Gibson was in, and he hated to put his friend in this spot—a spot that could potentially cost him his career.

As an officer of the law, it was his duty to follow orders. Instead, Gibson had a soon-to-be fugitive with him, and he was helping her evade law enforcement.

Duke stole a glance at his friend again. "Are you sure you want to do this?"

He knew he'd already asked that question, but it couldn't hurt to ask again.

Gibson's gaze remained fixed on the road. "I'm positive. I'm taking you both to a cabin about fifteen minutes outside of Fairbanks. No one should trace you there."

"Your cabin?" Duke asked, thinking through the implications. There was still a lot he didn't know about his friend, mostly personal details.

"No, the place belongs to an old friend who said I could use it whenever I wanted. I know the code to get in. We can stay there until we see how everything blows over."

If it blows over. But Duke didn't speak those words aloud. Even if his statement was true, there was no need to express the sentiment and remind everyone of the grim possibilities.

His thoughts continued to spiral as he tried to come up with some type of plan to protect Andi.

But there was still so much he didn't know.

He glanced at Andi beside him, and he didn't like the expression on her face. The hollowness. The exhaustion. The turmoil.

The two of them had been through a lot together. More than once, they'd been on the run for their lives. They'd been hurt. Threatened. Tested beyond belief.

But for some reason, this situation felt different.

It felt even more deadly.

Duke kept his eyes on the road behind them as Gibson drove, needing to be certain they weren't being followed.

They weren't.

Would Lockjaw tell the police that the woman he'd suspected of killing his son had been at the campground? Lockjaw would probably share Andi's name with the cops, which would then mean the police could label her as a person of interest and put out an arrest warrant for her. Eventually, the cops would find the car she'd driven. They would put two and two together.

The good news was that he didn't think Lockjaw had seen Gibson's face back in the woods.

They continued to drive farther and farther off the highway. It was hilly in this area with evergreens on either side of them. A stream played chase with the road, weaving in and out only to disappear then reappear again. At one break in the trees, a moose could be seen standing in a small field.

The sun had sunk low, but dusk still lingered casting grays and pinks around them. Complete darkness would fall at any moment.

Finally, they pulled up to a small log cabin in the middle of the forest.

"This is it." Gibson put his SUV into Park and stared at the building. "It's nothing fancy, but we should be comfortable here until we figure out a plan."

Duke's gaze traveled to Andi again. He needed to concentrate on her right now.

She'd just been through a nightmare . . . and there were no guarantees there wouldn't be a return trip.

———

Andi cleaned herself up in the bathroom at the cabin.

There was no hot water, but she'd found a washcloth and had wiped most of the mud off. Thankfully, she had some clothes in her backpack. The leggings and blue sweatshirt felt comforting right now. And they were clean.

She emerged from the bathroom, trying to appear normal and to conceal her injuries—both physical and emotional. The efforts felt futile, however. Her hands still shook from everything that had happened. Her body ached. Her mind wouldn't settle.

She glanced around the cabin and saw Gibson in the

small kitchen, preparing something in the microwave, which added a hum to the otherwise quiet solace of the place.

Duke waited for her at the kitchen table, a first-aid kit in front of him. As soon as he saw her, he pointed to the wooden chair he'd pulled out. She lowered herself onto the ladderback, knowing better than to argue.

She had several cuts that needed to be tended. One might even need stitches.

She didn't want to deal with any of that, but Duke wouldn't give her a choice.

It was better if Duke took charge a moment. She wasn't thinking clearly.

He gave her some Tylenol, along with a small cup of water.

After she'd swallowed, he doused a cotton pad with some antiseptic and dabbed the cut near her hairline on her forehead.

She tried not to flinch as the solution hit her wound.

"Someone did a number on you." His gaze narrowed as he studied her injuries.

It was more than that though. Anger simmered in his voice.

If he ever got his hands on the person who did this to her . . . it wouldn't end well. She appreciated his protectiveness, but she didn't want it to get him in trouble.

"It was actually a few people." After she said the

words, she realized she should have kept her mouth shut. The statement only added to Duke's fury.

"Who?" The word had come out of Duke's mouth as more of a demand than a question.

Andi sighed before running through how Victor and his crony had been in her apartment. Had threatened her and her friends. Had knocked her out cold.

Then she told him how she'd fled, first to the airport, then to the motel, where Skeeter had later shown up. She told him how Skeeter had tried to attack her. Then how she'd knocked him out and tied him up.

She ended with her encounter with Lockjaw at the campground.

Andi was used to fighting her battles in the courtroom, not with her fists.

She wished she was like those action heroes in the movies who could bounce right back after being beaten. But her body dictated otherwise.

"Andi . . . Skeeter was shot," Duke told her. "They found his body in a motel room."

Her eyes widened. "Shot? What? When I left him, he was alive. He came after me and hit his head against the wall. The impact knocked him out. But I didn't shoot him!"

"Someone must have come in after you then."

She shuddered at the thought. "But I'm the one who looks guilty."

"We'll get it sorted out." He squeezed her knee.

She tried to find reassurance in his words, but she knew how this looked.

Duke gently ran a finger along her jaw as he sat in front of her, his knee between her legs as he scooted closer to address her injuries. "That's a pretty bad bruise. Can you open and shut your mouth?"

Andi slowly moved her jaw back and forth. The motion didn't feel great, but it wasn't excruciating either. "I think it will be okay."

"None of this is okay." Duke's gaze darkened as he looked at her forehead again.

Gibson set two containers of microwaved ravioli on the table beside them, plastic spoons already shoved into the bowls. "It's the best I can do for now. Sorry."

"I appreciate it," Andi said softly. "Chef Boyardee was a staple for me in college."

She wasn't hungry, but she knew she should eat. She needed to keep her energy up. This battle wasn't over. It was far from it.

Gibson sat at the table behind them and began eating his own meal.

"Anything else I need to see or clean up?" Duke's gaze locked with hers, their dinner on hold until after this first-aid session ended.

"I don't think so." She didn't bother to tell him about the pain in her ribs.

She halfway feared he might insist she go to the hospital. She couldn't do that. But every time she took a breath, pain gripped her midsection and made her lungs ache.

She stared at Duke. Stared at the barely there beard on his cheeks and upper lip. At his determined gaze. His broad shoulders and strong arms.

She soaked in his surprisingly gentle touch. Basked in his attentiveness.

She was so thankful to have him in her life.

But everything had a flipside. Trouble was following her, and now the very people who cared about her were in danger.

Which made her wonder if being alone was the better choice.

Gibson's phone buzzed, and he set his fork down.

As he glanced at the screen, his face went pale.

Andi braced herself, certain he'd gotten bad news.

"Gibson?" Duke was clearly on the same wavelength as Andi.

"This is what I was afraid of." Gibson showed them his phone screen. "An arrest warrant was just put out for you, Andi. You're a person of interest in the murder of Billy Pitts."

AS DUKE HAD DOWNED his food, he watched Andi pick at hers.

He didn't force the issue. She'd been through a lot, and at least she was trying.

After he finished, he paced the living room of the cabin.

"Between the grainy security footage at the motel and whatever Lockjaw might have told the police, the cops must have figured out Andi had been in that motel room," Duke muttered.

"That's most likely how they put everything together." Gibson stood against the kitchen counter with his arms crossed.

"If her image is posted around the area, Victor will know Andi hasn't left the state." Duke rubbed a hand over his jaw, realizing he'd been gritting his teeth.

Andi pressed her eyes closed and lowered her head.

Duke hated to say the thought aloud, but someone had to. Sugarcoating the truth wouldn't do any of them any good right now.

Duke's gaze snapped to Gibson. "Are you going to report us?"

"No. Doing so would only put Andi's life in more danger. Besides, we need answers."

"Thank you, Gibson. I appreciate that." Andi shifted in her seat, flinching as she did. "In the meantime, we need to get burner phones to the rest of the team."

She was clearly in more pain than she wanted to let on. Hopefully, the medicine would kick in soon.

Duke let her maintain a measure of pride.

For now.

"Why burners?" He turned his attention back to her statement.

"It's the only way that we're going to be able to communicate securely, and I'm going to need the team's help if I have any chance of getting through this unscathed." Andi swallowed hard at the words.

"I'll go get them." Gibson said as he began to clear the table.

Duke turned toward him in surprise. "You will?"

"I make the most sense. If Victor has guys out there looking for Andi, then he's going to be watching for you too, Duke. We can't make it obvious the team is communicating with each other."

Gibson grabbed their food containers and spoons and placed them in the trash as he talked.

"But again, you're putting yourself in a bad position." Duke didn't want to beat a dead horse, but he knew what was on the line.

Besides, Duke *was* the one who'd called Gibson earlier.

If his friend lost his career over this, Duke needed to know his conscience was clear, that he hadn't pressured Gibson into doing any of this.

"Delivering burner phones shouldn't get me in trouble." Gibson dried his hands. "Besides, today is my day off, and buying burner phones isn't illegal."

Duke's gut tightened anyway. "You sure you don't mind?"

"I'm sure." He glanced at the time on his watch. "But I'm going to need to do that now before stores start to close. Leaving here means I'm leaving you guys without a vehicle. Are you okay with that?"

"We should be fine," Duke told him.

"I'll get some gas while I'm out." He pulled his keys from his pocket. "Then I'll pick up some phones and deliver them. I'll make sure everyone has each other's new, temporary number. That way you guys will be able to talk without anyone knowing. And I'm not only talking about the police. If Victor has all the connections you think he does, he could very well have people monitoring any phone messages or emails you guys are getting."

Duke couldn't argue. Victor was resourceful, and he had enough money to get whatever he wanted. No doubt he could hire people to trace the team's phones and communications.

They had to plan each of their steps very carefully.

A few moments later, Gibson left, leaving Duke and Andi at the cabin alone. As soon as he was gone, Duke turned to her.

She rose from her chair and stepped closer.

The next instant, Andi fell into his arms. She nestled her head into his chest, and Duke wrapped his arms around her tiny waist.

He couldn't be sure, but he thought she might be crying.

Andi hardly ever cried.

But it was healthy to get her emotions out, and Duke was honored she felt safe enough around him to do so. Even the mighty and fearless had breaking points.

He continued holding her, leaning down to plant small kisses on top of her head or to stroke her hair on occasion. As he felt a bump on her head, his gut tightened again.

One of Victor's men had done that.

Rage built inside him. However, he needed to hold that emotion at bay.

Later, all bets would be off.

Andi finally took a step back and wiped away the moisture beneath her eyes.

Duke's heart ached at her inner turmoil.

He gently pushed a hair behind her ear before

murmuring, "You know I always want to be there for you."

"I know." She used her palms to wipe below her eyes again before drawing in a deep but shaky breath. "I was going to contact you as soon as I could. But I had to sell the idea that I was leaving without telling anyone."

Duke supposed that made sense. She *had* set things in place so he could find her.

Her gaze met his. "I don't know who Victor has in his pockets. That means I don't know who I can trust—other than you, Gibson, and the rest of the gang. That makes this whole situation even more precarious. But I have to find those answers once and for all."

Duke didn't argue. He agreed with everything she said.

He was in this for the long haul.

Andi had risked everything for him more than once, and now he would do the same for her.

———

Andi and Duke caught up with each other while Gibson was gone.

Duke started a fire as a chill filled the cabin. As they waited for Gibson to return, they sat on the couch in front of the flames, and Andi placed her head on Duke's chest, wishing she could disappear into the moment.

If only it were that easy.

They talked about their respective trips home.

However, all the talk felt mundane considering the circumstances, and restlessness stirred inside her.

Two hours later, Gibson finally returned.

He'd brought snacks and drinks with him as well as burner phones for Andi, Duke, and himself. He'd delivered the other phones to each murder club member. All the numbers for each person in the group had already been programmed on the devices, so they should all be able to communicate.

He also explained that he'd daisy-chained the burners to everyone's actual cell phone. That way, everyone could still get their regular phone calls—if they chose to answer. If the whole team suddenly stopped answering their phones, people would get suspicious.

It was better this way.

However, it would be nearly impossible for anyone to track them if they tried.

Duke glanced at his new cell before shoving the device in his back pocket. "You're a real lifesaver, Gibson. Thanks."

Gibson remained near the table, his hands on his hips and his gaze serious. "I don't know about that. But I hope the phones will help for now. There's a lot of buzz out there."

"What do you mean?" Andi grabbed a water bottle and took a long sip before leaning back into the couch.

"People are talking about what happened, and

they're talking about you, unfortunately." Gibson frowned as if he hadn't wanted to say those words.

Andi's hand went to her neck, and she rubbed the tight muscles. "What are they saying?"

"They're digging up your past. Talking about the podcast. Someone even posted a reward if you're found."

Andi's eyes widened. "How much?"

"A hundred thousand."

Andi's gut clenched. A hundred thousand dollars was enough to motivate a lot of people to do some serious searching for Andi.

It wouldn't surprise her. Very little would at this point.

Andi's cell phone rang, and she startled at the sound.

She glanced at the screen. "It looks like it's Mariella. Maybe she's testing out our new system."

"Let's see." Duke leaned closer.

Andi put the phone on speaker. "Hello?"

"Andi?" Mariella's voice rang through the line. "Is that really you?"

Relief washed through her. "It's me."

"I'm so glad you're okay," Mariella rushed, her words coming out fast and high pitched. "People have already been calling me—on my regular phone, of course, which is being rerouted to the burner. Anyway, they're wanting to know if I know where you are."

Duke's eyes crinkled at the sides as he narrowed them. "What are you telling them?"

"I'm telling them I haven't heard from you, of course. Because I haven't." Mariella paused. "I'm really worried."

"We're doing our best to stay on top of this," Duke told her. "We're going to try to come up with a plan of how we can cut the snake off at the head. As soon as we know what we're going to do, we'll let you know."

"Okay. Of course. Whatever you need help with let us know. We're all so worried. I wish I could see you."

"We appreciate your concern," Andi said. "But I can't show my face right now."

"I understand." Mariella paused. "Wait . . . there is one other thing I thought you might want to know."

"What's that?" Andi said.

"I keep getting these weird messages. They're like pieces of a picture that are being sent to me in tiny sections. It's almost like a puzzle."

"What kind of images?" Duke asked.

"It's too soon to tell," Mariella said. "I'm still not sure what the total picture is going to be."

Duke and Andi glanced at each other, worry in their eyes.

Andi leaned closer to the phone. "Do you recognize the phone number?"

"No, it's an unknown number. But something about it just seems weird, you know?"

"It is strange," Andi said. "If you're able to put anything together, let us know."

"Will do. Stay in touch."

When they ended the call, Andi glanced up at Duke and Gibson. "I don't want to jump the gun here, but I fear it's already happening."

"What's already happening?" Gibson squinted in confusion.

"Victor already has a plan in place. If he knows I didn't obey his orders and leave, then he's going to make sure everyone in my life pays dearly for their involvement in my plan to take him down."

HECTOR PAUSED outside the bedroom at his aunt's house and hesitated.

He knew his mom was on the other side of that door in a small bedroom that smelled putrid.

The whole house smelled putrid. It had always smelled like cigarette smoke, unwashed dogs, and dirty clothes.

But today . . . today there was a new scent.

Hector wasn't sure exactly how to describe it.

A mix of dirty diapers and decay? However, there was no baby in the house. He supposed nothing was officially decaying either.

But the scents were still there—a reminder of the beginning and end of life. They were part of the reason why he dreaded coming to this place to visit his mom.

Everything around him made him want to vomit.

Yet he had an obligation to come. Despite his turbulent relationship with his mom, he couldn't ignore her now.

He knocked and heard a frail, "Come in," from the other side.

He opened the door and saw his mom laying in a twin bed with a Strawberry Shortcake comforter wrapped around her skeletal body.

A tray rose beside her, full of medicines and a glass of water. A TV blared from atop a dresser in the corner.

That was how Mama spent most of her time. Watching TV—Phil Donahue, Geraldo, and Oprah were her favorites. She was too weak to walk so there wasn't much else she could do.

"My son." She extended her frail hand toward him.

The words, coming from other mothers, would have sounded affectionate. But not coming from his mama. She might be able to fool others, but not him.

His entire life, she'd made decisions based solely on what was best for her. It had always been that way. Their future had been dependent on his mother's boyfriends. On the newest adventures. On the quickest way to make money.

Despite that, Hector wished he could take her to a better medical facility. But he couldn't afford it. He'd just finished high school and working at the cattle farm down the road barely provided enough money for gas.

Besides, people of their social status weren't important.

He'd known that for a long time, but his mother's illness had driven home the fact.

When people like them died, no one missed them. It sounded cold, but it was true.

Mama squeezed his hand before saying in a raspy voice, "I don't have much time left."

Hector's heart lurched into his throat. Even though he wasn't sure he loved her—or that she'd ever truly loved him—the death of his mother would leave a hole in his heart.

"I know," he said softly. "I'm sorry."

Her gaze met his. "Have you forgiven me yet for selling our home?"

Familiar anger surged through his veins. He'd thought about that moment nearly every day for the past nine years. Everything had changed that day. *Everything.*

"Things would have been different if you hadn't," he told her.

She squeezed his hand tighter. "I had no choice."

"You always have a choice!" His voice rose at the words.

He swallowed hard, trying to calm himself. He shouldn't get worked up right now.

"Life isn't fair." Her voice changed from weak into the harsh dictator she'd always been. "You need to learn that."

He said nothing. Who was *she* to give *him* advice? Yet a part of him craved it.

For so long, he'd wanted someone he could look up to. His mom had never been that person.

Now that she was on her death bed, she'd chosen this moment to dole out advice?

Yet her life had been one bad decision after another.

"That's the way of the world," she continued. "It's eat or be eaten. Do better than me, Son. Don't let men walk all over you. You be the one doing the walking."

His eyes widened. "Are you saying those are the only two choices?"

"Isn't that clear?" His mom's gaze met his. "There are no in-betweens."

"There has to be." He'd been at war with himself for so long. There was the person he thought his father wanted him to be. Someone with integrity.

Then there was the person he'd become, born out of experience.

He'd stolen in order to eat.

He'd pulled a knife on someone who threatened Tito.

He'd let some cattle roam free after being fired from another job when the owner had called him derogatory names.

Maybe he was more like his mother than he ever wanted to admit.

"There isn't an in-between," his mom continued. "You're a smart boy. You graduated at the top of your class, despite everything we've been through. Do you still have those scholarships?"

"I do." Hector was proud of himself. Despite the bad things he'd done, he'd never been caught. Very few people had seen past his polite outer persona—the one who followed all the rules, the one who was obedient, just as Mama had taught him.

He'd maintained his grades. Volunteered when needed. Played sports.

A counselor at school had helped him apply for scholarships—and he had more than one offer.

"Which one will you accept?" Mama asked.

"I'm not sure." He'd even gotten offers from a couple Ivy League schools.

Part of him knew it wasn't just his smarts that had gotten him those scholarships. It was also his financial status.

Despite the fact he should be honored, another part of him still felt taken advantage of. Felt as if he was being given these things because he was poor, not because he'd earned it.

That wasn't okay with him.

"I'll accept the best one, Mama," he told her. "I'll make you proud."

A weak smile fluttered across his lips. "What will you study?"

"Business." He'd watched the people around him. He knew that was where the money was. He didn't want to work for people. He wanted his own company.

He would rise above his circumstances. He didn't ever want to be poor again. He didn't ever want money to be the reason someone in his family died without medical care.

He was going to do better—even if he had to claw his way to the top.

Mama's face brightened. "I like that idea, my boy."

A second later, her eyelids drooped. She was getting tired and didn't have much time left.

Hector released her hand and stepped back. "I'll let you rest now, Mama. But I'll be back."

The truth was, he was leaving for college soon. He wasn't sure if he *would* make it back. Part of him didn't want to see her like this again.

He didn't want to care about her, though some part of him did.

He'd been staying at his girlfriend's place. He didn't really like her that much, but she was beautiful. She met a need.

His mother hadn't cared about seeing him until she'd received her cancer diagnosis, and only then it was because she needed someone to look after her.

Hector was her son. Maybe she thought that was his job.

But Mama's job had been to look after *him*, and she'd failed miserably.

Why shouldn't he do the same?

He gave her one last glance before leaving.

He was going to change his life.

And no one would stop him.

NINETEEN
NOW

AFTER THE PHONE call with Mariella and eating some snacks, Duke encouraged Andi to lay down.

It was late, and she hadn't gotten any sleep last night. Plus, she'd been through a lot—both mentally and physically.

To Duke's surprise, she didn't argue with him. Instead, she said goodnight, planted a quick kiss across his lips, and disappeared into the bedroom.

As soon as she was out of sight, Duke turned to Gibson. "Is there anything else you need to tell me?"

Duke couldn't help but feel like there was more to this story than his friend had shared.

Gibson paused near the door, almost appearing as if he would deny Duke's words. Instead, he let out a long breath and ran a hand over his face.

"I think someone I work with is dirty." His words sounded strained.

Duke's eyebrows shot up. He hadn't been expecting that.

"Why do you think that?" Duke paused in front of him, not wanting to miss a single detail.

"I don't know . . ." He rubbed a hand over his mouth and jaw. "It's just a feeling, really. There are certain cases that have been closed too early and other cases that aren't being given enough attention. Every time I bring it up, I'm shushed. Told to concentrate on my own cases. I don't like it."

"What kind of cases are these?"

"Several involve indigenous people." Gibson's gaze darkened. "I don't want to think any of this is on purpose or being done because someone feels like these people aren't as important. But it's been bothering me. I've been looking into things on my own, trying to figure out if my instincts are correct or not. So far, I haven't found any definite proof of anything."

"Do you know who might be calling these shots?"

"I'm afraid it might be my captain. He likes to climb the ladder. I fear he may be doing that now."

Duke's neck muscles wove together even more tightly.

He closed his eyes and drew in a deep breath.

The situation kept getting worse and worse. How many people were willing to turn a blind eye to the wrong doings of those in power?

Too many it seemed.

Sometimes, the battle felt futile, like he was running in circles.

Was there a connection between what Gibson had just said and everything else going on?

Duke wasn't sure. The idea seemed like a stretch.

But he couldn't dwell on those things right now. Instead, he needed to focus on what was in his control.

He opened his eyes again and studied Gibson. "Have you heard any Senator Glassine updates?"

Gibson let out a long breath. "Rescue crews can't find any wreckage or signs of where the plane went down. They're still looking."

"I don't think that's a coincidence." The woman was a key player in the whole Prometheus drama. If Glassine had decided to vote against the oil drilling, certain people stood to lose a lot of money.

There was enough at stake that someone—someone like Victor—might even resort to murder to get what he or she wanted.

"I don't think it's a coincidence either," Gibson said. "I'm still waiting to see what I can find out. I know they're interviewing people who knew the pilot and airport employees. They're trying to locate the black box as well, but the plane was flying over a remote area of Alaska—Gates of the Arctic National Park, actually— when it disappeared. It's going to take some time."

As silence stretched, a new sound filled the air.

Tires on gravel.

Duke bristled.

Had someone pulled up outside the cabin?

————

Andi awoke with a start, adrenaline pumping as her body went into fight or flight mode.

Something was wrong.

"I didn't mean to scare you," someone murmured.

She blinked, and Duke's face came into focus. He leaned over her, his expression stony.

Her shoulders relaxed—but only for a moment.

"I need you to come with me," Duke said.

Her eyes widened. She knew by his tone, his expression, and the fact he'd come into her room to awaken her that something was definitely wrong.

He didn't give her a chance to respond. Instead, he grabbed her wrist and tugged her out of bed.

He didn't let go. Instead, he led her toward the living room.

She scurried behind him. "What's happening?"

"We heard a vehicle outside," he quickly explained. "We don't know who it is."

Andi's heart pounded even harder.

Duke pulled her into the living room and opened a closet door.

This was the only space in the cabin without a window, she realized.

He nudged her inside. "Stay here until we know what's going on."

"Duke . . ." Her voice wavered with fear.

His gaze locked with hers. "It could be nothing. But we need to know for sure."

Andi stared at him another moment before nodding.

Before he closed the door, Duke leaned toward her and pressed his lips into hers.

Then he wrapped her fingers around something cold, hard, and heavy.

She glanced at her hand.

A gun.

Her heart continued to beat at a fast pace.

Even though she'd grown up on a ranch in Texas and she owned her own gun for protection, she didn't want to handle guns any more than she had to.

Everything went dark as Duke closed the door.

She pressed her back against the wall between coats and flannel shirts. She tried to listen so she could have some clue as to what was happening outside the enclosed space.

As she did, she gripped the gun Duke had given her, praying she didn't have to use it.

Silence stretched outside the closet.

She pressed her eyes closed and began to pray because right now, the silence felt scarier than any kind of noise.

DUKE AND GIBSON strode to the front of the house, guns drawn.

Remaining guarded by the wall, Duke barely moved the curtain so he could glance out the front window.

"I don't see anything," he murmured. "If a car was coming this way, the driver must have stopped farther down the lane."

Out of sight where they couldn't see him.

Maybe it was someone who'd gotten lost and turned around. But Duke knew that was unlikely.

They positioned themselves on either side of the front door.

With a nod to each other, Duke threw the door open.

He pivoted into the darkness, his gun pointed, a flashlight on top of it. He shone it around. Nothing but trees and Gibson's SUV appeared.

Gibson did the same, scanning the lane leading to the cabin for any sign that someone else was here.

They saw nothing.

If someone was on the road to the cabin, they'd parked farther out of sight. Had they then gotten out of their vehicle and come the rest of the way on foot?

It was a good possibility. They couldn't take that chance.

They nodded at each other again before splitting. Duke went one way around the cabin and Gibson went the other.

Duke kept his senses attuned to the sounds around him.

He saw and heard nothing.

Duke and Gibson met again at the front door. Gibson shook his head, letting Duke know he hadn't seen anything either.

But they'd both heard that sound of tires on gravel. It had been close enough to the cabin for their ears to pick up on it.

"Who's out there?" Duke called.

He waited.

There was still nothing.

But he couldn't let this go, especially if danger lurked close.

Another sound filled the air.

A branch cracking.

It came from the woods to his right, from somewhere deep in the shadows.

If Duke had to guess, that was no animal.

Some*one* was watching them right now, just waiting for the chance to strike.

———

Andi heard voices in the distance.

It almost sounded like Duke had called out to someone.

She gripped the gun as she waited, running through what-if scenarios.

What if Duke was hurt?

What if Lockjaw had found them?

What if Victor had found them?

What if unseen enemies were headed toward this closet right now, about to open the door and attack?

Andi's heart pounded out of control. She didn't like thinking in worst-case scenarios. But couldn't seem to stop.

She couldn't just hide here indefinitely, especially if her friends were in trouble.

Concentrate on your breathing, Andi. In and out. Keep it steady. Stay calm.

Then, swallowing hard, she pressed her ear to the wooden closet door.

It was quiet again.

Not knowing what was going on out there was driving her crazy.

She squeezed her eyes closed and continued to pray that neither Victor nor Lockjaw had found them.

But the silence felt maddening.

Suddenly, a new sound cracked the air.

Gunfire.

Her lungs froze as fear paralyzed her muscles.

Only one shot had sounded—so far . . .

Would there be more?

Her thoughts raced before stopping on one scenario.

One terrible, terrible scenario.

What if that one bullet had hit Duke or Gibson?

AS DUKE STEPPED CLOSER to the woods, a bullet split the air.

He ducked to the ground. Beside him, Gibson crouched behind his SUV.

"You don't want to do that!" Duke called into the woods.

"Who are you?" a deep voice called back. "What are you doing on this property?"

The voice was unfamiliar.

"I'm a friend of Morgan's," Gibson yelled back. "Who are you?"

"A concerned neighbor," the man replied. "How do I know you're telling the truth?"

"Call Morgan," Gibson said. "She'll tell you."

"Stay where you are while I do that. Don't make any sudden moves."

Duke wondered what would happen next.

To his surprise, an older man—probably in his early seventies—stepped from the woods. He wore blue jean overalls and had white hair and sunken cheeks along with many wrinkles.

He lowered his rifle as he raised his phone in the air. "Morgan? Is that you?"

He paused a moment and put the phone on speaker.

"It's me, Samuel. A couple of guys are at your place. One says he knows you."

"What's his name?" Morgan's voice came through the phone.

"It's me," Gibson called out. "Logan."

"Logan?" Surprise laced the woman's voice. "What are you doing there?"

"You said I could use your place any time I wanted. I needed a last-minute, quick getaway."

"Of course, you're welcome there." She paused. "Samuel, thanks for looking out for me, but Logan is a friend. He's okay. You don't have to worry about him."

Samuel eyed them anyway. "You sure about that?"

"I'm positive."

Samuel ended the call and glanced back at them. "I guess you're okay then. Sorry about that. I live about a mile away. I saw the smoke coming from the chimney, and I came by to make sure things were okay. When I called Morgan the first time, she said no one was supposed to be here."

Duke couldn't help but wonder who Morgan was and what her relationship to Gibson might be.

"Morgan and I go way back," Gibson explained, a more friendly tone to his voice. "She's a great lady."

"She sure is," Samuel said. "Well, I'm sorry for the trouble. But I saw you with your guns . . . and those ain't no hunting rifles. Something didn't feel right. That's why I fired that warning shot into the air."

"No, we're not hunters." Gibson lowered his weapon. "We were just being cautious when we heard a vehicle coming down the lane."

Samuel waved a hand at them. "I understand. I'll be getting on my way. People out here . . . they have to look out for each other, you know."

"You're absolutely right," Gibson said. "I'm glad you're keeping an eye on Morgan's place for her."

The man waved and began lumbering back through the woods, probably to wherever he'd parked his vehicle.

As he disappeared behind some trees, one thought remained in Duke's mind.

That man had seen that Gibson was with Duke. If the right people—or the wrong ones—began to piece together things, then Gibson would definitely be associated with Duke.

And maybe, by default, Andi as well.

The situation was looking more dire for Gibson.

Duke's lips flickered into a frown.

More dire for all of them, he supposed.

————

Andi gripped the doorknob.

Was that talking she'd heard? Or was she imagining things?

If she didn't hear from Duke by the time she counted to thirty, she was leaving this closet. She didn't care what she'd promised.

For all she knew, Duke and Gibson might never come back.

A lump formed in her throat. She didn't like that scenario.

She sucked in several deep breaths. *In and out. In and out.*

She had to keep a grip.

God, please keep my friends safe. Give me wisdom. Blind my enemies.

Her relationship with God was a fairly new thing. Talking to Him still didn't feel quite natural. But she couldn't stop herself from doing so either.

She opened her eyes and practiced her deep breathing another moment.

Then she twisted the door handle.

Before she could open the door, a voice sounded on the other side.

"Andi, it's me. Duke. Everything is okay."

Relief swept through her. She threw the door open and saw Gibson and Duke coming back inside, their weapons lowered.

She lowered her own weapon and set it on a table.

Duke pulled her into a quick hug.

"What happened?" Andi pulled away slightly from his hug.

Duke explained the situation.

"So someone saw the two of you here?" She glanced back and forth between Duke and Gibson. "Together? That's not good."

They both frowned. Neither of them appeared happy about the situation. How could they be?

"Most people who live off grid don't watch a lot of TV," Gibson said, his words cautiously optimistic. "We still should have some time."

In a way, his words were reassuring.

But still, they were on borrowed time, and they all knew it.

CHAPTER
TWENTY-TWO

DUKE HAD HARDLY SLEPT. He had too many thoughts keeping him awake. Plus, he had one ear open, listening for any signal that danger had shown up like an uninvited guest.

He didn't think Samuel would call the cops. Not yet. But they couldn't take anything for granted. There was still a possibility that could happen.

Before the sun rose, Duke stood from the couch and stretched. He'd let Gibson take the other bedroom. He folded his blanket and placed it on top of his pillow.

He found what he needed to make some coffee, knowing he'd need plenty today.

He grabbed a cup as soon as the percolator was ready and sat down at the table. He found an old Bible on a shelf. There was no better way to start his day than by reading scripture.

As he opened the pages, a picture fluttered out. He

snatched it from the floor and studied the photo for a moment.

It was a picture of Gibson—a younger Gibson, probably by at least five years. He had his arm around a woman with dark hair and a light brown skin tone. Maybe indigenous.

Her smile was bright—and so was Gibson's.

Duke stared at the photo another moment, wondering what the story behind it might be. Really, Gibson's past was none of his business.

Still, he pondered the image.

Was this Morgan, the woman who owned this house? Did the two of them have a romantic history?

It was hard to say. It could just be a friendly photo. But they both truly looked happy. What if this woman was Gibson's ex-girlfriend? Ex-wife?

For all Duke knew, she could be his current wife or girlfriend.

Maybe when this was all over, the two of them could have coffee. Could talk about things beyond investigations and police work.

Duke placed the photo back between the pages. Then he opened the Bible to 2 Corinthians 4. His gaze immediately went to verse eight.

We are hard pressed on every side, but not crushed; perplexed, but not in despair; persecuted, but not abandoned; struck down, but not destroyed. We always carry around in our body the death of Jesus, so that the life of Jesus may also be revealed in our body. For we who are alive are always being given over to death for Jesus' sake, so that his life may also be revealed in our mortal body. So then, death is at work in us, but life is at work in you.

The verse had never seemed so appropriate. Now more than ever, Duke understood what it meant to be hard pressed on every side.

Death is at work in us, but life is at work in you.

He'd read that verse before, but the words hit him differently right now.

Lord, help life be at work within me. Within all of us. You stood up for injustice. Stood up to those who were greedy and power hungry. Help us to right the wrongs of others.

After Duke muttered amen, he opened his eyes and saw Gibson step from his room. He was already dressed in jeans, boots, and a blue Henley. His hair was combed, and he appeared surprisingly alert.

His friend grabbed a cup of coffee and sat across from him. He placed his police radio on the table beside him before asking, "Anything new?"

Duke shook his head. "Not that I know of."

"We need another plan."

"Agreed." Duke grasped his coffee mug, finding comfort in the warm ceramic. "I've been thinking it through all night. I really wish that neighbor hadn't seen us."

"You and me both." Gibson pressed his lips together and shook his head.

Silence stretched, each of them lost in their own thoughts.

After a moment, Duke glanced at his phone. He'd been avoiding checking his messages. But he needed to.

Worrying about his business might seem strange considering the stakes of everything happening right now. But Duke was the boss, and he didn't want to disappear off the grid without so much as a word if he didn't have to.

After a hostage situation at his office six weeks ago, everyone was on edge. They'd lost some business, but Duke wasn't too concerned about that aspect. However, he wanted to check in with his employees and make sure they were okay—especially in light of everything that had happened.

There was no telling exactly what Victor planned next. Targeting Duke's business or his employees could very well be a part of it.

He opened his e-mail and scanned the messages but didn't see anything of importance from his office.

However, another message caught his eye.

One from Lane Sullivan, aka Sully, his former colleague with the Army CID.

As soon as Duke saw the man's name, his muscles tightened.

He hesitated before clicking on it.

The message filled the screen.

We need you to come into the office. An investigation into Operation No Name is being reopened, and the higher ups want to question you. I've tried to reach you on your phone, but you didn't answer. Don't make this any harder than it has to be. Come in today and things will go a lot smoother.

Duke was going to be brought up on charges based on what had happened, wasn't he?

His throat tightened. He'd thought all that was behind him. That the CID had moved on after discovering that Alpine Grist was behind everything.

The Army had experimented with some brain implants that would help people gain mobility—but in the wrong hands, the tech could practically be mind control. Some of the experimental testing data had disappeared, and it turned out that Celeste had stolen it from Duke.

The only reason she'd taken it was because she had an implant controlling her actions. The person behind everything was Alpine.

The man was awaiting trial on multiple charges.

But now the Army needed a scapegoat for the missteps on their end.

It sounded like they wanted Duke to be that person.

Did Victor have a hand in this? Or was that too far of a stretch?

Duke wasn't sure.

But the pressure closed in from every side.

———

Andi smelled the coffee and stepped out of her bedroom.

As soon as she saw Duke's face, she knew something was wrong.

She paced to the table and placed her hand on his shoulder. "What happened?"

Based on the way Gibson stared at Duke, the officer was also concerned.

Duke put his phone down and ran a hand over his face. Then he ran a hand over his face again.

"Lane Sullivan sent me an email," Duke said.

"The guy from the CID?" Andi asked. "He goes by Sully, right?"

Duke's expression remained listless. "He's the one. He wants me to come in for questioning about Operation No Name."

Her breath caught. "What? I thought that was over and done with."

"Apparently not." Duke's jaw hardened.

Andi's mind raced. The stakes of that operation had been high. What had happened afterward had resulted in the deaths of at least six people. If the person behind the experiments had gotten their way, this technology could have been used for even greater harm. To control political leaders and decision makers and people with power.

It was best that it had been shut down.

Then another thought slammed into her head.

What if this development was Victor's way of getting revenge? What if he'd somehow had a hand in this?

The man was powerful, and Andi knew he liked to blackmail people, to manipulate them into getting what he wanted. If he had information on someone who worked at the CID, Victor could have pulled some strings and pushed this to happen.

Her heart thumped in her chest. She didn't like that thought. But she couldn't ignore it either.

She turned back to Duke. "What are you going to do?"

"I'm not sure yet." Duke ran a hand through his hair. "I need some time."

"It doesn't sound like you have much time," Gibson said. "If you don't go into the office, my guess is that they'll put an arrest warrant out for you by tomorrow."

"Then there would be an arrest warrant out for both of us," Andi murmured.

Silence stretched a moment as they all let that sink in.

Before they could talk about it any longer, something crackled. Gibson had brought his police radio inside with him, and he'd kept it on low to monitor things.

"We have a possible location of our suspect in the murder of Billy Pitts," a staticky voice said. "A man west of Fairbanks thinks our suspect might be hiding out in the cabin next to his."

Andi's breath caught.

They were talking about her, weren't they?

Everyone in the room stiffened.

Then an address was called out.

This address.

Another officer responded. "I'm only fifteen minutes away. I'll go check it out."

"Use caution," the voice on the other end said. "Andi Slade could be armed and dangerous."

The three of them glanced at each other before shooting to their feet.

They had to move.

If Andi, Duke, and Gibson didn't get out of here soon, she would be arrested.

And probably Duke and Gibson as well.

DUKE, Gibson, and Andi grabbed their things in record time and were back in Gibson's Suburban.

Duke didn't know where they were going. He only knew they needed to get out of here. There was no time to waste.

Gibson sped down the lane away from the cabin back toward the main road. Instead of heading toward Fairbanks, he turned in the opposite direction.

Duke hoped Gibson's move might buy them some time.

"Samuel must have somehow seen the news," Gibson muttered, rubbing his jaw. "Maybe it was too much to hope he wouldn't."

"It was just a matter of time." Duke glanced over his shoulder to see if anyone was behind them. The road was still empty. "I was just hoping it wouldn't happen so quickly."

"I know what we can do," Andi said from the back seat.

Duke stole a quick glance at her. "What's that?"

"I was thinking about it all night, trying to come up with an alternate plan. I think I have one. But I don't want anyone to do anything they're not comfortable with."

He looked behind them again.

The coast was still clear, as the saying went. They must have left just in time.

"Duke, if you feel like you need to go into the CID office, then you need to go," Andi continued. "And Gibson, if you want out of this and you need to report me and what I'm doing, then you have to do what you have to do. I just ask that you let me have a head start."

"I'm already in this, Andi." Gibson's expression remained unchanged as he gripped the wheel. "I know something fishy is going on. I've asked for a couple more days off work—I had the time off banked. I should be okay unless someone reports me."

"How about Samuel?"

"It was dark outside," Gibson said. "Even though I said my name, I don't think he saw my face. He shouldn't put two and two together. Right now, I think I'm in the clear."

"And you know I'm with you." Duke's tone left no room for doubt.

"I don't want either of you to be arrested." Andi's

voice cracked under the emotional strain of the situation.

"I don't want to be arrested either. That's why we need to get to the bottom of this. We need to figure out who all the players are." Gibson glanced toward Andi. "So what's your plan?"

She explained her idea to them.

Duke listened carefully to everything she said. As he did, he continued to watch the road around them, acting as a second set of eyes for Gibson. He halfway expected police cars to appear in every direction or to hear sirens. But sirens would have alerted anyone at the cabin that the police were coming.

He remained on edge, knowing things could turn at any moment.

He considered Andi's strategy. Her idea was decent. More than decent, actually. It might work—at least for now. But the plan wasn't without risk.

"You really think we can do this?" Duke studied Andi's face, trying to get a read on her.

"Yes, I do," she told him. "But there are no guarantees."

Gibson turned off the main road and onto a road leading back to Fairbanks.

It looked like they'd scraped by this time.

But only by the skin of their teeth.

———

Nearly six hours later, Gibson pulled behind the Almost Halfway Trading Post.

Andi stared at the building as they approached it. This was the place it had all started.

Where the members of the Arctic Circle Murder Club had met for the first time. Where they'd bonded over the murder of true crime podcaster Craig Rogers. Where they'd decided to give the podcast a chance.

It only seemed fitting that this was the place where they wrapped up one of their biggest cases.

Hopefully.

This place was originally a pad of gravel where the Trans-Alaska pipeline had been staged. Now it was one of the only places a person could get food and gas for miles and miles on the isolated highway.

There was nothing fancy about it. In fact, the ceiling sagged in several spots. At one point, a beam had been close to collapse because of heavy snowfall, and a sturdy branch had been placed to hold it up until someone could come out and fix it.

Beyond the area with the guest rooms was a convenience-like area with prepackaged foods and rows of cafeteria tables where travelers could take a break and eat. There was usually a homemade soup and a few sandwiches on the menu—but once they were gone for the day, they were gone. Signs proclaiming "hello" in different languages decorated the walls.

Simmy had worked here a few years and had personally hired the people who'd taken her place. The out of the way location had been perfect for her when she'd been trying to keep a low-profile.

Two other cars were already parked back here. Andi didn't recognize them, but she thought she knew who the drivers were. The whole point was not to be recognized.

As soon as Duke parked, the back door to the grungy, beige building opened.

Simmy and Ranger stood there.

For a split second, Andi felt safe and at home. She knew the feeling wouldn't last long, but she would enjoy it while it did.

She rushed toward them and threw her arms around Simmy. She even hugged Ranger, though he wasn't normally a hugger. This moment seemed like an exception.

"Glad you guys made it." Ranger extended his hand to Duke, then Gibson.

"Glad we're here too," Duke said.

"Is everything secure?" Andi glanced back and forth between Ranger and Simmy, knowing they couldn't let even a single detail fall through the cracks.

"Yes," Simmy assured them. "Giselle is working. We can trust her. But I didn't tell her any details."

Giselle had taken Simmy's place when she'd left the trading post. Simmy had handpicked the woman, who'd come from the Ukraine.

"She's not going to see you," Simmy continued. "I told her I needed three rooms because I was planning a surprise for my friend. She shouldn't be suspicious."

Relief washed through Andi, and she squeezed her friend's arm. "Thank you for doing this."

"Of course." Simmy smiled softly. "You know I'd do anything for you."

"Where's Anastasia?" Andi was primarily concerned about the young girl. She couldn't stomach the thought of Ranger's daughter being hurt.

"I had a friend recently retire from some deep cover work overseas. He owed me a favor, so I asked him to stay with Karen and Anastasia at an undisclosed location. He agreed." Ranger paused. "I wanted to keep her with me, but I knew she wouldn't be safe here. My best bet was tucking her away somewhere no one knows about."

Karen was Anastasia's nanny and practically a member of the family.

"I'm glad you were able to figure that out," Andi said.

Simmy ushered them inside and into one of the rooms. They weren't large accommodations. Each room —there were eight all together—had two cots with lumpy mattresses and a small table made out of pallets. A community bathroom was located down the hall.

They could hide out here for now. No one should look for them.

Andi had thought through all the details.

Using the new burner phones, she'd texted each

member of the Arctic Circle Murder Club. She'd instructed them not to bring their old phones or laptops or any other electronic devices with them.

She'd told them to borrow a car for travel. Alfonso probably had some extras in his collection.

Then they needed to come to the trading post to meet.

They'd all left at different times, making promises to check to see if they were being followed.

If anyone saw members of the murder club getting on the Dalton Highway, the trading post would be the most logical guess as to where they were headed.

They couldn't let that happen. They absolutely *couldn't* be spotted.

Andi trusted each member enough to feel confident they'd been careful.

If they were going to figure this out, they needed to meet face-to-face. They needed to come up with a plan and discuss all the details.

"There's something I want to tell you." Ranger stood near the wall, between two twin beds.

The rest of the gang stood around him in a tight circle. The space wasn't large, so they'd have to get up close and personal for the rest of their conversation.

"What's going on?" Duke crossed his arms as he waited to hear what Ranger had to say.

"Two things, actually," Simmy chimed in.

Then she held up her left hand.

A diamond sparkled on her ring finger.

"You're engaged?" Andi gasped. "Congratulations!"

"That's great!" Duke said.

"Nice to hear some good news," Gibson added.

They all hugged and gave the happy couple claps on the back.

"When's the big day?" Andi asked.

"Hopefully in a few months." Simmy smiled at Ranger, her cheeks glowing. "Neither of us want a big wedding. But we're both ready to tie the knot. Who knows? Maybe it will be even sooner."

"That's fantastic news." Andi was truly happy for her friends. They'd been through a lot to get to this point.

"There is something else." Ranger shifted before clearing his throat. "I've been asked to join in the rescue or recovery efforts for Senator Glassine."

Andi supposed the request made sense. Ranger had worked with the park service as well as the CIA, *and* he was an expert tracker.

The government would want professionals to search for the senator, her chief of staff, and the pilot.

It made sense that Ranger might be one of those people.

"The SAR team wants me to leave later today," Ranger told them. "But I wanted to meet with you first."

"I think you looking for Glassine is a great idea," Andi said. "She's involved with this whether she wants to admit it or not."

"I agree," Duke said. "She's a key player. If they can

find the plane, maybe there will be something on board to give us a clue about what happened. Plus, I have to wonder if that plane was tampered with, if none of this is a coincidence."

Ranger nodded stiffly. "Okay. But before we leave, we all need to talk."

"Do we know when Mariella and Matthew are arriving?" Duke asked.

The two were twins. Mariella was the social media/influencer brains behind the podcast, and Matthew was practically a computer genius. They'd come to Alaska for a travel piece and had stayed when true crime fell into their lives.

"Last time I heard from them, Mariella said they'd be here within the next thirty minutes." Simmy shrugged.

"I'm going to put our luggage in the room, and then we can get things squared away," Andi said.

"I brought some food for us all just in case we're hungry." Simmy was the nurturing, motherly one. "It's not much, but there are some sandwiches, chips, and drinks."

"They sound perfect," Duke said.

They would get settled in.

Then Andi would dive into the details of what had happened.

CHAPTER
TWENTY-FOUR

AN HOUR LATER, the whole gang had gathered in one of the small rooms at the trading post.

Mariella and Matthew had arrived driving an old Kia sedan that Alfonso let some of his handymen use. Apparently, he'd even left tools in the back, and the vehicle smelled like oil.

At least it was free transportation.

With everyone here, Duke made himself comfortable on the edge of a cot, ready to get down to business.

Normally, when they met, Mariella brought a murder board with her, one decked out with lots of bling and pink—both things that fit Mariella. When Duke had first met her, he'd thought of her as Malibu Barbie. But as he got to know her, he'd discovered she had much more depth to her.

"So I've been thinking about this for a long time." Everyone's attention turned to Andi as she started.

Gone was the vulnerable woman Duke had comforted yesterday, and in her place was the go-getter attorney who wouldn't back down or bow to pressure.

Duke liked both sides of her.

"What I really need to make this case is an eyewitness, someone from Victor's inner circle who we can flip. Someone we can get a testimony from. If I have that, I can go to the attorney general and make my case. However, based solely on the evidence I have right now, Victor could deny it all."

"That makes sense." Duke nodded slowly.

Andi's gaze met everyone's in the room. "I know I've said this to you before, but it bears repeating again. If anyone wants out, I understand. But now is the time to leave. Of *course* I want you all here with me. Your support means a great deal. But I don't know what this will all look like in the end. I know Victor has threatened to harm each of you if I don't drop this. I totally get it if you want to leave and deny your involvement with any of this."

"I'm in." Mariella raised her chin, almost defiantly. "The problem with people like Victor is that they intimidate others to get their way. If people continue cowering, then nothing will stop him."

"I'm in also." Ranger nodded slowly. "My only concern is keeping Anastasia safe. But if I can do that *and* help you, then I will."

"Me too." Simmy smiled sweetly.

"I've come this far." Gibson's words were steady and sure. "I'm not backing out now."

"I'm not out in the field much." Matthew pushed his glasses up higher on his nose. "But anything you need me to do from the computer, I'm more than happy to help."

That left Duke. Everyone turned toward him.

"You know I'm in." He grabbed Andi's hand, squeezing it. "Whatever you need."

Gratitude filled her gaze. "Thank you. That means a lot to me."

He'd meant the words. Andi had been there for him through one of the toughest seasons of his life, and she'd never hesitated to help him. He would cross oceans and scale mountains for her if that was what she needed.

"I was hoping you'd say that." The softness in her gaze only lasted a moment before Andi snapped back into professional mode. "Ranger, I need you to help the rescuers search for Glassine. If you find her plane, maybe we'll find evidence of what happened."

"I can do that." Ranger nodded slowly.

"Simmy, I need you to keep us all on track," Andi continued. "You're really good at that."

"Sounds right up my alley."

"Mariella." Andi turned to her. "Victor has a hairdresser who works out of Anchorage. She has a decent social media following. I'm hoping you can use your connections and influence to get to know her and find out if she knows anything."

"I would love to."

"Matthew," Andi continued. "I'm still desperately trying to hack into Victor's personal finances. I know it's risky. But I need to see where his money is going. I'm sure he's covered all his bases, but you're really good at what you do, and I'm hoping you can find anything we missed."

"I'll see what I can do."

She looked at Gibson. "Gibson, I think it's best if you're our inside connection. I know you probably don't want to go back to work, but I also don't want people becoming suspicious of you. While on the job, you can keep a pulse on this investigation. It's the perfect way to find out more about Glassine."

His cheek twitched as if he didn't like that idea. "I'm going to be at the mercy of my work schedule. If something happens, there's no guarantee I can help."

"I understand. But I think it's necessary."

"Then I'll do it," Gibson said.

Then Andi turned to Duke. "I need you to be my righthand man."

"Always."

The way he said the word made her breath catch.

"What about you?" Mariella stared at Andi.

Andi blew out a long breath. "I'd love more than anything to try to flip one of Victor's lawyers, but I know there's not a good chance that's going to happen. I have no doubt they all know who I am. Instead, I'd like to focus on one of his lawyer's paralegals, a man named Cody Gleeson. I've been researching him. He lives in Anchorage, and he likes pickleball."

"Sounds like we're going to be splitting up and going all over the state," Ranger said. "How are we handling the travel?"

"I'm glad you brought that up." Mariella sat up straighter, her eyes suddenly brighter. "I'm happy to say that our sponsorship for the podcast has continued to grow. Even without Alpine's support, we are doing really well. I don't have a problem using some of the profits to finance our travel right now. That is, if everybody else is in favor of it."

She glanced around the group, and everyone nodded.

"Great," Mariella said. "Then that's what we'll do."

"The subcommittee meeting has been rescheduled for two days from now," Andi reminded them. "Right now, they're planning on meeting even without Senator Glassine. We don't have any time to waste."

"If anyone needs any disguises, I'd be happy to help," Mariella said before shrugging. "I like that kind of thing. All my hair and makeup knowledge can finally pay off."

"We might need that." Andi knew Mariella would do a great job with that. She glanced at the group. "We all have our assignments. Now we just need God's grace and mercy to protect us and guide our steps."

A lull stretched in the conversation as everyone seemed to mull over what they'd discussed.

After a few moments, Simmy stood and stretched. "If you'll excuse me a minute, I'm going to run to the restroom."

She opened the door but paused, then quickly ducked back inside.

Her face looked paler as she turned back to them.

"Simmy?" Ranger asked.

"It's Lockjaw," she whispered. "He's here."

———

Andi's thoughts raced.

"Are you sure?" she whispered to Simmy.

Simmy nodded, not a hint of doubt in her gaze. "He used to come in all the time when I worked here. I'd recognize him anywhere."

Had the man followed Andi here?

She didn't think so. They'd been careful.

She and Duke exchanged glances. He'd become tense at the announcement.

He placed a finger over his lips, motioning everyone to be quiet.

They waited, listening for the sound of his footsteps coming to the door. Waiting for Lockjaw to barge inside. To get justice for his son.

Instead, a female asked, "Will this work for the night?"

Giselle. Andi recognized her voice and accent.

"Looks good." Lockjaw sounded gruff. "I know the rest of the routine, so you don't need to stick around. I've got a place to sleep, and that's all I need."

More footsteps sounded, and the door slammed shut.

Lockjaw had rented the room next door, Andi realized. Dread pooled in her stomach.

Maybe she shouldn't be surprised. She knew Lockjaw used this place going back and forth between Fairbanks and Prudhoe Bay.

She just hadn't expected him to be here *now*.

Everyone remained quiet.

Lockjaw couldn't find them. It wouldn't be pretty if he did. Plus, they had other things to worry about.

A moment later, his voice drifted through the paper-thin walls—walls they'd need to be painfully aware of. They couldn't let him hear anything they were talking about. It would ruin everything.

"I haven't found her yet," he muttered to someone. "I don't know where she went or how she got away."

Pause.

"I'm still working on things. Wait. What? You heard she might be heading up north?"

Andi's head spun. How had Lockjaw heard that?

"Believe me, she's going to pay for what she did." Anger simmered in his voice. "Nothing would bring me more pleasure than to squeeze the life out of her with my bare hands."

Andi's blood turned cold. She had no doubt his words were true. Lockjaw would hurt her and enjoy every moment.

Silence stretched. Lockjaw must have ended the phone call.

The murder club all exchanged glances.

"Are we all trapped here?" Mariella finally whispered.

"He shouldn't recognize our faces," Matthew said from his spot on the floor.

"Unless Victor hired him," Andi added.

"What?" Ranger squinted. "What do you mean?"

"Lockjaw is offering a hundred-thousand-dollar reward to anyone who gives information on finding his son's killer. Where did Lockjaw get that kind of money? Victor makes the most sense."

No one argued with her assessment. They knew her words were true. They knew that Victor had deep pockets and would use every means possible to find her.

If Andi had to guess, *Victor* was the one who'd set her up for all of this.

"Wait . . . what if he sees our cars out back?" A wrinkle formed between Mariella's eyes. "Then he'll know we're here, right?"

"He shouldn't recognize them since they're borrowed, but I can move them, just to be on the safe side." Ranger stood. "I'll be stealthy."

"I know just the place you can stash them," Simmy said. "Somewhere no one will look."

Andi hoped Simmy was right and that their presence wouldn't be discovered.

But nothing felt certain right now.

One wrong move could ruin them all.

CHAPTER
TWENTY-FIVE

THE SITUATION WAS TOO volatile for Duke to be comfortable.

If Lockjaw caught wind they were staying here, things would get ugly. Duke wasn't sure who would initiate the ugliness first—him or Lockjaw. Part of him wanted to give the guy a piece of his mind after what he'd done to Andi.

But that wouldn't be prudent right now. It would only create another headache.

Ranger returned from moving the vehicles and quietly shut the door behind him. In a muted tone, he said, "They're behind the shed and out of sight. We should be good."

He returned each of their sets of keys.

Then they all turned to each other.

"Remember, we all need to keep our voices low,"

Andi whispered. "If Lockjaw hears us, it's a death wish."

"Agree," Duke murmured.

Andi turned toward him, studying his face. "What are you thinking?"

Duke swallowed hard, deciding not to share all his thoughts. Instead, he said, "I'm thinking that nothing about this situation makes me comfortable."

Andi's lip pulled down in a half frown. "I feel like we're stuck here until he leaves."

"We're assuming he's leaving in the morning to go to Coldfoot," Gibson said. "But who knows what he'll do after that."

"You know what?" Mariella sat up straighter. "I think this is a good time to turn the tables."

Duke narrowed his eyes as he waited to hear what she had to say. "What do you mean?"

"I mean, his truck is obviously here. Maybe there's something inside that will give us a clue as to what he knows."

"That sounds risky . . ." Duke's shoulders tensed at the idea. He was all for taking risks—but only when they were necessary.

"Maybe if one of us lures him outside, someone else could check his room and see if he brought anything inside with him that's significant," Mariella continued.

"I think it's a great idea," Andi said before Duke could tell her that it was a terrible one.

"We'd be putting ourselves in a dangerous situation

if we did that." Warning stretched through Ranger's voice. "But I have to agree this could be a good opportunity to get some info."

"So we have someone stay inside and watch his room," Gibson said. "Then someone else can go out to his truck, and if he starts to leave then we can let you know."

Andi rose. "I want to check his truck."

Duke stood also. "I'll go with you."

"The rest of us will stand guard," Ranger said.

Duke's muscles hardened. He didn't like the idea of doing this. Yet they needed to use whatever opportunities presented themselves.

This was one of them.

Duke glanced at Andi once more. "You sure you want to do this?"

"I'm as certain of this as I'm sure it's going to snow in Alaska this winter."

———

Quietly, Andi opened the door and glanced up and down the hallway.

She saw no one.

Best she could tell, Lockjaw had fallen asleep. When she'd put her ear to the wall a few minutes earlier, she thought she'd heard him snoring.

She nodded to Duke, and he followed behind her as she slipped out the back door. Her cell phone was snugly in her pocket in case anyone needed to get in touch with her.

They scurried around the back of the building to the side parking lot where Lockjaw had most likely parked.

Right away, Andi spotted his truck. It was the same F-350 he'd been driving at the campground.

No one else was outside, which worked to their advantage.

They darted to his vehicle and tried the driver's side door.

It was unlocked, so Andi and Duke slipped inside.

Andi's heart pounded in her ears as she glanced around the truck. The cab was messy with fast food wrappers and trashy magazines littering the floor. Plus, the scent was horrific . . . like he'd passed gas while driving through a septic field.

She wasted no time. She went straight for his glove compartment and began to rifle through the papers there.

But there was nothing of interest. A couple of unpaid parking tickets. An old package of spearmint bubble gum. A half-eaten package of peanuts.

She slammed the glove compartment shut and then looked underneath the seat.

While she did that, Duke searched the driver's side, including the pockets in the door. He pulled out a pink knit hat, one that probably belonged to a woman.

Duke leaned closer and pulled off a hair—a long, dark strand.

Andi paused from her search to watch with curiosity. "Maybe Lockjaw gave someone a ride."

"Does he seem like the generous type?"

"Not really."

"Is he married?" Duke asked. "Does he have any kids besides Skeeter?"

"Divorced. Skeeter was his only child. As far as I know, Skeeter didn't have any children."

"So who does this belong to?" Duke stared at the hat then glanced at her.

A bad feeling roiled in Andi's stomach. Something didn't feel right about this.

Duke placed the hair back in the folds of the hat and shoved it into his pocket.

Andi's phone vibrated, and she jumped at the sudden feeling.

Then she let out a breath, realizing how ridiculous her reaction was.

She quickly answered.

"Lockjaw just left his room," Ranger said. "You guys need to get out. Now."

CHAPTER
TWENTY-SIX

DUKE AND ANDI darted from the truck.

They'd barely gotten across the parking lot when Lockjaw stepped out the back door.

Thankfully, he was looking at his phone.

Duke grabbed Andi's hand, and they detoured toward the shed.

There was no time to run back to the building. They'd be too easily spotted if they did.

Their best bet right now was to remain hidden.

They huddled behind the old structure, waiting with bated breath to see if they'd been discovered.

Duke watched as Lockjaw strode to his truck. He paused as he reached it and glanced around.

His gaze darkened. Despite that, he opened the door.

Did he know Duke and Andi were out here? It seemed far-fetched, unlikely that he could know.

The whole situation gave Duke bad vibes.

He continued to watch as Lockjaw searched for something. As he *frantically* searched for something.

Was it the hat?

Would Lockjaw realize someone had been in his vehicle? That they'd taken it?

Hopefully, he'd simply think he'd misplaced it.

It was hard to say.

The only thing Duke and Andi could do was to stay where they were and observe.

And to pray for the best.

———

Andi's stomach was in knots as she and Duke continued to watch Lockjaw.

He seemed to survey everything around him for hours—though it was only mere minutes.

Finally, the man climbed from his truck and slammed the door. Even though Andi couldn't actually hear him grunt, she knew that was exactly what he'd done.

As he gave the area one final glance, Andi and Duke ducked back behind the shed.

Andi was keenly aware of how close Duke was standing. Pressed up against his side, Andi closed her eyes and thought about how different this time alone with Duke was compared to what she had planned.

Andi had planned on returning from Texas and cooking him some barbecue—her family's secret recipe. Then they would enjoy an evening together.

Then all this had happened.

There was no one else she'd rather have fighting by her side, however. Duke had proven himself time and time again to be a class act.

The two of them waited, hip against hip, to hear what Lockjaw was doing.

Finally, Andi peered around the corner again.

Lockjaw was stomping back toward the trading post.

It didn't appear that he had seen them.

Praise God!

Andi pulled out her phone and texted Ranger:

> Let us know when the coast is clear.
> He's heading back that way.

Ranger responded:

> Will do.

Then she and Duke waited. Duke placed his hand on her shoulder and pulled her close, kissing the side of her head.

Side kisses were the best.

She wanted to lean into the moment and continue leaning into him, to forget their problems.

If only she could.

"Do you think Lockjaw knows we are out here?" Andi glanced up at him.

"It's hard to say for certain, but he almost seemed to be looking for that hat."

That was what Andi had thought too. But why would he have looked for the hat now?

A bad feeling rumbled in her gut. "I hope this doesn't make him suspect we're here."

"I can't imagine he has any idea we're here. That doesn't even seem possible. Not unless someone told him, and I can't imagine anyone in our group doing that."

Andi agreed.

Her phone buzzed. It was Ranger.

He's back in his room. Be careful.

Wasting no more time, she and Duke darted back toward the trading post.

They paused at the exterior door, hesitating a moment.

Then Duke cracked it open and peered inside.

Then he gave her "the coast is clear" sign.

They hurried back to the room, where everyone waited.

Lockjaw hadn't seen them.

Andi leaned against the door and hauled in several deep breaths, her heart still racing. "That was close."

"You can say that again." Mariella raised her eyebrows as she nodded. "But we have news."

"What kind of news?" she asked.

"I went into Lockjaw's room while he was gone," Mariella whispered. "And I found a bag full of cash."

Andi's breath caught. "You went into his room?"

"Focus on the cash," Mariella told her.

Good point. "How much cash?"

"Thousands of dollars." Ranger raised an eyebrow.

Andi let that thought settle for a moment.

Duke shifted and crossed his arms over his chest. "I wonder if one of Victor's men somehow got that cash to him."

That was Andi's exact thought.

Victor must have had one of his men following her. He'd known she had left the airport, despite her best efforts.

Victor's guy must have seen Andi go to the motel and then seen Skeeter spot her there. As soon as she'd left, this person must have finished Skeeter off and made it look like Andi was responsible.

Why hadn't this person just killed her? Was this a game to Victor? Did he consider Andi a formidable foe, someone he wanted to conquer rather than kill?

She wasn't sure.

However, Andi had practically laid all the groundwork to make it incredibly easy to frame her.

Having the police on her tail would certainly slow her down and make her investigation harder. Victor knew that. In fact, he was counting on it.

He must have approached Lockjaw and offered to help him, knowing it would be yet one more roadblock preventing Andi from finding answers.

Her jaw hardened.

Whatever Andi did, she could *not* let Victor win.

But he was already leaps and bounds ahead of them.

TWENTY-SEVEN

EARLIER

JUST LIKE HIGH SCHOOL, Hector graduated at the top of his class from college. Afterward, he'd had multiple job offers.

He sat at his desk and looked at all the offers in front of him. Many were lucrative. Enough to change his life. Some even offered to pay off the little bit of college loans he had.

But there was only one offer that stood out.

C.W. Wells. Hector had been offered a position as a project manager with the company.

He stared at the paperwork.

He'd had other, better offers.

But this one was personal.

This was the one he would accept.

Hector had thought about that man every day for the past twelve years. Had thought about what it would be like to get to know him. To ask him questions. To find out how this man could live with himself knowing everything he'd done, all the hurt he had caused.

Hector's mother had passed away during his first month in college.

Passed away was a merciful way of saying her suffering had ended.

He hadn't been able to take it anymore.

When his aunt wasn't looking, he'd messed with her medications. He'd ensured that it wouldn't be long until the poisoned pharmaceuticals ended her pain.

He didn't stay in touch with anyone in town.

Not even Tito.

Especially not Tito.

Tito had turned on him. But that was fine. He didn't need Tito.

He'd just used him for his car and for his sister.

But when things had gone south with Donna, Hector had told Tito he couldn't speak of what had happened. If he did, then Hector would tell everyone how Tito had broken into some houses. How one of those break-ins had resulted in a homicide.

The two hadn't spoken since.

If Hector took this job, he'd be working about an hour from where he'd grown up. Things felt as if they were coming full circle.

He would get to know C.W.

Then he would enact the revenge he'd been formulating ever since the man had bought his house for mere pennies on the dollar all those years ago.

A smile teased his lips at the thought.

TWENTY-EIGHT

NOW

"I HAVE AN IDEA," Duke started. "It's risky. But I think it will work."

The team had been sitting in the room for the past hour, feeling as if it were a prison cell.

However, they'd agreed they couldn't risk Lockjaw seeing them.

His presence had made this situation entirely more complicated than needed.

The room was already small with two twin beds against the wall, with maybe four feet of floor space between the beds. Andi and Duke sat on one bed, Ranger and Simmy on the other, Mariella and Matthew were perched on the floor against the wall, and Gibson stood near the door.

"What's your idea?" Andi studied Duke's face as she waited for an answer.

"I'm going to go outside and call Lockjaw," Duke

said. "I'm going to tell him I saw a post on social media about what happened and the reward, and that I might know where you are."

Andi's eyes widened. "What? Are you sure that's a good idea?"

"If Lockjaw is as determined as he claims to be, then a tip might get him out of here. I think we all agree that's what we want right now. We need him gone. Just having him here is oppressive, to say the least."

"I can't argue with that," Andi murmured with a slight shake of her head.

"Wait . . . what kind of clue are you going to give him?" Mariella tilted her head as she waited for his response.

Duke blew out a breath. "It needs to be believable. We need to make sure he buys whatever I'm trying to sell right now."

"Maybe you can tell him you're a teacher at one of the villages," Ranger suggested. "Tell him a woman matching Andi's description has been seen there. You heard some of the kids talking about her. Mention she's wearing a disguise, but the kids keep talking about her pale skin and blue eyes."

"I think he would buy the idea that I might run to a village." Andi nodded. "It would be a great place to hide out—if the people there accepted me."

"I agree," Duke said. "I think that story would work."

Andi's gaze caught his. "But when you call him, you need to be careful. If he has any clue that it's you . . ."

"I will be. There's no room for mistakes right now."

No one argued with his statement.

———

Duke had been gone ten minutes. Andi was keeping track of the time, just waiting for something else to go wrong. She prayed that wasn't the case while trying to prepare herself for the worst.

What if someone caught Duke outside? What if Lockjaw picked up on what they were doing?

She sat with her ear pressed against the wall so she could hear whatever happened in the other room.

She heard Lockjaw's phone ring. Heard him answer. Heard him asking questions. Grunt. Ask more questions.

Then the call ended.

Seconds later, Lockjaw spoke again.

He'd called someone else, Andi realized.

"I just got a tip," Lockjaw said, his voice gruff. "This man thinks some people he knows saw Andi. He sounds legit. She's apparently wearing a dark wig and going incognito at an Indian reservation or village or whatever people call them around here."

Pause.

"This guy said she always says, 'Am I right?' Sounds like that annoying catchphrase Andi always used."

Yes, the smoking gun.

Would Lockjaw fall for it?

Andi waited, nervously rubbing her fingers together.

"I'm going to head out and see if I can catch her," Lockjaw finally said. "There's no time to waste."

Another pause.

"I'll go now. I don't need a lot of sleep. With any luck, I'll be back this way so I can talk to my friend in Coldfoot by tomorrow."

Movement sounded inside the room. A moment later, the door opened then closed. Footsteps sounded.

The team glanced at each other.

It appeared Duke's plan had worked.

Lockjaw was leaving. They could all let down their guard—just a little at least.

But Andi refused to relax until she knew Victor was behind bars.

AN HOUR LATER, the team turned in for the night.

Duke had come back inside, and Andi gave him the update on what had happened with Lockjaw. They confirmed the man's truck was gone.

It had been a long day for each of them, and they needed to get some shut-eye, especially because they had big plans for tomorrow.

They still had a few things they needed to work out as far as transportation, but they could discuss those final details in the morning.

While Simmy went to talk to Ranger, Duke slipped out of his room and into Andi's. He needed a moment alone with her.

As soon as he closed the door behind him, Andi practically fell into his arms. They embraced for several minutes, simply holding each other and not saying anything.

If Duke could, he'd never let her go.

Too bad that wasn't realistic.

He refused to be the one to pull away and instead waited for Andi to do so.

He wasn't sure how much time had passed before she took a step back and glanced up at him. A strange mix of worry and determination captured her features.

He gently nudged a lock of blonde hair behind her ear. "This is all risky, you know."

"I know. But I've come this far. I can't back down now."

"I get that. I'd like for us to stick together, however. Being alone out there won't do either of us any good."

A frown tugged at the corners of her lips. "But if we're together it might be more noticeable."

"I think we need to take that chance," Duke said. "We can both wear disguises. See what we can get done together instead of separately."

"Makes sense." Andi nodded slowly as if thinking through his words. "It sounds like we have most of our details in place. Now we have to hope it all works."

Just then, his phone buzzed, and he pulled it from his pocket.

He frowned at the number on the screen.

Sully with CID.

Instead of answering, Duke let the call go to voicemail. When he saw that a message had been left, he put it on speaker and hit Play.

His friend's voice rang through the line. "Duke, I

gave you the chance to come in on your own. I know you said you're not in town, but rumor has it that you're lying. The director is breathing down my neck. If you're not here at the office first thing in the morning, I'm going to have to send some guys out to look for you. Don't make me do that. Please."

———

Andi didn't like the sound of that voicemail.

It appeared that by tomorrow morning, both she and Duke might have arrest warrants out for them.

That would make it even more complicated to get a pilot to fly them to Anchorage. They could drive, but from the Almost Halfway Trading Post it would be ten or twelve hours. Flying made the most sense.

"What about Blaze?" Andi asked.

Blaze Andrews was in his early thirties, outgoing, and a bit of a daredevil. Neither she nor Duke knew the man very well, but he'd helped them out in a tough spot before when Ranger needed help rescuing Anastasia.

Plus, the man knew Alaska better than anyone.

"That's a great idea," Duke said. "I like Blaze. He has both guts and a good moral compass."

"Maybe we can get in contact with him."

Before she and Duke could talk any longer, a knock sounded on the door. Mariella barged inside before they could answer, her eyes wide and almost frenzied.

She held up her phone. "I finally know what those images are. The pieces of the puzzle came together."

Andi stepped closer, not liking Mariella's distressed tone. "What is it?"

"It's a picture of me." Her voice cracked. "From back when that incident happened with Mark."

Mark Scott was Mariella's ex-boyfriend. He'd posted some compromising pictures of Mariella as a means of ruining her reputation. Mariella had been a different person back then.

The incident had completely changed her.

Andi looked at the picture, and her eyes widened. She turned the phone away from Duke, knowing Mariella wouldn't want him to see something like this—even though the photo would be available for the whole world to view online soon, if not already.

"They're going to post this." Mariella's voice cracked again as her pleading gaze looked up at Andi. "I thought I'd put all of this behind me, but everything is coming back to the surface."

Andi knew what that meant.

Victor's threat was materializing.

He was beginning to bring them all down one-by-one.

And she felt powerless to stop him.

CHAPTER
THIRTY

THE NEXT MORNING, Duke and the rest of the gang awakened early to do each of their respective tasks.

They had one last meeting with breakfast provided by Simmy as they chatted. She'd brought several different types of homemade muffins with her. Planning ahead was one of her superpowers.

Afterward, they hugged, wished each other the best, and departed.

Everyone except Matthew, who would stay at the trading post to work. Since this place was in the middle of nowhere, he was safest here. The internet allowed him to do most of his work from his room.

He was a complete techie. He'd even met his girl-friend online—though the gang joked that she might not be real since none of them had met her. Mariella had even kidded that the woman was AI or an avatar.

Still, working alone was usually Matthew's first choice. He was the total opposite of his sister.

Meanwhile, Duke, Andi, Mariella, and Simmy headed toward Coldfoot, where they would catch a flight to Anchorage. Ranger was heading north to search for the senator. And Gibson had left to go back to work.

Sully had left Duke another voicemail this morning. Duke had ignored it.

He knew what it said. That CID agents would be looking for him.

He'd worry about that later.

He pulled up to the airport and saw a man with thick, dark hair double checking a small airplane near the runway.

Blaze.

Duke and the others exchanged silent glances as they climbed out and strode toward him.

This was it. There was no going back after this.

"Duke McAllister." Blaze extended his hand, half shaking and half slapping Duke's. "Good to see you again."

Andi stepped closer and lowered her voice before saying, "You shouldn't tell anyone we're here. For your own good."

Blaze went still, other than his eyebrows rising with surprise. Then, just as quickly, he returned to his laid-back demeanor. "I think I can manage that. I'm just happy to help. And how about this? I won't ask any questions. It might be easier that way."

"For sure," Duke said.

"Well, the plane's all ready. Let's get you all inside."

———

As Andi stared at the mountains and clouds around them, she couldn't help but think about Glassine and what she must have been through before her plane crashed.

Was there any hope the senator was still alive?

Andi wasn't sure. Most likely not.

Those moments before the plane went down must have been terrifying.

Andi didn't have much respect for the woman and thought she might even be crooked. But a plane crash would be a terrible way to go.

Not long ago, Andi had dug into the woman's finances and discovered that Victor had made large contributions to Glassine's campaigns. That was just the tip of iceberg. Andi knew for a fact that Glassine had been having secret meetings with Victor.

Now there was the vote coming up.

A vote that could change everything.

A vote that could mean Victor would get his way.

The plane rattled just then, and Simmy sucked in a breath. She was terrified of flying, especially in small planes.

Andi squeezed her hand from across the aisle. "It's going to be okay."

She nodded but still looked pale.

The aircraft dipped again, lower this time. Andi's stomach rose.

"Blaze?" Duke called.

"Just some turbulence," he yelled. "Nothing to worry about."

Was that what Glassine had thought as well?

Andi pressed her eyes closed and prayed for a safe flight.

CHAPTER
THIRTY-ONE

TWO HOURS LATER, Blaze landed the plane at a small executive airport—which was ideal for keeping their presence in the area on the down-low.

They climbed out and took a deep breath of the clean, crisp air. The temperature today in Anchorage was a balmy sixty-eight degrees, and the sun was shining.

Duke would take whatever blessing came his way.

The group paused on the runway and faced each other.

"This place keeps a few cars on hand for pilots to use," Blaze started. "I already had arranged to borrow one. I can get a second one from my sister while everyone is in town if needed."

"That would be amazing," Duke said.

The man had been a real godsend.

They all wandered toward an old white Crown Victoria Blaze pointed to.

Duke turned toward Blaze. "Listen, would you mind staying with Mariella and Simmy?" He frowned apologetically at the ladies. "I'm not saying the two of you can't take care of yourselves. I would just feel better if there was someone else with you, especially considering the stakes in this operation."

"I get that." Simmy didn't look offended in the slightest. "Personally, I'd feel better if someone else was with us also."

"Is there any chance Jason could come up?" Mariella's voice perked, though her gaze still bore the signs of her earlier distress after seeing that picture. Her eyes were red and much of the light had disappeared from their depths.

Jason was her boyfriend, and he lived on the Kenai Peninsula in a town called Salmon-by-the-Sea.

"I'm afraid someone might be keeping an eye on him and follow him up to meet you." Duke lowered his voice compassionately. "I hate to say it but having him come feels too risky."

Mariella didn't bother to hide her frown, but she nodded anyway. "I understand."

"I would be happy to stick with you guys." Blaze placed his hands on his hips as he turned toward the wind, which ruffled his wavy hair. "I plan on being in town until you guys need me to take you somewhere else or you tell me that you're done with me."

"We appreciate that," Duke said.

"And just in case you need shelter, my sister has a place here in Anchorage," Blaze continued. "It's not huge. She's a photographer, and she uses Anchorage as her home base. She just happens to be out on the Aleutian Islands right now taking pictures for some magazine. I'm sure she'd be fine if we stayed there."

"That would be perfect," Duke said. "If you're sure she wouldn't mind."

It was another answered prayer.

"My sister is one tough cookie," Blaze said. "I'm sure she wouldn't mind."

"Great." Duke offered a definitive nod. "I think that should be our plan."

"So I'm guessing you won't all want to stick together?"

"Probably not," Andi said.

"I'll drive you all to my sister's place, where I can pick up her car then," Blaze said.

Duke glanced at Andi. "Sounds good. That way Andi and I can keep our eye on someone and figure out how to coincidentally"—he used air quotes around the last word—"make our paths cross."

That person was Cody Gleeson. Duke and Andi had looked up everything they could about the man. He appeared to be in town. Now they had to figure out a way to become friends with him.

They all climbed into the car and took off down the

road. Ten minutes later, Blaze pulled up to a small house, and Blaze, Mariella, and Simmy got out.

Blaze gave Duke the keys to the Crown Victoria before ushering Mariella and Simmy toward another vehicle in the driveway.

Duke and Andi wasted no time heading toward downtown Anchorage where Gleeson had an office.

Thanks to his social media, Duke and Andi knew exactly where he liked to hang out, what he liked to do, and what his routine was.

They needed to use that information to their advantage.

As Duke took off down the road, he glanced at Andi. "You ready for this?"

"As ready as I'll ever be." She said the words with subdued confidence.

That was probably a good sign. None of them should be gung-ho right now, not in a situation this dicey.

Duke found a parking space in downtown Anchorage.

Before getting out, Andi pulled on a mousy brown wig that came to her shoulders, as well as sunglasses, leggings, and tennis shoes. Duke donned a baseball cap and running shorts. He hadn't shaved this morning, so his beard was thicker than usual.

They jogged toward an office building that housed one of the most prestigious law firms in Anchorage.

The two of them paused near a bench outside of the

six-story building and took long sips of water, biding their time and trying to blend in.

They'd arrived just at the right time—close to the lunch rush. Ten minutes later, Cody Gleeson stepped out of the building. He was a man of routine. His social media proved it.

Not only did he post at the same time on most days, but his posts confirmed that he had a schedule that he liked to keep.

The late twentysomething was dressed in khakis, a white shirt, and a dark blue blazer. He had light brown hair that was cut short around his ears and neck, and he had an oval face.

He headed toward his favorite sandwich shop—the Mile High Sub. He'd mentioned how much he loved the place online several times.

Duke and Andi gave him a few minutes before following behind, walking hand in hand toward the restaurant as if they were just getting lunch.

By the time they stepped inside, Cody was already at a corner booth scrolling on his phone.

The place was busy, obviously popular with businessmen and women in the area. Duke and Andi ordered their sandwiches and then paced toward the pickup counter.

There was nowhere else left to sit.

Which just might fit according to their plan.

Duke glanced at Andi, and their conversation was unspoken but clear.

It was showtime.

———

Thankfully, talking to strangers came naturally to Andi, so she took the lead.

"I just have to ask." She paused by Cody's table. "What sandwich is that you're eating? I've *got* to try it next time I'm in here."

Cody glanced up, not looking the least bit annoyed at this interruption.

"It's the Beefeater." He didn't even bother to swallow before answering. "It's the best. I mean, it's *really* the best. I've tried them all."

"I'm going to have to try that one," Andi continued. "I always get the same thing when I come here. The Italian Stallion. The ham, salami, and pepperoni get me every time, not to mention the banana peppers."

"That's another good one. You pretty much can't go wrong with any of the sandwiches here." He raised his Beefeater in the air. "But this one is the best."

"I'll definitely try it. My boyfriend here, on the other hand, looks as if he likes eating meat, but he's really a huge fan of the BLT."

Duke shrugged. "In my defense, I usually order two."

Cody laughed. "There's nothing wrong with that. BLTs are a classic."

Andi shifted, trying to remain casual looking as she

pointed out a paddle on his lapel. "Say, is that a pickle-ball paddle by chance?"

He touched the gold jewelry. "Yes, as a matter of fact it is. I'm in a league, and I won the championship last year. I got a trophy and this pin. Didn't know what I would do with it at first. Didn't know if people actually wore pins on their lapels anymore. But I figured I could bring them back into fashion."

Andi laughed warmly. "I like that. My boyfriend and I love pickleball as well. Don't we, honey?"

"Love it almost as much as listening to Kenny G as I stare at the stars at night."

Their order number was called, and Duke grabbed their tray. Then he looked around helplessly—all as an act, of course.

"We should have gotten here earlier," Andi murmured loud enough for Cody to hear. "Maybe we could take our food and eat on the bench outside."

"Don't be ridiculous," Cody called. "Why don't you sit here at the booth? There's plenty of room. Anyone who loves pickleball is a friend of mine."

"Are you sure?" Duke's forehead knotted with hesitation. "I feel like we're intruding."

"Not at all. Have a seat."

"Well, then . . . if you don't mind." Andi shrugged at Duke, who shrugged back.

They slid into the booth with their sandwiches. Duke handed her an Italian Stallion then grabbed his two BLTs.

"I'm Olivia, by the way," Andi started. "This is my boyfriend, Rick."

"Nice to meet you. I'm Cody. I work at the lawyer's office right across the street."

Andi widened her eyes as if impressed. "You're an attorney?"

His cheeks brightened. "Not exactly. But I'm working my way up. Right now, I'm officially a paralegal."

"It still sounds pretty impressive," Andi said. "What kind of stuff do you do?"

"Whatever my boss tells me." He let out a laugh before taking a bite of his sandwich. Then he continued to talk, not slowing down to swallow. "But I do get to do some interesting things. We have some fascinating clients we work with."

"Anyone I'd recognize?" Andi tried not to stare at the masticated food in his mouth, but it was hard not to.

Gross.

He thought about it for a moment, still chewing heartily. "We've been doing work on the drilling proposal up north. That's been interesting. Speaking of which, we're all in shock over Senator Glassine."

"I can only imagine." Duke held his sandwich raised in the air but didn't make any moves to eat it. "I hope they're able to find her. What do you think the odds are that she's still alive?"

"I don't think anyone is holding out hope for that." Then Cody flinched. "That sounds harsh. Maybe they *are* holding out hope, but it doesn't seem like the smartest idea to do so."

"The whole situation is crazy." Andi snatched a banana pepper from her sandwich and popped it in her mouth. "Especially with that vote about oil drilling coming up in that Senate subcommittee. The whole proposal has caused so much division, hasn't it? I can only imagine what it would be like to be in the middle of it all."

Andi could see while talking to Cody that his ego inflated every time she sounded impressed.

"It *is* kind of interesting being in the middle of it all." He shrugged, but the action didn't look as nonchalant as he probably wanted. "I don't really mind it though. I guess if I hated conflict, I shouldn't have gone into law, right?"

She laughed. "I guess that's correct. You're an interesting guy."

"I try." He kept his attention on her. "How about you two? What do you both do for a living?"

Thankfully, she and Duke had already discussed this.

"We're in the process of trying to open a record store here in town," Andi said. "We're scoping things out and trying to find the perfect location."

His eyebrows flickered up. "Interesting."

They knew through research that Cody collected vintage records. Their "career choice" had been purposeful.

They talked and chitchatted a while longer. Though Andi would like to get to the heart of the matter and dive in with questions about Victor that might lead to answers, she knew she had to be more subtle than that.

Being too aggressive would only scare him away. So for lunch, they stuck with chitchat.

Fifteen minutes into their conversation, Cody looked at his watch. "Unfortunately, I've got to get back to work. It was really good getting to know the two of you."

"You're pretty fun to talk to as well," Andi said. "And if you're ever looking to match up against someone new for pickleball, we were actually the pickleball champions back in Atlanta."

Cody raised his eyebrows. "Is that right? I'm always up for a good challenge on the pickleball court."

"We *love* a good challenge also," Duke said. "Name the time and place."

Cody took another bite of his sandwich and didn't swallow before asking, "How about tonight? I'm a member at a local country club, and I have the court reserved. We could play doubles."

Andi tried not to make a face as she noticed the chewed-up bread and mayo in his mouth. Instead, she stole a glance at Duke. "We would love that. We love beating people, don't we, hon?"

"Yes, we do."

Cody laughed. "I'm afraid *that* won't be happening."

Andi winked at him. "We'll see about that."

He let out another good-natured chuckle.

Other than being full of himself, Cody seemed like a nice guy—which made this whole farce harder. Tricking bad people into sharing information wasn't as guilt inducing.

The stakes were too high right now to care too much about that.

Cody rattled off an address and a time, and then he grabbed his trash to leave.

As soon as he was out of sight, Duke and Andi exchanged glances.

That had gone surprisingly well. They just had to make sure to find out the information they needed tonight.

CHAPTER
THIRTY-TWO

DUKE AND ANDI continued to eat their sandwiches after Cody left.

"You were fantastic back there," Duke said, washing his BLT down with a swig of lemonade.

"You weren't too shabby yourself." Andi pushed the rest of her sub away. "But tonight is when we really need to pull this off."

"I think you can handle it."

"I hope so." She smiled. "You ready to get out of here?"

"Let's go."

They threw their trash away and stepped outside. As soon as they did, Duke's muscles tightened. The reaction was born of experience and instinct.

He kept one hand on Andi's arm as he turned around.

"What is it?" Andi's voice switched from warm to tense.

"I feel like we're being watched."

"I don't see anyone. No one should know we're here. Only the rest of the gang and Blaze know we came to Anchorage."

"That doesn't change my gut feeling right now." All his focus turned to his surroundings. He had to be sharp. He couldn't let himself miss anything.

Not when lives were on the line.

Andi grabbed his arm and tugged him. "Maybe we should keep going if that's the case."

"Probably a good idea. I don't want to go to the car. Not yet."

"Where do you want to go?"

"Keep walking. Stay public."

"Got it." But Andi's voice didn't sound as relaxed and easy as it had only moments earlier.

He hated to put her on edge, but he needed her to know what the stakes were.

What Andi had said was correct. No one *should* know they were here. They'd covered all their tracks. Their cell phones were untraceable. They weren't in their normal vehicles.

So how would someone know they were in Anchorage?

Duke didn't like the fact he even had to ask that question.

"Where are we going?" Andi asked as she hurried to keep step with him.

"I thought we could talk to Helena. I think she could be a valuable asset. I think we can trust her."

Helena Gray was a local reporter who'd helped them solve one of their cases a few months ago. The woman was smart and resourceful. She seemed to genuinely care about justice more than receiving a byline or an award.

"Let's head toward her office." Andi slipped her hand into the crook of his arm.

Duke continued to scan everything around them as they walked.

So far, so good.

But he hadn't been imagining things.

Just before they reached the newspaper office, Andi's cell phone rang.

She glanced at the screen. "It's Mariella. Maybe she has an update."

They paused beside the building, their backs toward it. It was the safest place they could be right now.

Andi put her phone on speaker. "What's going on?"

"I called the hairdresser and told her I was an influencer doing a story on the zaniest hair stylist stories. I asked if she wanted to be featured, and she jumped on the opportunity. I mean, she jumped on it. Cleared her schedule for me even. Apparently, she looked me up and was impressed."

"Did you find out anything?" Duke leaned closer.

"She was chatty. As the conversation progressed, she mentioned that there is one rich guy whose hair she cuts, and he is so arrogant. He thinks everyone should be at his disposal. But she keeps cutting his hair because he tips well."

"Did she say Victor's name?" Andi asked.

"No, but I think we can assume that was him," Mariella said. "In fact, I asked her what this guy did for a living to make that much money, and she said that he was in the oil business."

Andi and Duke exchanged a look.

"Anything else?" Andi asked.

"We kept chatting. I told her it was interesting to have someone in the oil business as your client. Asked if he was always talking about things for work or if he seemed normal. She said he mostly kept quiet. But one day while she was cutting his hair, he was texting someone, and her eyes skimmed one of the messages."

"Did she say what it said?" Andi asked.

"I asked her. She said it read, 'The plan has been enacted.'"

A chill ran down her spine at those words.

"Good work, Mariella," Duke said.

The two of them had a blow up a while ago, but their friendship was slowly being restored.

"Thanks," Mariella said. "We're going to go back to Blaze's sister's house for now. How about you guys?"

"We have one more stop to make, and then I think

we'll head there," Andi said. "But we lined up that pick-leball game for tonight, and we'll need to get ready."

"Makes sense. Keep me updated and stay safe."

"You too." Andi hit End and put her phone away.

Now it was time to talk to Helena.

———

Andi was thrilled when Helena had agreed to meet them. In fact, the reporter had sounded excited and asked if they could meet right away at a coffeehouse down the street from her office.

Andi and Duke arrived at the eclectic coffee shop first. The walls were painted bright orange and purple and filled with local artwork. Acoustic music played on the overhead speakers, and succulents decorated any other free space.

Duke ordered them both a coffee, and they sat down.

Helena stepped inside a moment later. She was close to Andi's age with dark, thick hair and a muscular body that made it clear she liked to spend time at the gym.

She smiled at Duke and Andi, and then glanced around as if on edge.

Strange, Andi mused. Why would she be on edge?

She gave them both quick hugs before sitting down.

She wasted no time starting as she turned her gaze toward Andi. "You know people are looking for you."

Andi tried to keep her expression neutral, despite

the blunt comment. "I was afraid of that. What are they saying?"

"They're saying you killed a man," Helena whispered. "I saw your picture on a news release that was sent out by the state police department up in Fairbanks."

Andi locked her gaze on Helena's before stating, "I didn't kill anyone."

"I know that. Or I figured if you did, it was in self-defense or something."

"It's a really long story," Duke said. "But we're in trouble right now. It's all because of Victor Goodman."

Helena's eyebrows shot up. "That man is always trouble. I just wish I could find evidence to nail him. I know he's corrupt."

"So do we, and that's what we've been trying to do as well," Andi said. "But the harder we push the more he attacks us. That's why we're in the situation we're in now."

"You need help?" Helena glanced from Duke to Andi and back to Duke.

"We'd *love* your help," Duke said. "It's going to take all of us working together if we want to bring this man down. Is there anything you can share with us about Victor?"

Helena let out a breath. "I'm not sure. I mean, there are always rumors circulating. There have been protests and petitions and death threats even. What do you need to know exactly?"

Andi glanced around to make sure no one was listening before saying, "I've heard rumors about him and Glassine. I heard Glassine was in Victor's pocket."

"I've heard that shooting was politically motivated, and that the guy who's on trial for it was paid to pull the trigger. In fact, someone told me the man has cancer. It made sense to me. I was like, what kind of guy would take the fall for someone else like that? The man is facing life in prison. But if he had a terminal cancer diagnosis then maybe he figured he didn't have anything to lose."

"That's interesting," Andi murmured.

"I'm trying to find out if he received a large payout for it, and if so, where that payout went. I believe he has a daughter living somewhere in the Lower 48. I've been working on finding her, but my editor isn't very eager for me to pursue this. She said if I go after Victor, he could cause a lot of trouble for us."

"She's telling the truth." Duke crushed his paper coffee cup and tossed it in the trash.

"I know." Helena frowned before raising her chin. "But since when do journalists back down to bullies?"

Andi *definitely* liked this woman.

"However, something you may not know is this: Victor bought up the majority share in the newspaper last year," Helena said.

"What?" Andi's voice rose with surprise.

Helena nodded. "It's true. He asked us not to make a big deal about it. But talk about conflict of interest . . ."

"You can say that again," Andi murmured.

"Speaking of Glassine." Helena shifted. "I'm actually interviewing one of her staffers tomorrow. It's about the plane crash and how everyone's coping and what this means for Alaska."

"If you don't mind me asking, when and where are you meeting with this person?" Duke asked.

Helena narrowed her eyes. "You're not going to try to crash the interview, are you?"

"No," Duke reassured her. "But if I just happen to be close and overhear a few things . . ."

Helena's eyebrows shot up. "You want to hear what this person has to say, I take it."

"Yes, I guess I do." Duke paused. "What do you think?"

Helena hesitated a moment. "I'm not sure how much you're going to get out of this interview."

"We know you." Andi leaned closer. "You ask the tough questions. Maybe we could even add a few of our own if you're open to it. Because we haven't told you everything we know yet."

"You going to share?" Helena asked.

Andi and Duke exchanged glances. "As long as we set some ground rules first."

Helena stared at them both before slowly nodding. "I like where you're going with this. And I think I'm okay with your plan. But we need to talk everything out."

So that was exactly what they did over the next hour.

DUKE AND ANDI stayed in the coffee house for a few minutes after Helena left. Duke ordered another coffee for each of them. They both needed the caffeine.

The feeling that someone was watching them had faded. But Duke wasn't going to let down his guard. At least he and Andi now had a solid plan—in part, thanks to Helena.

They had three hours before they were supposed to meet Cody and play pickleball.

Duke didn't bother to tell Andi that he'd never played pickleball before. They would get to that detail soon enough.

"We just need one or two people to flip on Victor." Andi crossed her arms and shook her head. "That's all it would take to bring him down. But whoever that person is, Victor will try to off them. That's what he does."

"I know. That's when we're going to have to bring in

some type of law enforcement. We're not set up to give twenty-four-hour protection to any of these witnesses. You know that, don't you?"

Andi nibbled on the side of her lip as if fighting a frown. "I know. There are all kinds of different angles we need to look at here."

Duke glanced to the corner where a TV played. A story there caught his eye, and Andi followed his gaze.

It was about a woman's body that had been found near Fairbanks. Duke was surprised the news was reporting on her death all the way down here.

Had they reported about Skeeter down here as well?

Duke kept listening.

The woman was named Sarah Diaz, and she was twenty-seven years old and from Anchorage.

That explained why the local news was covering this.

Her body had been found off the Dalton Highway.

A picture of the woman flashed on the screen.

Duke and Andi both sucked in a breath when they saw her face.

In the picture, the brunette was wearing a pink stocking cap . . . just like the one they'd found in Lock-jaw's truck.

———

Andi wasted no time calling Gibson with the update. She made sure to mention that not only the hat, but the woman's hair color and length matched the photo as well.

"I've been so distracted today with everything else going on, that I hadn't even heard about this woman," Gibson said. "It's not on my caseload."

"How's everything going there?" Andi asked.

Gibson lowered his voice. "My boss has been asking a lot of questions."

Her heart beat harder. "Are they onto you?"

"I'm not sure. But I'm going to need to be careful."

"Anything else you can tell us?" Duke asked. "Any updates on the Skeeter situation?"

"Apparently, Andi's fingerprints were found on the phone cord that bound his arms and legs together. She's definitely the prime suspect. In fact, I'm almost certain they're not looking at anyone else."

Her throat tightened. Why would they look for anyone else? Andi had been set up as the perfect suspect.

"Are there any other video cameras around that motel?" Andi asked. "Someone knew he was in there. Knew I left. They jumped on the opportunity to make me look like a killer."

"I know," Gibson agreed. "But the only video we have right now is the one of you checking into that motel room."

"There have to be more," Andi murmured. "There has to be something that we're missing."

"I'm going to see if any of the other businesses

within a thirty-minute radius picked up on anything," Gibson continued. "There's a gas station about twenty minutes north. It should give a record of all the cars coming and going. I'm going to see what I can find out —but I have to do it all on the DL."

"Let us know what you find out." Andi's voice cracked. "Please."

"Will do."

They ended the call, and Andi and Duke rose. They tossed their empty coffee cups into the trash and then stepped toward the door.

Andi noticed Duke was still studying everything around them, looking for any signs of danger.

They'd only taken a few steps when Duke paused and grabbed her hand. "It's Devou."

Devou was a hitman who'd previously been hired to take them out. He'd disappeared for a while, but somehow, he'd found them again.

Andi followed his gaze and saw the thirtysomething, all muscles man standing across the street staring at them. Something dark stretched through his gaze. As he shifted, his jacket moved, revealing his gun.

"We have got to get out of here," Duke muttered.

He began to pull her at a fast clip down the sidewalk . . . with Devou on their heels.

IN DIFFERENT CIRCUMSTANCES, Duke might have confronted Devou. But not here on the streets of downtown Anchorage with so many civilians around. Not when he and Andi were trying to keep a low profile.

If the police came, Andi would be arrested. Maybe Duke as well.

The best the two of them could do right now was to take off and get away from Devou.

He still had no idea how this guy had found them.

Duke pulled Andi around the corner and cut through a small parking lot. They emerged onto another street.

He quickly glanced back and forth.

They could run toward the bay in the distance or toward the highway.

Neither seemed like a good choice right now.

"Duke?" Andi's voice wavered as she said his name.

He was taking too much time.

Still gripping her hand, he took off across the street.

A plan formed in his mind, one that was risky. But it might work.

He sprinted into a parking garage.

Not slowing down, he darted up two flights of steps, Andi keeping pace with him.

Then he pulled Andi behind an oversized truck, and they crouched there.

"Is this really a good idea?" Andi whispered, quietly heaving in deep gulps of air from their sprint.

Duke wasn't sure. This could go one of two ways.

He knew which way he hoped it would go.

The one that ended in his favor.

Devou had seen them come in here. He should be following any time now.

Downstairs, a door closed.

Devou was in the stairway, wasn't he?

Would the man check each floor? Duke wasn't sure.

For now, he waited. Anticipated. Braced himself.

Then he heard footsteps.

Coming toward them.

Duke pressed his gun into Andi's hand. "Use this—but only if you have to."

Her eyes widened, but she nodded.

Duke crouched closer to the edge of the truck. He ducked his head so he could see underneath the vehicles in the garage.

He saw legs and feet as the man carefully scanned the area.

Devou was two cars away.

His footsteps kept coming.

Right before the man reached the truck, Duke burst from his hiding spot and lunged at the man, his shoulder hitting his abdomen.

Devou put up a good fight—just like Duke expected.

But Duke had braced himself.

Instead of ramming the guy into the wall, Duke flipped him over his shoulder and onto the ground.

Wasting no time, Duke pinned him down.

But Devou still had his gun in hand.

Before he could use it, Duke slammed the man's hand into the ground.

The weapon flew from Devou's grip, and Duke grabbed it.

Then he rose to his feet, took a few steps back, and aimed it at Devou.

The man froze on the concrete floor and raised his hands.

Certainly, Devou had to know he was trapped.

Duke hauled in a deep breath.

Finally, the ball was in Duke's court.

———

Andi saw everything play out from her position behind the truck—she couldn't help but watch.

Duke's moves were impressive.

After several minutes of feeling as if she couldn't breathe, Andi watched as Duke subdued Devou and had raised a gun to him.

But she was too smart to let down her guard.

The tables could turn at any moment.

She rose from behind the truck, Duke's gun still in her hands. She kept it slightly lowered, but still within view, just to let Devou know that she had it. Even if the man were to somehow get away from Duke, he'd still have to face her.

"Why are you following us?" Duke demanded as he continued pointing the gun at the man.

"I'm just a hired gun," Devou sneered.

"What did Victor tell you?" Duke continued. "Why did he tell you to kill us?"

"It's like I said, I'm just doing a job." He said the words through gritted teeth.

"You could use your skills for better purposes," Duke said.

Devou's expression remained stony. "You have to do what you have to do."

At those words, realization hit Andi. She stepped closer. "Victor has something on you, doesn't he?"

She watched his face carefully.

His jaw hardened, and he averted his gaze. "I don't know what you're talking about."

Andi knew better. "He's threatening you or someone

you care about. Why else would you be pursuing us in broad daylight with so many people around?"

Devou didn't say anything.

But she knew that her words were the truth.

In fact, maybe Devou could assist them. Was she being too optimistic by thinking that?

She wasn't sure. But it wouldn't hurt to feel him out.

She stepped close enough to see his gaze.

"I know we're on opposite sides of this," Andi said. "But I'm not sure if you're on the opposite side by your own free will. My guess is that you've been forced into this position."

Still no response.

"Let us help you," Andi told him. "Stop letting Victor have this power over you. He's a tyrant who uses people before tossing them aside like yesterday's trash. He'll do the same to you. So let's talk."

As Andi waited to hear his response, she held her breath and prayed for the best.

DUKE KNEW Andi was onto something.

What she'd described was simply the way Victor operated, through coercion and manipulation. He got dirt on people. Threatened people.

It was the only way for him to ensure that the people around him remained loyal—if forced loyalty was considered loyalty.

"Tell us." Duke stared down at Devou. "Let us help you."

Was Devou going to speak? He hadn't responded to anything they said.

So they waited.

"No one can help. If I don't finish you two off—" He cut off the statement abruptly as if he'd said too much.

Duke's breath caught. "Then what?"

Devou ran a hand over his face. "They're going to

kill my brother. He's disabled and living in a group home in New York."

Shock ran through Duke. He'd known there had to be *something*. But it never ceased to disgust him just how far Victor would go.

"Is that what Victor told you?" Andi asked.

Devou nodded. "He didn't say it directly. He has people to do all his dirty work. But they sent me a picture of Tommy and made it clear I had no choice."

"You're saying you're not a hitman by choice?" Duke asked.

His gaze darkened. "I've done some jobs before. But I always took out bad people. I don't think you folks are bad people."

"Let us help you," Andi said. "If we go to the police with this, it's reason enough to arrest Victor."

Devou shook his head. "I have no proof. It's my word against his—and I've done some awful things. No one will believe me."

Duke wanted to argue with the man's assessment, but he couldn't. His words were probably true.

He had a feeling Devou was behind some other recent incidents. Duke just hadn't known the man had been coerced into doing those things.

"Maybe we can help you," Andi said. "I just need more details. Signed sworn statements. Something that will prove this. Maybe your story alone won't be enough, but we're collecting other evidence as well."

Devou's gaze remained skeptical until finally his countenance relaxed. "You really think you can bring the guy down?"

"We're *going* to bring him down," Andi told him. "If it is the last thing that we do. Right now, you just tell him we got away and you're still trying to track us."

"Then what?"

"In the meantime, we find out what you know," Duke finished. "We get either a written or a video statement. Then when it comes time to nail this guy, you'll have helped your brother be safe."

———

Andi hoped they didn't regret it.

But they let Devou go.

What were they going to do? Take him to the police where she and Duke would most likely be arrested?

That didn't make any sense.

Besides, they had a pickleball game to get ready for.

Devou had agreed to meet them at a local park at sunset so they could talk more.

Meanwhile, the two of them stopped at a department store and bought the appropriate clothing for pickleball, as well as some paddles—paying for it all in cash. They needed the right attire if they wanted to look like they knew what they were doing on the court.

"I guess I should mention I've never played this

before," Duke said as they headed toward the country club.

Andi glanced at him. "Are you for real?"

"Absolutely."

"We are supposed to be champions, so I hope you're good at faking things."

"I played football in high school, but I'm not sure how much that will help me play pickleball."

"I'm not sure either. We may have our work cut out for us tonight."

She explained the basics of the game and how to keep score as they continued the drive.

Andi hoped that this plan worked. If she could find out something from Cody and combine that with whatever Devou was willing to share, then maybe they had a chance.

This would be a great start at least.

They pulled up to the country club. Just as Cody had promised, he'd left their names at the entrance. They followed the signs back to the pickleball courts.

As soon as they walked in, Andi saw that Cody was here early.

Along with his partner.

Andi plastered on her best smile as she approached them.

But as soon as she saw who Cody's partner was, her grin faded.

Andi only knew a few people in Anchorage.

Dabney, the attorney general.

Helena, the reporter.

And Emilia Daughtry, a woman with whom she'd gone to law school and a one-time sworn enemy.

Of all the bad luck Andi could have . . .

Emilia was Cody's pickleball partner.

CHAPTER
THIRTY-SIX

ANDI'S HEART sputtered out of control as she stared at her former classmate, the one with sleek blonde hair and impeccable makeup.

The two of them had never been friends. When Andi had found out one of her professors was sleeping with a student, she'd confronted the man. He'd eventually been fired. The student he was sleeping with wasn't Emilia but a friend of hers.

Andi didn't care if she ever saw the woman again. But then she'd learned Emilia had moved to Alaska. When Andi had found herself in some trouble not long ago, she'd called up Emilia.

The woman might not be a good person, but she was an excellent lawyer.

Andi hadn't seen her since.

Until now.

"You guys made it," Cody started with a wide grin. "I'm looking forward to a good challenge tonight."

Andi let out a feeble laugh. "That's exactly what you'll be getting."

Emilia continued to stare at Andi, her eyes narrow.

But Andi gave her a look, praying Emilia got the message. So far, she hadn't said anything.

"This is my friend, Emilia," Cody started. "Emilia, this is Olivia and Rick."

Emilia's gaze flickered. "So nice to meet you . . . Olivia and Rick."

"You too," Andi said, keeping her voice warm and friendly.

Andi wasn't sure how long Emilia would remain quiet, nor was she sure what her relationship with Cody might be.

Pickleball partners? Friends? Or more?

Depending on the depth of their relationship, that could change everything.

Cody glanced at his watch. "We have five minutes until the court's ours."

"If you don't mind, I'd love to run to the locker room really quick." Andi cast Emilia a glance. "Would you mind showing me where it is?"

Something flashed in Emilia's gaze. "Not at all. Follow me."

They began walking toward a door in the distance.

This was Andi's chance to talk to her.

Before Andi could start, Emilia turned toward her,

her gaze all business as she demanded, "What are you up to, Andi—or should I say, Olivia?"

"I'm in the middle of a deep investigation," Andi whispered. "I'm begging you not to blow my cover right now."

"Why shouldn't I?" Emilia said as they kept walking, her voice full of attitude and even a touch of malice.

"There's a lot on the line, and I believe Cody has information I need."

Emilia stole a glance at Andi. They reached the locker room, and Emilia shoved the door open, ushering Andi inside.

Emilia glanced under each of the stalls, checking for anyone else.

There was no one.

She turned back to Andi. "I'm going to need more than that if you want me to keep my silence."

Andi had known her former classmate would say that. How did she know that? Because that was exactly what Andi would have said if she were in Emilia's shoes.

"We are investigating Victor Goodman," Andi rushed. "He's responsible for a string of deaths, uncountable extortions, and manipulations. If I had to guess, he's responsible for what happened to Senator Glassine as well. All this has been done to get that drilling approved up in Prudhoe Bay. We have to stop him."

Emilia narrowed her eyes but didn't argue with

Andi's statement. Instead, she crossed her arms. "What do you hope to learn from Cody?"

"We're trying to find definitive proof, and Cody works for the lawyer who works for Victor. I know Victor's lawyer won't crack. But Cody might."

Emilia only grunted.

Andi studied her face, trying to figure out what she was thinking. "Is Cody your boyfriend?"

"Cody?" She let out a scoffing laugh. "No. The man talks with food in his mouth and can't keep a secret. I'd *never* date someone like that."

That sounded exactly like Emilia.

But Andi had other things to discuss—life-changing types of things.

Andi locked her gaze with her former classmate. "Emilia, my friends' lives are on the line right now. I have to do something."

"You'd have better luck asking me to help you find out something from Cody. He's been hounding me to go out on a date with him. He'll open up to me before he will to you."

Andi raised her eyebrows. "You would do that?"

Emilia shrugged. "Victor Goodman thinks he's the smartest man in the room. He thinks he owns everything and everyone he encounters. I can't stand people like that. Plus, my real interest has always been in environmental law, and I've never been in favor of more oil drilling."

"So you're in?" Andi held her breath as she waited for the woman's response.

She paused before nodding. "I'm in."

———

Duke glanced over at Andi as she and Emilia emerged from the locker room. He tried to get a read on the situation.

Would Emilia sell them out? If so, that would give Victor more ammunition against them. But the two women seemed surprisingly pleasant as they walked toward the court.

Andi took her place beside Duke and gave him a reassuring look.

If only she could explain right now. But she couldn't.

"Let's get this game on!" Andi shouted, her voice full of enthusiasm.

For the next hour, the four of them played as hard as they could.

Cody and Emilia won two games while Andi and Duke won two.

Duke surprised himself by enjoying the game. Maybe he and Andi could play this in Fairbanks when they returned.

If things ever returned to normal.

Everything was on the line right now.

"So you're both lawyers," Andi murmured as they

all walked toward the locker rooms, towels around their necks.

Emilia cast her a look.

"I think that's amazing," Andi continued.

"I don't feel like talking about work right now." Cody's phone buzzed, and he stopped to check the message. "In fact, I need to go into the office and handle something. Sorry to cut this short."

"Is everything okay?" Duke asked.

He pulled his gaze away from the phone. "I guess you could say that. But when your boss calls, he calls. Maybe we'll get to play again sometime." Cody glanced at Emilia. "Same time next week?"

"I'll be here," she murmured.

As soon as Cody hurried away, Emilia turned to them and lowered her voice. "I'll see what I can find out."

"You'd do that for us?" Duke questioned.

Emilia nodded. "As I told Andi earlier, yes. I'd do it to bring Victor down. I'll keep in touch."

Duke hoped she was telling the truth.

Otherwise, this whole pickleball match had been for nothing.

THIRTY-SEVEN

"WELL, at least that wasn't a total waste of time," Andi whispered to Duke as they walked outside toward the Crown Victoria.

"What happened with you and Emilia back there?" Duke asked.

The two of them still hadn't had a chance to talk about the locker room conversation yet.

Andi gave him the update.

"Of all the people to be his pickleball partner." Duke shook his head in disbelief.

"You can say that again." Andi let out an exasperated breath. "Maybe we're inching closer to finding answers to all of this."

"Hopefully Devou will have the final answer we need."

Andi glanced at her watch. "We have just enough time to meet him."

They climbed into the car, and Andi plugged the address into the GPS. Then they took off toward a local park.

The place was popular with tourists who liked to see the sun set behind the mountains and watch moose meandering in the distance. At this time of year there should be enough tourists that people shouldn't notice Duke or Andi.

Andi still wore her wig, which had astoundingly stayed on during the pickleball game. She'd been worried she might have a mishap.

Overall, Cody seemed clueless as to who she really was. Or maybe he didn't know about her at all. It wasn't as if Victor was broadcasting Andi's face and declaring her as a sworn enemy that everyone in his inner and outer circles should stay away from.

Andi and Duke found a parking space and climbed out. Then they casually began to walk toward one of the boardwalks over the marsh.

She glanced around. She, Duke, and Devou hadn't exactly clarified *where* they would meet, only that they would find each other.

"You think he's going to come?" she asked Duke as they lingered near a sign detailing some of the area's history.

"It's hard to say." Duke's voice sounded tense. "Maybe he'll show up. Maybe he won't show up. Maybe he will turn up dead. Maybe he will turn on us."

The only option Andi liked was the one where they got Devou's full cooperation.

"Let's walk toward the back," Duke suggested. "It makes the most sense to meet there. It's more private, and not as many tourists know about it."

They nonchalantly walked that way, careful not to draw any attention.

The sun continued to sink on the horizon, and the mosquitoes were out in full force. But Duke and Andi ignored them as they walked toward the back of the park.

They paused at one of the last platforms on the boardwalk and leaned on a railing overlooking the marsh to wait.

It really was beautiful here. If only they'd come to enjoy the view instead of trying to stop a killer in his tracks.

Duke continued to glance around, afraid to let down his guard.

But Andi didn't see Devou anywhere.

She paced toward the other end of the viewing area and paused. She squinted as she saw something on the railing.

"Duke . . ." Her voice quivered.

He walked toward her and glanced at what she pointed at.

It was a red substance. And it was fresh. Still liquid.

"Oh no . . ." Duke muttered.

Andi followed his gaze.

She glanced deep inside the marsh where she saw a hand and a foot sticking up above the reeds.

As she followed the lines, a face came into view.

Devou's.

She swallowed the cry that wanted to escape.

Someone had silenced the hitman.

It sounded like the perfect title for their next true crime podcast.

———

Duke reached for Andi.

Devou had been shot—and it had happened recently.

Really recently.

He glanced around, looking for any signs of the shooter.

No one else was hanging around at this end of the park—which was both a good and a bad thing.

"We should report this." Andi squeezed Duke's arm.

"We can't. If we report him, then the police will show up here. They're going to want your driver's license and name. They're going to figure out who you are. The fact that you're now linked with two dead bodies? It won't be good for you."

Andi opened her mouth as if to argue but shut it again. She knew his words were true.

"So we just leave him here?" she asked.

Duke shrugged. "Somebody will find him, if not

tonight then in the morning. An investigation will be launched. We just need to hope Devou doesn't show up on any security footage following us."

Andi didn't bother to hide her shudder.

Neither of them could deny the precariousness of the situation.

Just as that thought went through his mind, a bullet split the air.

He barely heard it. Someone was using a silencer.

But he felt the bullet whiz by and heard it embed into the wood post behind him.

"Get down!" Duke shouted.

He and Andi dropped onto the wooden planks of the boardwalk.

"Where are we supposed to go from here?" Andi turned to look at him. "There are railings on three sides of us and if we run toward the parking lot, we'll be running toward the shooter."

Duke tried to come up with a viable plan that would get them both out of the situation safely.

Another bullet flew, nestling into another piece of wood behind them.

Whoever was firing wasn't going to back down.

"We have to make a run for it," Duke said. "We have no other choice."

"How do we run without getting shot?"

ANDI'S HEART raced as she tried to figure out how to get out of this situation.

Even though it seemed impossible, she knew it wasn't. She and Duke just had to use their brains.

A group of people started walking their way.

Her heart lurched into her throat when she saw them.

This could be their opportunity to get out. But if the shooter was brazen enough, more people could get hurt.

Either way, they couldn't let these people catch sight of them. If they saw Devou's dead body, and they saw Andi and Duke . . . they'd report them to the police.

Duke and Andi's investigation would come to a screeching halt.

Duke seemed to be thinking along the same lines as he grabbed her hand. "We need to go. Now."

They ran to a nearby tree, knowing it would offer them some cover.

Andi wasn't 100 percent sure which direction the shooter was located. But she thought it was from near the back of the parking lot.

She and Duke waited near the tree, listening for any signs that more shots were being fired.

There was nothing.

The large group coming toward them was laughing and boisterous. Their gregariousness could muffle the sounds of a bullet.

"Let's walk casually away from here," Duke whispered in her ear. "We don't want those people to see our faces."

It took every ounce of her strength to move from behind that tree, to not run, to remain calm. But with Duke holding her hand, it was a little bit easier.

They walked from the tree to the sidewalk and kept walking calmly.

No more shots were fired.

Maybe the group of people had scared the gunman away.

They kept their steps steady as they walked. Andi didn't dare release the pent-up air in her lungs until they reached the car.

Then she began to move quickly.

She ducked inside, and Duke wasted no time starting the motor and backing out.

But Andi knew there were no guarantees that this shooter wouldn't follow them.

———

Duke repeatedly glanced in the rearview mirror, but he didn't see anyone.

Had he and Andi lost the shooter that easily? It didn't seem possible.

But he wasn't going to complain right now either.

He headed down the road, knowing he couldn't take a direct path toward the house owned by Blaze's sister just in case they were being followed. He couldn't lead the killer to the others.

"None of this is making sense," Andi said. "How does someone know where we are and what we're doing?"

"That's a great question, and I'm not sure. But someone knew we were supposed to meet with Devou. They got there first and silenced him—permanently."

"We could have really used his firsthand account of what Victor was doing to him." Disappointment cut deeply into her voice.

"Devou's statement was going to put him in danger no matter how we looked at it. But I didn't mean to get the guy killed either."

"Me neither. If that bullet had been just one inch to the left, you might not be here." Andi reached for Duke's hand and squeezed it.

She didn't have to tell him that. Duke had already thought about it plenty.

Devou hadn't been the only person Victor had hired to do away with them. How many more were out there?

Part of him didn't want to know.

Duke circled the city, making several random turns for the next thirty minutes until he was certain no one was following them.

Then he headed to Blaze's sister's house.

Maybe someone else had discovered something.

CHAPTER
THIRTY-NINE

BLAZE'S SISTER lived in an ordinary looking home with black siding and white trim. The place, though small, appeared to be newer, and it was in a neighborhood with similar houses.

As soon as they arrived the door opened, and Blaze ushered them inside.

Andi sensed everyone was anxious to hear each other's updates.

She knew she was ready to hear if her friends had discovered anything.

She prayed for the best.

They all sat in the living room. Simmy had prepared some coffee for everybody, and even though it was late, Andi decided to have some. She also nibbled on one of the chocolate chip cookies Simmy had set out.

Andi and Duke, at everybody's insistence, started with their updates. They told the gang about meeting with Cody. About Devou. About the pickleball tournament. About the shooting at the park.

Devou's death was a big hit. So much had been riding on him being willing to come forward. Now that wouldn't be happening.

"Do you really think that we can trust Emilia?" Mariella asked. "You said she wasn't very nice when you were in school together."

"She wasn't," Andi answered honestly. "And I'm a little anxious about it to be truthful. But when she told me how much she disliked Victor, I believed her."

Then it was everyone else's turn.

"I've already been getting hate mail." Mariella rubbed her arms as if chilled. She still wasn't acting like herself. "The picture has been posted online, and people are calling me all kinds of nasty names that I won't repeat for you."

"I'm sorry." Andi truly was.

Mariella wasn't perfect—none of them were—but she didn't deserve to be exploited like this either.

Mariella shrugged as if she didn't know what to say, which was another sign something was wrong. Mariella always knew what to say.

"I talked to Ranger not long ago," Simmy said, her voice soft. "They're still searching for the wreckage."

"I talked to Matthew," Mariella added. "He's still trying to find some financial records."

"I know I'm not officially a part of any of this," Blaze chimed in. "But I talked to some of my friends who've worked with Bob before. He was the pilot flying Senator Glassine. Bob is a righteous guy and a fantastic pilot. I have a hard time believing the crash was because of any error on his part."

"Was anyone else around the plane before it took off?" Duke asked.

"That's the question of the hour, right?" Blaze shrugged. "I asked some of my friends, but no one knows. Sorry I couldn't be of more help."

Simmy's phone buzzed. As she glanced at the screen her face went pale.

"What is it?" Andi asked.

She held it up. "It's a picture of Anastasia. According to this, it was taken this morning."

———

Simmy had managed to get in touch with Ranger, who then got in touch with his friend who was watching Anastasia. He confirmed his daughter was safe and that the photo was merely a scare tactic.

Hearing that was a relief to all of them.

But Andi knew that relief wouldn't last long.

After she heard the updates, the gang talked for a little while longer. Then Andi had decided to turn in for the night. She was exhausted, and her body was demanding some rest.

She had said goodnight to Duke before disappearing into the room she shared with Mariella.

Mariella was on the back porch, talking to Jason. Andi could hear snippets of their conversation, though she tried not to listen.

She knew that Mariella was having a tough time with the picture that had been posted.

It was yet another hit on the team—but mostly Mariella was taking the brunt of it.

After going through her nighttime routine, Andi climbed under the covers. But as soon as her head hit the pillow, her brain wouldn't shut down.

Had Devou's body been discovered? Would Victor frame her for yet another death?

She knew it was a possibility.

Andi also knew that trusting Emilia could be a huge mistake. Even though she thought Emilia had been sincere earlier, her former classmate had always been the type to do what was best for herself instead of others. Emilia would stab someone in the back to get the top grade in the class—Andi knew because she'd seen it happen on more than one occasion.

The woman couldn't be trusted.

Yet Andi had to do just that right now.

She hoped she didn't regret it.

THE NEWS PLAYED on the screen.

Oil tycoon and founder of Wells Oil Company, C.W. Wells, was found murdered in his home. The police are still looking into his death, but it is believed to be a robbery gone bad. Wells is remembered for his legacy in the area. Through the foundations he set up, he started multiple children's hospitals, built schools, and is even responsible for opening four museums.

A man came on the screen and began talking about the legacy Wells left behind and how the community would never be the same now that he wasn't a part of it.

Afterward, they talked about the man's humble beginnings. His business smarts. How he was a fixture on the social scene in the area. How he'd been married four times. That he had no children.

That was why Hector was taking over his business.

He was twenty-eight now, but he'd worked his way

up through the ranks in the company all the way to vice president.

He'd learned everything he could under C.W. The man had thought of him as a mentee. And Hector had acted like C.W. was his mentor.

But the man had been clueless. It was either eat or be eaten.

That was what Hector's mother had told him. He still remembered those words. She didn't have much good advice, but that was some of it.

She had told Hector there was no in-between.

That was what he'd taken with him into business. He'd learned to become ruthless.

It was the only way he could succeed.

Just two weeks ago, C.W. had told Hector that he wanted him to take over the company one day. He'd already met with his lawyer and the board about it.

Now, if Hector's plan continued, he would soon become the president of Wells Oil.

Once he worked that position for a while, he'd change the company's name so he wouldn't have to remember the vile man who'd started the business more than thirty years ago.

Hector would never forget the look in C.W.'s eyes when he'd told the man he'd been poisoned. As Hector told C.W. who he really was. As he told C.W. what he'd done to Hector's family. How his mother was dead because of his selfishness and greed.

C.W. had begged Hector to call 911, to save him.

Instead, Hector had taken the hula girl from his pocket and held her up so she too could watch the life slip from the man.

The hula girl had reminded him of Robert—another man who had died an "accidental" death five years ago.

Hector had tampered with the man's brakes, so when Robert drove home after a late night of drinking, he'd run off the road.

The man got what was coming to him.

Hector left the hula girl on the table where she could watch Wells's body turn cold.

It only seemed fitting.

Now Hector would take over his company.

He had plans. Big plans. And nobody was going to stop him.

He would finally get what he deserved.

Just like C.W. had gotten what he deserved.

AS DUKE DRANK some coffee on the back patio the next morning, he couldn't help but think how everything seemed so surprisingly normal—if just for a moment.

However, he knew things wouldn't stay that way for long. They'd gone through some storms already, but more were coming.

Before he'd come outside, he'd listened to the news. All the local stations were reporting on the dead body in the park. Police were asking anyone with information to come forward.

Devou's face had been plastered on the screen.

The sight of it made Duke's stomach churn. He didn't like the man. In fact, Devou wasn't even a good man. But he'd been killed to keep his silence.

He'd simply been another pawn in Victor's game.

Duke took another sip of his coffee as he tried to swallow that thought.

"You want to eat?" Simmy stuck her head out the patio doors. "I made breakfast."

"I'd love to." Duke rose. "I thought I heard someone else moving around inside."

He stepped inside and, sure enough, the rest of the gang was up. Simmy made some pancakes and more coffee. She insisted they needed to eat.

They all sat together, again the moment feeling strangely normal. Even their conversation was normal as they talked about the weather and their favorite restaurants. Blaze regaled them with stories of being a Navy pilot. A Blue Angel, for that matter.

The mental break was good for all of them.

By the time they finished eating, it was time for Duke and Andi to leave. He stood and glanced at her. "You ready?"

Andi nodded and rose. "I'm ready to nail Victor to the wall."

"That's my girl."

In one hour, Helena would talk to the person who had worked for Glassine. Duke wanted to get to the restaurant early to hang out and acclimate to their surroundings.

Duke hoped this eavesdropping session would prove to be fruitful.

———

Andi sipped on her smoothie as she listened to the conversation next to her. Every once in a while, she and Duke pretended like they were talking between themselves, just so they wouldn't look suspicious.

They were close enough to overhear, yet far enough away that some things that were said sounded mumbled.

The woman whom Helena was meeting was in her early forties with short, brown hair and glasses. She wore a suit and appeared to be all business. Andi had overheard her say her name was Kelly.

Everything the woman said had clearly been rehearsed.

Politics . . .

Most of what was said was perfunctory but not necessarily interesting. Kelly said lots of nice things about the senator. Talked about how important it was to locate her. Noted all of her accomplishments and how much she was missed right now. She also mentioned Charles Sudan, who had been a faithful aide to the senator since she had been in office.

Andi couldn't wait, however, for them to get to the good stuff.

Finally, forty-two minutes—yes, Andi was keeping track—into the interview, the subject shifted.

"I've heard rumors that maybe this plane crash wasn't an accident," Helena said. "What do you think about that?"

Kelly's eyebrows shot up. "Where did you hear that?"

"Several people."

"Well, that's most likely a conspiracy theory. You know that airplane accidents happen all the time here in Alaska. We have no reason to believe this is anything but that."

"So you don't think there's any reason that someone would want the senator dead?"

"I didn't say that. Based on the volume of correspondence we get from people who oppose her, there is always the threat that somebody would want her dead. And I'm sure you haven't forgotten what happened only a few months ago when the senator was shot. So I think we both know the answer to that question."

"The new drilling prospects up north have put her on many people's radars," Helena continued.

Andi appreciated the woman's straightforward response and the way she didn't back down.

"Of course," Kelly said. "But there's no reason to think somebody would have killed her over that."

"I understand this trip to Prudhoe Bay was a surprise."

"That's right. I didn't even know about it myself until after the accident."

"But someone did, right? She had to have told someone what she was doing."

"Well, obviously." Kelly let out a chuckle. "Sarah, our legislative director, was aware of it."

Andi's eyes widened.

Then Kelly shook her head, squeezing the skin between her eyes. "I shouldn't have said that. I'm usually more on the ball than this. I'm sure Sarah doesn't want to be questioned."

"Why do you say that?" Helena asked.

"She's been very upset by this whole thing. Just because she knew about the trip doesn't mean anything. There were probably others who knew that I'm just not aware of." Kelly shifted. "Anyway, can we get back to talking about the senator's accomplishments?"

As the conversation shifted, Andi's thoughts wandered away from what was being said.

She wanted to find the legislative director, this Sarah woman. Andi needed to find out what she knew.

As Helena continued the interview, Andi and Duke glanced at each other and stood. There was no time to waste.

Based on the fleeting look Helena gave them, they would need to talk to her about this soon. Andi had no doubt the reporter didn't want anyone to get a jump on this story.

"DID YOU FIND OUT ANYTHING?" Duke asked Andi as they sat in the car.

Andi was already on her phone, researching Sarah.

"Here she is," Andi announced, a triumphant sound to her voice. "Her name is Sarah Mason, she's twenty-seven, and she works as Glassine's legislative director."

"Have you looked at her social media?"

"Doing that now," Andi muttered, her thumbs flying over her screen.

Ten minutes later, they knew everything they needed about Sarah.

The woman was single. Bright. Had graduated from the top of her class at Purdue. She had begun to work for Senator Glassine right after college graduation. Some even thought the senator was grooming her to go into politics one day.

"So where can we find her now?" Duke shifted toward Andi from behind the steering wheel.

"Turns out that she's also an author, and she's having a book signing today here in Anchorage. Her book is named *Gobbledygook*. It's a book about understanding politics for kids. According to her book bio, she couldn't decide between teaching and political science. This book allowed her to combine both."

"I guess she didn't cancel the signing after Glassine's plane went down?"

"It doesn't appear so."

They headed toward the bookstore and parked.

After walking inside, Duke and Andi stood in the back of the crowd. Probably twenty people were in line to get an autographed book. Sarah, meanwhile, smiled from behind a table with a navy-blue cloth draped over it, and an American flag stretched behind her.

She looked happy and friendly on the surface—and not like someone whose friend was possibly just killed in a plane crash. However, her gaze seemed shifty, almost as if she were anxious about something.

It could simply be the grief over what had happened to Glassine.

Or it could be something more.

What did this woman know?

It was time that they found out.

———

Andi and Duke made sure they were the last in line to talk to Sarah.

Her bright smile faltered when she saw them, almost as if she sensed they weren't regular constituents or her target readers.

"Can I help you?" She tilted her head, her voice soft but bubbly. "Would you like an autograph?"

"Can we talk to you?" Andi started. "In private."

"I'm afraid I have a busy schedule." Sarah glanced at her watch as she seemed to scramble to make up an excuse.

"It's about the senator," Duke said. "We don't believe her plane crash was an accident."

Sarah's face paled. "Why would you say that?"

"For a variety of reasons." Andi leaned on the table as if to drive home her point. "We think you know something about it."

Something switched in Sarah's gaze, and she lifted her chin. "Well, you're wrong. I don't know anything. I'm just as broken up about what happened as anyone."

"Is that your official statement on this?" Andi narrowed her eyes as she continued to openly scrutinize the woman.

Sarah tilted her head. "What do you mean?"

"We're actually podcasters with *The Round Table*," Duke explained. "Maybe you've heard of it? We're at the top of the charts right now. We're doing an episode about Glassine. When we talk about the senator, we want to include the fact you were one of only a handful of people on staff who knew she was taking this trip."

Sarah's face went paler. "You can't say that."

Andi crossed her arms. "Maybe we won't—if you'll tell us more."

Sarah glanced around. The paleness of her cheeks was suddenly replaced with red. She was clearly anxious.

She glanced back at them and lowered her voice. "What do you want to know?"

"Why didn't Glassine want anyone to know she was going to Prudhoe Bay?" Andi asked, the question ready on her tongue.

"Because she's been getting threats. She wanted to go up there to talk to people about both the environmental and cultural impact of oil drilling."

"Do you know what her conclusions were at the end of her visit?" Duke asked.

Sarah glanced around again as if double checking no one was close. "The senator was going to vote against the new oil drilling. But she didn't want anyone to know that yet, not after that man shot her."

"So you did know about her trip as well as Charles and the pilot," Andi said. "Anybody else?"

Tears suddenly filled her eyes. She wiped her manicured fingers beneath her eyelids and glanced away, her eyes fluttering with moisture.

"You can't tell anybody," she started.

Andi's heart quickened. "Tell anybody what?"

Sarah's gaze met hers again. "I'm afraid that her accident is all my fault."

DUKE'S BREATH CAUGHT. "Why is it your fault?"

Sarah's face pinched with emotional agony again. "The senator asked me not to tell anyone about the trip, and I had no intentions of breaking my promise. I knew she trusted me, and I didn't want to let her down."

"What happened?" Andi crossed her arms, her body language still showing skepticism.

Sarah drew in a shaky breath, looked upward at the ceiling as if gathering herself, and then looked back at Andi and Duke again.

"The night she left, I went home after work," Sarah explained, her words strained. "A man was waiting for me outside of my apartment."

Duke's heart thumped harder. "What happened?"

"He said he knew Glassine was planning something, and I needed to tell him what it was. He had a gun."

"Was it this man?" Duke pulled up Devou's picture on his phone.

Sarah gasped when she saw his face. "Yes, that's him. How did you know?"

"Just a hunch." Duke slid his phone back into his pocket. "What did you do?"

"I really thought this guy might shoot me. I panicked. I always thought in a scenario like that one, that I would be strong. That I'd hold out despite whatever fear I felt. But it wasn't like that. All I could see was that gun pointed at me." Her voice quivered.

"So you told the man what the senator was planning?" Andi's voice softened slightly as she clarified.

More tears fell, and this time Sarah didn't wipe them away. Instead, she nodded. "I did. I made him promise he wouldn't hurt her. He said he wouldn't. Looking back, I realize that the emphasis in that statement was on *him*. That man *himself* wasn't going to hurt her. But that didn't mean that someone else wasn't."

Duke's thoughts continued to race.

If they found out the senator was going on the secret trip, then Victor must have had one of his men go to the airport, find the plane that she would be on, and sabotage it, ensuring that it would crash.

And if Glassine was out of the picture, then maybe somebody else would be placed on the Senate subcommittee who would vote for the oil drilling.

Then Victor would get everything he wanted.

A sick feeling swirled in his gut.

How could someone be that depraved?

"Please." Sarah lowered her voice as she glanced around. "Don't tell anyone I said this."

"Don't you think the police will want to know?" Andi asked. "They need to find the person who did this."

"It will be career suicide!"

"Anyone in your shoes might have caved," Andi said.

"No one will ever trust me again." Her voice turned to a whimper.

"Isn't finding justice for your boss more important than your future career?" Duke asked.

Sarah pressed her fingers to her eyes. "It is. But . . ."

"But what?"

"I'm afraid if I talk to the police, then I'll be next. That I'll have some kind of unfortunate accident, and no one will think anything of it." Her hand went to her stomach. "And I just found out I'm pregnant. I can't risk my child."

———

Andi and Duke climbed back into the car and looked at each other with loaded gazes.

"What should we do?" Andi crossed her arms and let out a long breath. "Should we report her?"

"Not yet," Duke said. "It's important right now that we have this information. But none of it directly points back to Victor."

"If Victor thinks that Sarah knows more than she should, Sarah might be right about meeting with an unfortunate accident." Andi frowned, hating the truth in her words.

"Do you think we're ready to talk to Dabney?" Duke asked. "Do we have enough evidence yet?"

Andi sucked on her lip before shaking her head. "Honestly? I'm not sure. I feel like we're getting close. I just need that one person who can be a valid witness for all of this. Right now, so much of this is circumstantial and hearsay. Victor is a smart man and good at covering his tracks."

Andi's phone rang. It was Emilia.

"Maybe she has something for us." She answered and put the phone on speaker. "Hey, Emilia."

"Hey, yourself." The words weren't said in a friendly, warm manner. Emilia almost sounded irritated. Then again, she *always* sounded irritated.

"So Cody and I talked last night," Emilia continued. "We went to a bar down the street and had a few drinks. That's really the best way to get him to loosen up."

"Did he say anything of importance?" Duke asked.

"Maybe." Emilia paused, her voice frosty. "What's in this for me?"

Frustration rose in Andi with enough force to make

her feel choked. "I thought you wanted to bring Victor down just as much as anybody. Isn't that enough?"

"So you get all the fame and glory while I just remain in the background?"

Andi bit back a retort. "How about when we break this story, we'll be sure to interview you for your part?"

"That's a start."

"Are you saying that's not enough?" Duke asked. "You're saying you want compensation, and we don't even know what kind of information you have."

"I suppose that's true enough."

"Emilia, I just need you to do this because it's the right thing," Andi said. "I'm not doing it to get attention or ratings on the podcast. I'm doing it because Victor is a bad person. He has hurt a lot of people. He's willing to hurt the state of Alaska if that's what it takes to get his way. If he continues to grow his power the way he is, he's going to be unstoppable."

Emilia was silent for a moment, and Andi wasn't sure if her little speech had helped or hurt.

Finally, Emilia said, "Okay, fine. I got Cody talking about some of his clients. Eventually, Victor came up."

Andi's breath caught, and she and Duke exchanged a quick look of victory.

"He mentioned something about a village near the site of the oil drilling," Emilia continued. "The people in the village had initially been adamantly opposed to drilling."

"But then . . . ?" Duke prompted.

"Then Victor offered a lot of money under the table," Emilia continued. "That changed people's minds. But everyone had to sign a statement saying they were okay with what was happening. The amount Victor offered them wasn't necessarily a lot in today's economy. But to those living in the village, it was more money than most of them had seen before. But Cody thinks that the majority of them didn't know exactly what they were signing."

Andi had suspected that much might be true.

"Let me guess," Andi continued. "None of them are allowed to talk about any of this, right? That was part of the agreement."

"Of course." Emilia's tone was dry. "That's the way lawyers work."

"And everyone in the entire village was on board with it?" Andi asked.

"Here's the interesting thing. There was one woman who was outspoken against what was happening. She put up a good fight, but Victor said that if everyone in the village didn't agree that no one would get the money."

Sounds like an ultimatum Victor would make. "What happened?"

"This woman disappeared, and no one has seen her since."

Andi's breath caught. "Was she murdered?"

"Cody didn't say," Emilia said. "Maybe she was run

off. Or maybe she *was* killed. I have no idea. But if you're looking for someone who might be able to bring Victor down, I would say this woman is your best bet."

Anticipation zinged through Andi. "Did he give you a name?"

"As a matter of fact, he did. Talise Cummings."

NEARLY AS SOON AS the call with Emilia had ended, Helena called.

Duke put the phone on speaker.

But before he even said hello, Helena's voice stretched through the line. "You *cannot* break this story before I do."

The normally calm reporter sounded agitated.

"That's *not* our intention," Duke explained. "But I think you know that."

"Did you already talk to this staffer?" Helena continued, almost as if she didn't hear him. "To Sarah?"

"We did." Duke shared what they'd learned.

"I'm going to talk to her too, you know." A touch of territorial frenzy filled Helena's voice.

"She's guilt-ridden and pregnant," Duke continued. "And she doesn't know what to do."

"Pregnant?" Surprise laced Helena's voice.

"Yes, and she'll protect her baby whatever the cost." Duke couldn't blame the woman for that.

"I guess I can understand that. But maybe I can help. Maybe I can frame it so she's a hero instead of a villain. After all, it's not like she sold out the senator for money. She was threatened."

"We believe that too," Duke said. "We appreciate you letting us sit in on that interview. I know it wasn't ideal, but as you know, there's no time to waste right now."

"I know. That's the only reason I agreed."

"We're still working on this together, right?" Duke asked.

"That was our agreement," Helena said. "I might not be able to run this story in the newspaper, but I *will* do something with it."

"Thank you for your help," Duke said.

He considered whether he should share what Emilia had told them. But he decided not to. Right now, the fewer people who knew that information the better.

They ended the call, and Andi said, "I think we know what we need to do. We have to find Talise."

"I agree. But how are we going to do that?"

"We're going to have to put our heads together. I have a feeling our work here in Anchorage is almost done. We'll need to head up north again soon. For now, we should go talk to Dabney Eldridge."

"Then let's get going."

———

Andi paused outside the door of Dabney Eldridge's recently renovated home—or should she say restored? A fire had eaten away at much of the structure not long ago.

The last time Andi and Duke had been here, they had rented the house beside his. A house fire had almost claimed the life of his daughter, but Duke had rescued her.

As a result, Dabney had promised that he owed them one.

Andi prayed he'd meant those words.

His wife answered the door after they rang the bell. The caution in her eyes was quickly replaced with recognition.

"I remember you two," the woman said. "You saved my daughter, Sophia. Duke and Andi, right?"

"Yes, ma'am," Andi said. "Sorry to stop by unannounced like this. We wouldn't have done it if it wasn't important. But we wondered if we could talk to your husband about something."

"He actually just got home. Give me a minute and let me see if he's available."

"Of course," Duke said.

She closed the door, and Andi and Duke waited.

Enough time passed that Andi wondered if Dabney's wife would return. Maybe she'd simply closed the door and hoped they'd eventually go away.

But finally, footsteps sounded, and then Dabney opened the door.

The man was in his thirties with a ruddy complexion and reddish hair. He wore dress pants and a white button up shirt that had been loosened around his neck.

"If it isn't Duke and Andi." He tilted his head in surprise. "I wasn't expecting you two to show up."

"We just happened to be in town," Duke explained. "Do you have a moment by chance?"

As Dabney hesitated, Andi wondered if the man had somehow heard there was a warrant out for her arrest. Or that the Army was looking for Duke.

She couldn't be sure, but the man was definitely acting a little cagey.

Then another thought hit her. What if it had taken Dabney so long to come to the door because he had called the police? What if they were on the way here now?

As if on cue, a siren began to wail in the distance.

Her body stiffened.

Andi had to figure out if she was going to engage in fight or flight.

DUKE SAW Andi's eyes widen with concern.

Had Dabney called the police on them?

They both stood there, frozen as they tried to decide what to do.

Duke glanced at Dabney again, but the man didn't appear alarmed.

"Would you like to come inside?" he asked instead.

Duke needed to make sure that wasn't a fatal mistake.

The sirens got closer.

Then they passed.

Duke released the breath he'd been holding.

The cops hadn't been coming here. Dabney hadn't sold them out.

Relief spread through his chest.

Duke turned back to the man. "If you wouldn't mind, we would love to come inside."

Dabney gave him a nod, and they stepped inside.

The attorney general directed them to his office and closed the door. Then he took his seat behind his desk, offering them the two chairs in front of the desk. "What can I help you with?"

"After I rescued your daughter from that fire, you said that if you could ever return the favor, to let you know," Duke said. "And we have a pretty big favor to ask of you now."

"What's going on?"

From there, Duke and Andi explained everything involving Victor Goodman, including the speculation about Senator Glassine.

Dabney listened, occasionally letting out some grunts and jotting down a few notes. He didn't interrupt them except to ask clarifying questions.

They told him about how Victor would do anything to get this project through the Senate subcommittee. How he'd already invested millions. How it seemed anyone who got in his way was expendable. How there was a string of dead bodies tied to him.

When they finished, Dabney let out a long breath and rubbed his chin. "I have to admit, I've never liked the idea of doing more drilling up there. But I do like the idea of being an oil independent nation. The issue is complicated."

"We understand that," Andi said.

"If Victor Goodman is up to no good, then he needs

to be brought down. But a lot of what you've told me is hearsay. I can't prosecute someone on hearsay."

"We believe we know the name of a witness who was offered a bribe by Victor in order to give approval for drilling in the native village," Duke said.

"Is this person willing to come forward?" Dabney asked.

"We're going up to find her and ask her," Andi said.

"Once you know that she's willing to talk, come back to see me. If this guy is as nefarious as you say, then he does need to be stopped and held accountable for everything that he's done."

Hope soared in Duke's chest. Maybe there was a possibility that the end was really in sight.

But first they had to find Talise.

————

Back at the house, Andi and Duke explained everything to the rest of the gang, including Blaze.

The bush pilot was beginning to feel like an official member of their group, Andi realized. He was definitely an asset—maybe not for the podcast itself but for the investigation.

"So what now?" Mariella tucked her legs beneath her in the overstuffed recliner. "How do we find this Talise woman?"

"I'm hoping either Matthew can look online and find something or we can talk to Gibson and he might know something," Andi said. "But either way, we need to head back north."

"I'd be more than happy to take you that way." Blaze held his coffee cup in the air as if making a toast.

"How quickly can you be ready?" Andi glanced at Blaze, waiting for his response.

He shrugged. "We can get to the airport probably within the hour."

"Perfect," Andi said. "My gut is telling me we need to go immediately."

"Then let's get moving."

Ten minutes later, they were all in the Crown Victoria they'd borrowed, headed back to the executive airport.

Once there, Blaze checked out the plane.

Apprehension stretched through Andi as she watched him.

No doubt, the pilot of Glassine's plane had also done this. He'd thought the aircraft was okay. But it wasn't.

Andi prayed for safe travel for them.

Despite her reservations, the gang climbed aboard the Cessna a few minutes later and buckled up. Not long after, they were racing down the runway and then were airborne.

The hum of the motor seemed especially loud, making talking to each other more of a chore. But right now, it also felt necessary.

Something had been bothering Andi, something she hadn't wanted to bring up before.

But she didn't have much choice at this point.

She glanced at the group around her, getting their attention.

"Something has been on my mind," she started. "Victor has been one step ahead of us this whole time. He knows what we're planning and where we're going to be, and I don't understand how he knows this. How he knew we'd come down to Anchorage. How he knew to hire Devou to find us. How he knew that Devou was about to turn on him."

"What are you suggesting?" Duke asked.

Andi hesitated again. "There are a few things that could be happening, I suppose. But no one should be tracking our phones, right? And we all switched vehicles."

"Right," Simmy said slowly, her brow pinched with concern. "So how?"

"I don't believe any trackers have been placed on us," Andi continued. "I've switched bags and gone through my things. It just doesn't seem possible."

"So where does that leave us?" Mariella crossed her arms, her eyes narrowing.

"I don't even want to say this out loud. But there's no need to beat around the bush." Andi's gaze met everyone's in their circle. "What if we have a mole?"

Mariella gasped. "Do you think one of *us* is talking to Victor?"

"I don't know what I'm saying," Andi said. "I just know that Victor has a way of putting the pressure on.

And I'm not saying that anyone in our circle would want to willingly give up information. But Victor knows how to leverage things to get what he wants. I'm wondering if that's what he's doing now."

"I haven't talked to Victor," Simmy said. "And I know Ranger wouldn't."

"Neither have I," Mariella said.

She glanced at Duke who gave her a look. "I think you know me well enough to know it's not me."

"I'm clueless about everything that's going on," Blaze called from the front. "Part of me still wants to keep it that way."

Andi nibbled on the side of her lip. She believed all of them.

But what if she was wrong?

She couldn't get the thought out of her head.

If the mole wasn't anyone on this plane, that only left her with Matthew and Ranger. She didn't want to think of either of them as being guilty either.

But if they all wanted to get out of this situation in one piece, Andi couldn't stick her head in the sand and pretend like nothing was happening.

Somehow Victor was finding information on them.

Which meant Andi was going to need to be very careful about exactly what she said and to whom.

CHAPTER
FORTY-SIX

DUKE COULDN'T STOP THINKING about Andi's theory.

She had some valid points.

But he didn't want to believe there was a mole in their tight-knit group. However, Victor's power was far-reaching. Maybe he *had* managed to get someone to sell them out.

That made this entire situation even more complicated.

They needed to figure out how to handle this wrinkle. They also needed to figure out how to find Talise.

If she'd run from the native village, there were uncountable possibilities as to where she might have gone. Finding her would be like finding a needle in a haystack, as the saying went. Alaska was a huge state—if she'd even stayed here.

If she was even still alive.

The rest of the plane ride was fairly quiet, and Duke was certain they were each lost in their own thoughts. Between the mole theory and Talise, they all had a lot to think about.

They landed safely in Coldfoot, something he was relieved about. Duke wasn't normally given to paranoia, but considering the stakes and the lengths of depravity Victor was willing to go through to get what he wanted, safety was only an illusion right now.

The car they'd left at the airport was still there.

Duke checked it to make sure there were no trackers and that it hadn't been tampered with. Again, they couldn't afford to take any chances.

Everything was fine.

They gathered on the small airstrip near the plane and turned to Blaze.

"Thank you so much for your help," Duke told him.

"What else can I do for you?" He sounded as if he earnestly wanted to help.

"You're still willing to help us?" Andi asked. "Are you sure? Because I'm not sure when this will all end—or how it will end."

"I'm always up to be a part of the fight of good versus evil. It sounds to me like that's exactly the way you all are too. I'm going to hang around here for now. If you need me, you let me know. Okay?"

"We will," Andi said. "Thank you again for everything, Blaze."

They all shook hands with him before climbing into the car.

But the mood remained somber as they headed back to the Almost Halfway Trading Post.

Like always, Duke scanned the road and everything around him as he drove. He didn't see anyone who might be watching them. In fact, the road was desolate.

Twenty minutes later, they pulled up to the trading post. Lockjaw's truck was nowhere to be seen.

At least that was good news.

They hurried inside to meet Matthew.

Maybe their resident tech genius had figured out a way to find Talise.

———

Andi noticed Duke wasn't acting like himself. None of them were really.

She wished she hadn't had to bring up the possibility that someone in their group might not be trustworthy. But how could she not?

Still, she hated the awkwardness between them as they all sat in the small room at the trading post together.

"By the way, I set up security cameras here in the parking lot and in the store area," Matthew told them. "That way, I've been able to monitor everyone who's coming and going. After all, I had to leave the room sometimes to get to the bathroom. This was the only option I could think of, and Giselle agreed."

"Smart thinking," Duke said.

Andi cleared her throat, knowing they still had other things to discuss. "Were you able to find out anything about Talise, Matthew?"

Matthew shook his head. "No one in the village is going to talk to you. If Talise had stayed there, then everyone would have lost the money offered to them."

"Doesn't she have anyone on her side?" Andi asked. "Family or a boyfriend or a best friend or . . . *someone*?"

Matthew shook his head again. "Her family wasn't particularly close from what I can gather."

"How did you find out all this information?" Duke asked.

"I talked to someone who used to be a teacher in this village. I found him online, and he agreed to chat. He told me most of what I know. But that's as far as it went. He was an outsider. He wasn't privy to everything. And as soon as Victor Goodman came around, he was fired."

"So how are we going to find her?" Andi asked.

"That's the question of the hour." Matthew shrugged before glancing at Duke. "By the way, some guy with the CID stopped by here looking for you."

Duke's eyes widened. "What? What did you tell him?"

"I said you weren't here, and I didn't know where you were. It was the truth. I mean, I knew you were in Anchorage, but that was *all* I knew."

Andi glanced at Duke and saw the tautness in his gaze.

Mariella had a revealing photo placed online.

Duke could be brought up on charges with the Army.

Andi had an arrest warrant out for her.

Ranger and Simmy had been sent pictures of Anastasia.

It felt like they were all walking on thin ice . . . ice that could break at any minute.

"One more thing," Matthew continued. "While I wasn't able to figure out anything more on Victor's finances, I did discover something interesting about him."

"What's that?"

"His past appears to be fabricated."

"Come again?" Andi stared at him.

Matthew nodded. "It's true. On paper, it's all there. But when you dig into the fine details, nothing matches up. I'm fairly certain Victor Goodman isn't even his real name."

HECTOR HAD FOUND his niche in the business world and thought he had everything figured out.

Business was nothing more than a complex game. There were many players for each round. Everyone else was your opponent, and strategy was everything.

Using those insights, he'd continued his career trajectory.

Because after C.W. died, the board had voted not to let Hector take over.

That was when he had to get creative. To prove himself.

One way of doing that was by making his colleagues look bad—sometimes when they hadn't even done anything wrong. It was all about the way you framed things.

He'd gotten some people fired.

Then there was that one board member, Cecil Whitten, who was never going to vote for Hector.

It had taken some creativity for his next strategic move.

He'd also poisoned Cecil, and Hector knew that would look suspicious.

So he'd purchased a plane ticket in Cecil's name and paid with his credit card. Then he'd sent fake emails and texts that made it seem as if the man was having a nervous breakdown. In those emails, Cecil had resigned from his position so he could have a new lease on life. He had the plane ticket to Aruba to prove it.

First, Hector had dumped Cecil in a river tied down by weights ensuring he would never be found.

Then he'd taken Cecil's car to the airport and had left it in a long-term parking garage. Hector had worn some of Cecil's clothes as he had gone into the airport. He'd ditched that clothing and left.

The trail had all matched when the police looked into it.

It had gone swimmingly well. Every detail had been a great move on Hector's part.

Because everyone believed this guy had just gone on a vacation to avoid a mental breakdown.

Without Cecil in the picture, Hector had taken over as the president of the oil company.

Checkmate.

Little did Hector know that that strategy would continue to serve him well throughout his career.

He hadn't fought his way to the top. He hadn't even clawed his way to the top, even though some people might say it like that.

The truth was, Hector was the smartest person in the room. No one would ever tell him differently.

It was exactly why he'd changed his name before he went to college.

Hector wasn't the name of a winner.

But Victor was.

CHAPTER
FORTY-EIGHT
NOW

A BAD FEELING simmered in Duke's gut, and he couldn't sit still any longer.

He needed to stretch his legs.

As he excused himself to get some water, he heard Matthew scurrying behind him.

"Why is everyone looking at me like I'm backstabbing them?" Matthew whispered as they walked down the hallway. "I wouldn't do that."

"We're all on edge."

"I can sense that. But I don't know why I'm being targeted."

Exhaustion pressed on Duke, and he didn't want to explain himself. But Matthew was in obvious distress right now.

"We're just trying to figure out how information is being leaked," Duke said. "That's all."

They stepped from the lodge area and into the main

part of the trading post. Before going too far, Duke scanned the place for any signs of danger or trouble.

No one was inside except Giselle, who smiled sweetly at them from behind the counter.

Duke went straight toward the refrigerated drinks and grabbed a few bottles of water since others on the team might want one too. Matthew paused near some snacks and began browsing them.

Just as Duke stepped toward Giselle to pay, the front door opened.

A woman with long, honey-blonde hair stepped into the trading post.

She didn't look like the typical Dalton Highway traveler in her tight black dress and heels. No, she looked like someone headed out for a night of clubbing.

Duke's shoulders bristled as he waited to see if anyone else came inside after her.

The next moment, he heard Matthew say, "Lucy? What are you doing here?"

Duke's heart thudded in his ears.

Lucy? Matthew's mysterious girlfriend?

What was she doing here?

————

Andi glanced at the monitor and saw Duke and Matthew step into the store area.

Emotions were running high right now, and she'd sensed Duke needed some breathing room.

However, Matthew apparently needed some reassurance.

As she studied the men on the monitor, a woman walked into the trading post. Someone who looked out of place for this area.

But based on the way the woman strutted in as if she owned the place and glanced around, she was on a mission.

Andi's breath caught when she saw Matthew approaching her.

Did Matthew know that woman?

"Wait . . . oh . . . my . . . goodness," Mariella muttered as she hopped to her feet. "That's Lucy."

"Matthew's girlfriend?" Andi asked. "She's real?"

"Yes, she's real." Mariella shook her head as she stared at the screen. "But what is she doing *here*?"

"We need to find out." Andi stood.

She quickly looked at the monitor showing the outside of the trading post, just to make sure the coast was clear.

She didn't see anyone.

Andi rushed into the retail area—Mariella and Simmy on her heels—just in time to see Lucy throw her arms around Matthew.

They surrounded the couple, none of them bothering to hide the irritation from their expressions. Lucy didn't seem Matthew's type. She was too social, too prissy, too . . . high maintenance.

Matthew, however, appeared oblivious to his friends'

irritation as he turned toward them, keeping one arm around the woman. He was practically beaming. "Everyone . . . this is Lucy, my girlfriend."

Lucy smiled sweetly. "Hey, guys. Sorry to come uninvited. But I just *had* to see Matthew."

"How did you know where he was?" Andi didn't bother with niceties.

"Matthew told me, of course." Lucy rested her hand on Matthew's chest and grinned again.

Red filled Matthew's cheeks, but he didn't deny her words.

"Matthew?" Mariella turned toward him. "You knew we weren't supposed to tell anyone where we are. Jason doesn't even know where I am, and he *definitely* wouldn't just show up here if he did!"

Matthew's gaze darkened. "Why are all of you over-reacting? All of you have someone to talk to. I don't have anyone. So Lucy has been helping me. She's the reason I got that lead on Talise!"

Andi turned toward Lucy, not buying Matthew's explanation. "You shouldn't be here."

"That's rude." Matthew scowled. "You can't talk to her like that."

Andi turned to him. "Don't you know everything that's at stake? Have we not made it clear that people's lives are on the line? This isn't just about a podcast anymore!"

Before he could answer, another realization hit her.

Andi physically took a step back as she reeled at the thought.

"Andi?" Concern stretched through Duke's voice.

But her gaze was focused solely on Lucy. "You're the mole, am I right?"

Lucy blinked innocently. "I don't know what you're talking about."

"You've been siphoning information from Matthew and sharing it with Victor. Everything finally makes sense." Andi raked a hand through her hair. How could she not have seen this before? "It's been you all along."

"Stop talking to her like that!" Matthew stepped closer, his cheeks still flaming.

"Why would I ever do something like that?" Lucy blinked again, her clueless, innocent act growing old.

"Open your eyes, Matthew." Andi's gaze burned into his. "It's not a coincidence she showed up here right now. You know it's true. Don't be blinded by your feelings."

Lucy crossed her arms, her demeanor changing from friendly and innocent to irritated and put out. "I'm only trying to be supportive. I have no idea what kind of little conspiracy theory you're trying to come up with. Matthew said you're all drama queens."

Despite the words—and the deflection—Andi could see right through the woman.

"Is this what you all think?" Matthew scanned their faces.

Quiet stretched a moment—a quiet plumb full of

unspoken accusations. No one wanted to be the first to agree with Andi, it seemed.

"I hate to say it, but it makes sense." Mariella finally broke the silence, fire flashing in her gaze. "How much have you been sharing with Lucy?"

Matthew turned sheepish, and Andi knew the answer.

He'd been sharing *everything*.

Nausea swirled in her gut. How could he have done this? His betrayal felt like a knife in the back—even if it hadn't been totally on purpose.

"Lucy isn't like that." Matthew sliced a hand through the air. "None of you know what you're talking about."

Andi barely heard him. Instead, her gaze zeroed in on Lucy. "How long have you worked for Victor?"

Her expression remained neutral. "Who's *Victor*?"

"Really?" Andi shook her head, still not buying her act. "That's what you're going with?"

Matthew turned to Duke as if looking for support. "Is this what you think too? That my girlfriend is only with me because she's using me?"

Duke nodded, his expression solemn. "I'm sorry. But it makes sense."

Matthew glanced at each of them before slowly shaking his head. "I can't believe this. I thought you were all my friends."

"Some friends . . ." Lucy murmured with a half eye roll.

"I've given up everything to help you out," Matthew continued. "I've bent over backward. And this is the thanks I get?"

"Matthew—" Mariella started.

Matthew grabbed Lucy's hand. "Come on. Let's get out of here."

Mariella's shoulders slumped. "Matthew, don't leave. You don't want to do this."

"Are you coming with me?" He paused, Lucy's hand still in his, and stared at his twin. "Or are you on their side?"

"It's not like that."

"I think it is," Matthew told her. "So what's your choice?"

Mariella remained quiet a moment before saying, "I'm not leaving."

Matthew scoffed and slowly shook his head. "I should have known. You were the ones just using me. Lucy was right. She told me you all were treating me like hired help. I should have listened."

Mariella's nostrils flared. "She's trying to turn you against us!"

"You're wrong. Lucy is the only one on my side." An equal amount of fire flashed in Matthew's gaze. "Let me grab my things. Then we'll get out of here. I'm done with this."

Andi had never seen him like this. He was usually so quiet and passive. She considered trying to talk some sense into him. But she didn't have it in herself to do so.

Maybe Matthew *should* go. He was proving himself to be a liability.

Thankfully, the team hadn't discussed what their next course of action would be. If they had, Lucy would find out, which would have set them back even further.

But they all needed to decide how they would proceed from here.

This was one setback they didn't need.

CHAPTER
FORTY-NINE

DUKE STILL FUMED over the Lucy situation.

How could Matthew have been so careless? Not only had he put the team in danger, but he'd put himself in danger as well.

But Matthew wouldn't listen to reason.

That had been clear when Matthew had left with that woman. If Lucy truly did work for Victor, then Matthew was in a very precarious spot.

Now they were all compromised and needed to get out of here.

But first, they needed a plan.

Duke could only think of one person to turn to for help.

He excused himself from the rest of the gang, who all stood in the trading post in shock, and stepped into the hallway near the sleeping quarters.

He called Gibson.

Gibson answered on the first ring, and Duke told him about Talise.

"Funny you bring this up because I actually worked Talise's case," Gibson said.

"What?" Duke's voice rose.

"The teacher who was working in the village called the state police when Talise went missing. I was assigned to look into it."

"And?"

"And . . . I investigated her disappearance—or if it could be more than a mere disappearance. I feared she might have been killed."

Duke's breath hitched. "Did you discover anything?"

"That's the unfortunate part. Just as I started digging into things, my captain told me I needed to drop it. He said we had more important cases to handle."

"What?" Duke's voice rose with indignation.

"I know. That's how I felt as well."

"Before the case was dismissed, did you get any inkling as to where she might have gone?"

"Just because my captain told me to stop didn't mean that I did."

Duke sucked in a breath. He knew there was a reason he'd always liked Gibson.

"And?" Duke asked.

"Last I knew, she left the village and went to a place called Beedoye. She'd met a man from that area when she lived in Fairbanks for a summer. The two hit it off and stayed in touch."

"Where is Beedoye?" Duke asked. "I've never heard of it."

"It's about an hour west of Coldfoot. As soon as I confirmed Talise was safe, I didn't ask any more questions. My hands were tied. My impression was that she wanted to start a new life."

"Thanks for sharing that," Duke said. "It's very helpful."

"Let me know what else you need," Gibson said. "I'm committed to this with you."

"Will do." Duke ended the call and stepped back into the store area. Everyone turned and looked at him expectantly. "Good news. I know where we might be able to find this Talise woman."

"Oh yeah?" A knot formed between Andi's eyes. "Where?"

He explained to them what Gibson had said.

"What's the best route to take?" Andi asked.

"We'll go to Coldfoot to meet Blaze," Duke said. "I just need to call him and confirm that works with his schedule."

"Then let's do it," Andi said. "Time is not on our side."

"Duke, you'll never believe this!" Mariella rushed toward him as they all gathered to leave.

He paused, hoping she had good news.

"Matthew forgot to take some of his notes," Mariella explained. "I started looking through them, just curious as to what he was working on. He was onto something!"

Duke crossed his arms. "What do you mean?"

"Remember how Matthew said it appeared that Victor Goodman isn't his real name?"

Now Mariella had his full attention. "Go on."

"I mean, the man did a great job creating a new identity. But Matthew was able to dig deeper. This must have been what he was talking about earlier. His real name was Hector Jones. He grew up in a poor town in Texas that was bought out by big oil. But he was smart and resourceful, and he turned his life around. Went to a prestigious school and graduated top of his class."

He rubbed his chin. "Really?"

She nodded. "Yes, really. This is big!"

It was big. It gave them more of a psychological profile on the man, explained a little about why he might be the way he was today.

He couldn't believe no one had uncovered this yet.

But it was like Mariella had said—the man was good at covering his tracks. It was how he'd gotten this far in life.

And it was another reason why he was so dangerous.

"I DEFINITELY WANT to look into that more," Duke told Mariella. "This could be the break we've been looking for. But right now, we've got to go."

"Right. I just wanted to let you know ASAP."

"I appreciate that."

Thirty minutes later, they all climbed into the sedan Alfonso had let Mariella and Matthew borrow.

As they started down the road, Duke started sorting through all the new information.

First, he wondered about Victor's real identity. There had to be more to that. They just needed to dig more.

Matthew, even though he'd essentially failed them, had done some good work. He only wished things hadn't gone as they had.

Then his thoughts shifted to Talise. If they could only find her, then they might have some of the answers they needed.

Otherwise, they were just spinning their wheels, trying to move forward yet going nowhere.

He prayed that wasn't the case.

He settled in for the drive, heading north on the desolate road.

A few minutes later, a vehicle appeared in the distance, coming toward them. Normally, that wouldn't be a big deal.

But this vehicle was hard to forget.

It was a large F-350 with antlers on the grille.

Lockjaw.

He was headed toward them on the highway.

"Everybody get down!" Duke told them.

Then Duke pulled his hat down close to his eyes to shadow his own face.

———

Andi ducked below the windows, squeezing her eyes shut.

She'd seen the truck. She knew what was happening.

How in the world had Lockjaw found them?

Then she realized that he *hadn't* found them.

He must be heading back down south. The timing of their paths crossing couldn't be worse.

Maybe—hopefully—he wouldn't recognize them in this vehicle.

"Duke?" Andi was anxious to know what he was seeing right now.

"I don't know anything yet." His jaw hardened. "In theory, we should be fine. Lockjaw shouldn't recognize this vehicle. Shouldn't expect us to be up this way."

Andi prayed he was correct.

But she could hardly breathe as she continued to wait.

Lockjaw had to be almost upon them by now. Andi used every ounce of her self-control to keep her head low and not peek to see what was happening.

Finally, she heard the truck rumble by.

He hadn't stopped. Hadn't slowed.

He must not have recognized them.

Praise God!

She let out the breath she hadn't even realized she was holding.

They'd just barely scraped by on that one.

"I think we're clear," Duke said over his shoulder.

At those words, everyone slowly rose from their hiding positions.

Andi glanced behind them, wanting to see for herself that Lockjaw was gone.

When she did, the truck's brake lights lit.

The next moment, the vehicle skidded, then did a quick U-turn.

Andi's heart thudded in her ears.

Even though the reaction was delayed, Lockjaw had somehow recognized them.

The next moment, the truck engine roared.

Even as Duke hit the accelerator, Andi knew it was

only a matter of time before Lockjaw caught up with them.

Then what would happen? After all, he had vowed revenge for his son's death.

DUKE GRIPPED THE WHEEL.

This section of the Dalton Highway was narrow and straight. There were no streets to turn on.

It was an open road and nothing else. He could pull into the boggy tundra around them, but his vehicle was too low, and Lockjaw's was high. They wouldn't stand a chance.

No, he needed another plan.

He glanced in the rearview mirror again.

Lockjaw quickly gained on them.

"Can't you go any faster?" Andi kept her neck craned toward the back window.

"I'm trying," Duke muttered through gritted teeth.

But it didn't matter how hard he pressed the pedal. Lockjaw's vehicle was faster. If his truck hit the back of their sedan, it could send them veering off road. If that didn't hurt them, Lockjaw would make sure they all suffered on his terms—which would be even worse.

"Anyone have any ideas?" Duke asked the question through gritted teeth.

"Divine intervention?" Mariella suggested, grasping the door and ceiling as they barreled down the road.

"I'm always in favor of that," Duke muttered.

Lockjaw's bumper collided with theirs.

Their car lurched forward.

Mariella screamed.

Andi and Simmy braced themselves.

A couple more of those, and they'd tumble off the road.

Duke's jaw hardened.

They could use that divine intervention anytime now.

———

Andi wasn't going to go down like this.

No way.

There had to be something she could do.

That was when inspiration hit.

She turned toward Duke. "I've got an idea."

"I'm up for anything." Duke's grip remained white-knuckled on the steering wheel.

Before he even finished his statement, Andi began to climb into the back seat.

"What are you doing?" Duke's voice rose in surprise.

Andi squeezed between Simmy and Mariella and tugged at a tab on top of the middle seat.

It was a shortcut into the trunk. She'd had a car like this in high school, so she knew the ins and outs of the vehicle.

"Going into the trunk while Lockjaw is slamming into our rear is *not* a good idea," Duke exclaimed.

He had a point, but going into the trunk was the only way.

"Trust me." Andi climbed into the dark space and grabbed her phone, turning on her flashlight.

She searched the contents of the trunk.

Finally, she saw a box.

Mariella and Matthew had said the vehicle had belonged to one of Alfonso's construction teams and that tools had been left behind.

She needed to see what kind.

"Andi?" Duke called. "Lockjaw is about to ram us again."

She braced herself. The next moment, there was another nudge. More than a nudge, actually. Andi had felt the hit with her entire body.

She didn't have much time, she realized.

Working quickly, she searched through the tools before stopping on a box of nails. She pulled her knees up beside her so she could move more freely.

Then she found the latch to open the trunk. She tugged on it until a crack of light and crisp wind filled the space.

Grabbing the nails, she poured them out onto the road.

She prayed her plan worked because after this, she was all out of ideas.

Before she could shut the trunk, she caught a glimpse of the truck behind them.

Lockjaw charged toward them. At any moment, his truck would hit them again.

She had to get as far away from his bumper as possible.

She scrambled from the back of the vehicle and climbed in between Simmy and Mariella.

"Here he comes again!" Tension stretched through Duke's voice.

Andi squeezed her eyes shut as she waited for the impact.

This just may be the one that did them in.

CHAPTER
FIFTY-TWO

DUKE GLANCED in the rearview mirror again.

He had no idea what Andi was up to. But he trusted her. He just didn't want her to get hurt.

The truck was so close that Duke could no longer see the antlers on the grille. And he could clearly see Lockjaw's crazed expression as the man gripped the wheel.

He'd lost his mind, Duke realized as he braced himself for the impact.

His muscles remained tight as the seconds ticked by.

But there was no crash.

Duke glanced in the rearview mirror one more time, and he saw the truck begin to swerve.

Lockjaw was losing control of his vehicle.

But how? What kind of sorcery had Andi enacted?

A moment later, the oversized truck bounced off the road and onto the tundra before lurching to a stop.

From what Duke could tell, the man's tire had blown out.

"You can sit up now," he told his passengers.

Andi drew herself upright into the seat and let out a long breath.

"What happened?" he asked.

"I remembered there were tools in the truck and found some nails. I dropped them on the road and prayed that one or two might pop Lockjaw's tires."

Admiration filled his chest. No one could accuse Andi of being unintelligent. The woman had some great critical thinking skills.

"Good job," he said, pride in his voice.

"Thanks." She shrugged as if it were no big deal as she climbed into the passenger seat. "That was close, to say the least."

"We bought ourselves some time," Duke said. "But Lockjaw could still call backup so we need to be on guard."

"You're absolutely right," Andi said. "Thankfully, we're only about fifteen minutes from Coldfoot. Hopefully, once we're in the air, Lockjaw won't be able to find us. Even though Blaze will need to file a flight plan, Lockjaw shouldn't be able to access it."

"He shouldn't. But there's a big difference between what he should and shouldn't be able to do."

Less than an hour later, the team had loaded into Blaze's plane.

Thank goodness he'd been willing to help them out again. Without Blaze, they wouldn't have been able to accomplish as much as they had so far. And thanks to the money the podcast was bringing in, they could reimburse him for all his time.

Andi's thoughts wandered as she looked out the window. She hoped this lead paid off. But she also knew it was a longshot.

The best-case scenario investigation-wise would have been if the group split up. But considering everything that happened, it didn't seem safe to leave Simmy and Mariella at the trading post. Not after Lucy had shown up.

They needed to stay together.

Andi was still worried about Matthew. He'd made the choice to leave. He didn't believe the team when they had tried to warn him about Lucy's intentions. Yet if Lucy truly did work for Victor, then Matthew could be in danger right now.

Andi prayed he'd stay safe. Maybe once they talked to Talise they could track him down and talk some sense into him.

But she needed to eat this elephant one bite at a time, as the saying went. If Andi looked too much at the big picture she would be overwhelmed as she faced this giant. Her strength rested in focusing on the details.

Without incident, they landed in the small village of Beedoye.

After Blaze had secured the plane, they climbed out.

As Andi stretched on the runway, she glanced up at the sky. She was no weather expert, but those clouds in the distance looked ominous. Were they coming this way?

She repressed a shiver.

"So how do we get into town from here?" Mariella glanced around at the tundra surrounding them. It was split by the gravel runway path and nothing else. Buildings rose up in the distance, probably a mile away. "Is there another airport car we can borrow?"

"Nope," Blaze said. "Looks like we'll need to walk."

This community was much like some of the other villages Andi had seen. Poor and desolate. Not without hope, necessarily, but there was a sense of oppression in the air.

Andi couldn't exactly put her finger on the feeling she had. However, she knew many people who lived in these villages felt stuck without resources and jobs, without proper medical care or education.

Many wanted to stay and preserve their culture and community.

But most wanted their lives in their native land to be better.

As the team—including Blaze—walked down the lane, houses began to appear. They were mostly clapboard, small, and rundown. There were no trees or flowers to make things look homey. Everything was either white or beige, colors that only added to the bleakness of the area.

A few ATVs were parked near the houses and trashcans were out front of several.

As they walked, people stepped onto their stoops and watched them wordlessly.

Maybe they didn't get visitors here very often. She knew their little group stood out.

But she wasn't sure if that would work in their favor or not.

As if to answer her question, four men stepped into the middle of the street.

For a moment, Andi felt as if she'd stepped into an Old West showdown.

As she stared at the animosity on the men's faces, she braced herself for what felt like an oncoming gunfight.

CHAPTER
FIFTY-THREE

DUKE DIDN'T LIKE the way this looked.

The men in front of them were *not* happy to have Duke and his friends in their village. They were outsiders—and potentially viewed as enemies.

He had to calm the situation before it got worse.

"We're not here to cause trouble," Duke started, pouncing the air with his hands. "We're just looking for someone."

"Who?" one of the men called back.

The two groups stopped in front of each other, facing off in the street while the crowd around them watched.

The opposing group's spokesperson was a man in his early forties with a brawny build and dark eyes. The scars on his face spoke volumes about his life experiences.

"Talise Cummings," Duke stated. "Do you know her?"

"Never heard of her," the man said.

Andi stepped closer. "She's in her early thirties. Probably single. She's not from this village, but she lives here now."

"Like I said, never heard of her." The man sneered, a mean look in his gaze. His hands were fisted.

Another man held what appeared to be a switchblade.

"We're doing a true crime podcast," Mariella said. "We think we can help her. That's all we want to do—to help."

The man's gaze remained icy. "I'm sorry you came all this way for nothing. She's not here. You should leave."

Duke bit back his disappointment. These guys weren't going to help.

It seemed a shame Duke and his team had come all the way here for nothing.

"We're sorry to have bothered you," Duke said.

"You should go now." The man pointed at the sky. "Before the snow starts."

Duke had seen the clouds. It seemed early to have a snowstorm—it was only September. But he knew this far north, snow was a definite possibility. However, a storm like that would make the flight back to Coldfoot more difficult and dangerous.

Duke directed everyone to turn around.

Andi glanced at him, her expression incredulous. "We're just going to give in that easily?"

"These people aren't going to help us." Duke kept his voice low as he said the words.

"But maybe we could reason with them!" Andi didn't bother to remain quiet. No, she was fired up.

"They're not interested in reasoning," he pointed out.

"How can you be so sure?" Mariella asked.

"Because I've seen those looks before," Duke told her. "They're protecting her."

Andi's eyes widened. "You think Talise *is* here?"

"I do," Duke said. "But talking to those men wasn't going to get us any closer to finding her. We need to come up with another plan—and fast."

———

Andi's thoughts raced. They couldn't have come all the way out here for nothing.

Especially if Talise really was here.

She could appreciate a community being protective of one of their own. But there was so much more at stake right now. If they could just talk to her . . .

She slowed her steps, trying to buy more time. There had to be another way.

Money obviously didn't motivate this woman. Did fame? Justice?

Justice, Andi would bet.

"It's too bad we can't find her," Andi said loudly.

"She's the hero we've been looking for, the only one who can stop this."

Duke gave her a look before catching on to what she was doing. "If she wants to hide, there's nothing we can do. We'll have to find someone else who's brave enough to come forward."

"Now Victor is going to get everything he wants," Andi continued. "How are we going to stop him?"

She hoped that Talise might be nearby. That she might hear something.

That she might feel compelled to do the right thing.

They reached the edge of town, the last house.

Most of the crowd had gone back inside. Or maybe they still watched from the windows. Andi couldn't be sure.

Had that little setup worked?

As they stepped beyond the last house, someone emerged from the shadows. A heavy-set woman in her early thirties with long, dark hair and an intelligent gaze.

Her arms were crossed over her chest as she stared at them. "I heard you're looking for me."

Talise.

They'd found her.

Or more accurately, Talise had found them.

DUKE STARED AT TALISE, his pulse quickening.

Maybe this trip hadn't been for nothing after all.

"We need to talk to you." Duke stepped closer. "Please, hear us out, at least. There's a lot on the line, and we've gone through a lot of trouble to get here."

Talise glanced around. "I don't want people here to know we're speaking. If you stick around too much longer, they will find out."

"It's important that we talk with you," Andi said. "Really important. We wouldn't have come all this way if it weren't."

Talise stared at them, not bothering to hide the skepticism in her gaze. "Who are you again?"

"We're with *The Round Table* podcast," Andi explained. "We're trying to bring Victor Goodman down, and we think you can help us. Maybe you're the *only* one who can help us. No one else is willing to come forward."

Talise's icy glare remained on them a few minutes before she finally asked, "You flew in, correct?"

"We did," Andi said.

"I'll meet you at your plane in twenty minutes."

Blaze glanced at his watch. "We need to take off within thirty. I can't fly out of here in a snowstorm, and I don't think anyone in this town is going to offer us room and board for the night."

"I will be there as soon as I can," Talise said. "But we need to do things my way."

Duke didn't like this. Didn't like all the elements surrounding them. The storm. The abrasiveness of the village people. The fact Talise was reluctant to talk to them.

But they had to try. They hadn't come this far to give up.

They continued through the tundra to the small airstrip where Blaze's plane waited.

They all paused there, knowing their time was running out.

Duke glanced up at the sky again, then he looked at Blaze. "Is this storm supposed to be a doozy?"

"It's not this storm I'm worried about so much." Blaze glanced up and frowned. "This one's going to breeze in and out and bring some flurries. It will make flying difficult because of the cloud cover but nothing else. But another system is coming in right behind it. I *definitely* don't want to fly through that one."

Duke could feel the apprehension thrumming through the air. They were all on edge now.

How long had it been since they'd run into Talise? At least ten minutes. Duke had been praying that the woman would be early instead of late.

Andi paced near the plane. Duke could see her mind racing. No doubt, she was rehearsing everything she needed to say to Talise, how she could convince her to help.

Because if Talise agreed to help them, she'd essentially be giving up everything. She would be a target. Her life might not ever be the same.

Andi glanced at the time on her phone. "It's been twenty minutes. Talise isn't here. What if she doesn't show up?"

Duke had already thought about that also. It was a possibility the woman wouldn't come.

"Let's give it another few minutes," Duke said. "If she didn't want to talk to us, then she wouldn't have made herself known when we were looking for her."

Andi held his gaze for a moment before nodding. "You're right. I'm just on edge."

"We all are," Duke told her.

Five more minutes passed. Each of the seconds seemed to crawl by with uncertainty.

The sky grew darker. Blaze continuously checked the radar. Andi continued to pace.

At what point did they admit defeat and leave?

Maybe that was what Duke should suggest. After all, the safety of the team was more important than this meeting.

But just as Duke opened his mouth to say the words, a figure on a bicycle pedaled toward them, heading from the village.

His breath caught.

Was that Talise? This person wore an oversized coat, one that made it almost impossible to tell if it was even a man or a woman.

It could be one of the men coming to make good on his threats.

Duke's muscles bristled as he waited to see who it was.

———

Andi watched anxiously as the person on the bike came closer.

She hoped this wasn't a trap.

A moment later, the biker stopped and threw the hood off.

Talise stared back at them.

Relief swept through Andi at the sight of her.

"I'm sorry I'm late," Talise started, swinging her long hair behind her. "But I didn't want anyone to see me."

"We're just glad you came." Andi stepped closer. "We know you're taking a risk by doing so."

"You have no idea." She laid the bike on the gravel and paced toward them. "I know this isn't ideal. I only have a few minutes to speak with you."

"We're trying to bring down Victor Goodman, and I think you have information that could help us." Andi swallowed hard. "Would you be willing to talk to us about that? About what happened in your village up near Prudhoe Bay?"

Her gaze darkened. "I'm still angry about it. I was disowned, and I came here to hide out. I'm still not sure how you found me."

Andi glanced at Duke. "It was difficult, but we're thankful it worked out."

Talise crossed her arms over her chest. "Yes, Victor Goodman paid off everyone in my village. Made us promises. Everyone fell for it. Everyone but *me*. But it was all or nothing. Everyone had to sign a contract stating they wouldn't speak to anybody about the terms listed in their deal."

"Sounds crooked," Duke said.

"It *was* crooked." Her eyes narrowed. "What we all stood to make in the deal was what Victor Goodman stands to make in one week of drilling. The payout was pathetic. But when you have nothing, an amount like the one he presented to us seems too good to be true."

"Since you've come here, you haven't spoken to anyone about this?" Andi continued.

"No. I fear what Victor might do to my family if he were to find out. My family rejected me, but I still don't want anything to happen to them. They don't deserve that."

"We could help you," Duke said.

She stared at him defiantly. "That sounds too good to be true."

"I don't want to make you promises I can't keep. But I do think it's possible for us to hammer out all the details so this can be a win for everybody. We can use discretion and be smart about this. We have the attorney general on our side, as well as a state trooper and a reporter. Not only that, but our podcast has millions of listeners. We have the right platform to make this work." Duke paused. "What do you think?"

DUKE WAITED for whatever Talise might say.

The tension in the air was as thick as an Alaskan bog.

"Guys . . . I hate to cut this short." Blaze's voice sliced into their conversation. "But we need to be on this plane and taking off soon."

Duke looked back at Talise, hearing the mental timer ticking in his head. "What do you say?"

Her lips pulled into a tight line. A moment later, she said, "With the right stipulations in place, I'll tell you what Victor did to my village. Because I did not sign anything. But I need to know that my family will be safe. That my village will be safe. They don't deserve any of this."

"If we're able to bring attention to what's going on through our podcast and then something happens to any of those people, Victor has to know it's going to point back to him," Andi said. "He's not that stupid. In fact, he's very smart."

"Okay, if you're sure . . . here is my number." Talise pressed the paper into Andi's hands. "Now, I must go before anyone sees me with you. Call me, and we can discuss more details."

Andi slipped the paper into her pocket.

As Talise rode away, the whole team looked at each other.

The victory in their gazes couldn't be denied.

———

Andi knew this was their ace in the hole.

If they could just get Talise to agree to their terms, then they'd have all the evidence they needed against Victor.

It almost seemed too good to be true.

"You guys." Mariella stepped toward them, waving at snowflakes now drifting from the sky. "We've got to go."

Andi snapped from her thoughts and nodded. She headed toward the plane with the rest of the crew so they could gear up and get out of here before the snow got any worse.

But her thoughts remained on this isolated village. Her thoughts remained on Talise.

"This is what we've been looking for, guys." Simmy

snapped her seatbelt in place. "Maybe we can put all of this behind us."

"Let's hope," Mariella said. "I can start getting stuff ready for the podcast as soon as you give me the go ahead."

Andi's thoughts continued to race through everything they needed to do, everything they needed to happen. To start with, they would need an official written or recorded statement from Talise about what had happened.

Andi hoped that maybe Talise had saved the contract Victor had offered her. The contract itself may not be illegal but paying off people to get what you wanted was.

As Blaze got the engines going, Simmy glanced at her phone. She was probably able to hop onto Wi-Fi here in town. Cell phone coverage—other than satellite phones—was nearly nonexistent in many parts of Alaska.

She looked at the screen, and her face went pale.

DUKE KNEW something was wrong with Simmy. But Blaze, from his position in the cockpit, was unaware. He told everyone to buckle up as they started down the runway.

But Duke's gaze remained on Simmy. "What's going on?"

She turned the phone toward them so they could see a photo.

It was Ranger.

Blood spread across his chest as he lay in the snow, his eyes closed. He looked . . . dead.

Duke's heart beat harder.

"It says we all need to find him at these coordinates by seven a.m. tomorrow or he is going to be left for dead. They'll keep him alive until then." Simmy paused and swallowed hard. "And that we can't tell anyone."

Going to a secluded location at Victor's demand seemed like a terrible idea. But what choice did they have?

"It says we all have to go," Mariella murmured.

"What about Matthew?" Simmy rubbed her throat as if fighting back emotions.

Silence fell as they lifted into the air.

It was a good question.

There was no way they'd be able to get him to come back up here and meet at those GPS coordinates.

Duke was especially worried about Simmy and what she was probably going through.

Quickly, he searched the coordinates, needing to know exactly what was being asked of them.

He found the location. It was worse than he'd thought.

Ranger had been left practically in the middle of nowhere.

The team had to decide now. There was no time to waste.

Duke leaned toward Blaze. "Slight change of plans. Is there any way we could land closer to Gates of the Arctic?"

"Let me see what I can do," Blaze murmured.

———

Andi's heart pounded in her ears.

She couldn't get that picture of Ranger out of her mind.

She didn't think that the photo was faked. It looked real.

If it was real, then Ranger was in serious trouble.

According to the location that had been sent, Ranger had been left near Gates of the Arctic National Park, the same area where crews had been searching for Glassine's plane. It was also one of the vastest wildernesses in the world.

What if Victor had somehow found out what Ranger was doing, and he had sent someone after him?

Wouldn't the search and rescue team have contacted someone to let them know what had happened? To report that Ranger was missing?

Andi wasn't sure how that worked, but communication in this area was sketchy at best.

If they were going to head out to find Ranger, they had some other details they'd need to address as well.

This wasn't a terrain that just anyone should venture out in. Not only were there wild animals and the elements of snow and ice, but the landscape was unforgiving. People needed to be in top shape to traverse some of those mountains.

The team was between a rock and a hard place.

No doubt Victor had known just that when he'd set all this up.

The thought left a foul taste in her mouth. She was

more than ready to expose Victor for the monster he was.

Duke grabbed her hand and squeezed it. She sent him a smile, grateful he was here.

They'd butted heads when they'd first met. But then their respect for each other had grown along with their friendship. They hadn't rushed anything. They'd wanted to do things the right way—to wait until there was resolution with Celeste.

Now they were finally together. Happy.

But her gratitude turned to dismay once she thought about Simmy and everything her friend must be feeling right now. This was no time for Andi to revel in the love she'd found. Not when Simmy was facing a potential loss.

She glanced out the window.

All she saw were clouds, metaphorically and physically.

They were currently flying *through* the clouds. Thick clouds. She knew Blaze would have to depend on his navigation system to get them where they were going. Visibility was bad.

As was the turbulence.

Heavy winds rocked the plane, making the aircraft rise and fall and shake back and forth.

Everyone was quiet as they anticipated what might happen next.

They had to make it safely to Gates of the Arctic.

Otherwise, who would find Ranger? Everything was on the line right now.

Victor had them exactly where he wanted.

Whatever happened, Andi could not let that man win.

WHEN THE PLANE finally touched down on the runway, Duke breathed a sigh of relief.

Things had felt precarious for most of the one-hour flight.

Now that they'd landed on a small airstrip, he saw that the pregnant gray skies had given birth to a snow shower.

His chest tightened at the thought of the reduced visibility.

He wanted to go alone to find Ranger. The women with him weren't equipped to deal with these kinds of things.

He had been in the Army. He had training.

But Andi was a lawyer, Mariella a social media influencer, and Simmy was the nurturing, motherly type.

The hike to find Ranger would be grueling.

Yet he also knew that he wouldn't be able to talk any

of them out of this. Besides, Victor had said that they all needed to come.

Which put them in an interesting dilemma when it came to Matthew.

There was no way that Matthew was going to catch up to them out here. Even if they were able to track him down, he wouldn't be able to get up here in time.

As they stepped off the plane, the wind had turned sharper. Duke wished that he had worn something heavier. But when he started the day today, he'd never anticipated coming this far north.

"What now?" Blaze asked.

"We have to hike to this location to help our friend," Duke said.

"I can come too," Blaze offered.

As much as Duke liked that idea, he knew it was a bad one. "Our instructions were that we needed to come alone. As much as I could use your backup, you'd be better off staying here."

Blaze looked as if he wanted to argue, but he didn't. Instead, he stepped back and nodded. "I understand. I can remain on standby in case you need assistance."

"That sounds good. Do you have your satellite phone?"

Blaze nodded. "Sure do. You can always call me in an emergency."

"We're going to need some water and food. Maybe some blankets. Any idea where we can get any of that?"

"I have a few supplies in the back of my plane you can use," Blaze said. "It's not much, but it should help."

"Perfect," Duke said.

He looked through what Blaze had and grabbed some granola bars, beef jerky, and water. There were also some blankets and a first-aid kit.

Duke stuffed them in his backpack.

With everything in place, Duke nodded toward a trail in the distance. "If everyone's all ready, then we need to get started."

—————

Andi's muscles burned as she climbed the side of the mountain. Thankfully, they didn't have to travel all the way up.

The trail meandered on the side of the range, and the elevation grew higher with every step.

But she worried more about Mariella and Simmy.

Mariella was already shivering and an alarming shade of white. Simmy looked full of grief but determined to push forward.

Knowing Victor, Andi felt as if they were walking right into a death trap.

But they didn't have much choice. And that was exactly what Victor had wanted. He'd wanted them to reach this place with no return.

She took comfort in knowing she'd been able to text Helena, and it appeared the message had gone through.

That way, if anything happened, Helena would know their destination. Maybe she could report on what had happened.

Maybe this wouldn't all be in vain.

Duke led the group, but he continually looked back to make sure everybody was okay as they trekked forward.

One hour passed. Then two. Then three.

But no one complained or lagged far behind.

They were operating on a deadline here.

Once darkness fell, Duke paused. "I know we all want to keep moving, but it's not safe to do so in the dark."

"But Ranger . . ." Simmy's voice cracked.

"That text said they would keep him alive until seven a.m.," Duke said. "I'm assuming there has been someone keeping an eye on him, giving him a blanket and some meds."

Andi squeezed Simmy's hand. "Besides, if we all get hurt, then we're not going to get to him either. We have to be smart here. It's what Ranger would want."

Tears welled in her eyes, but she nodded in understanding. "I trust you guys. But I just want to help him so much . . . What if we're too late?"

Andi hugged her friend. She could only imagine Simmy's emotional agony. And she would do anything she could to make her friend feel better.

But right now, they couldn't act based on their emotions. They needed to be practical.

As they set up camp for the night, Andi continued to lift up prayers for Ranger's safety.

But if Victor had lured them out here to rescue Ranger . . . what else was he planning? Was he watching them now, just waiting to strike again?

Whatever they did, they couldn't afford to let down their guard.

CHAPTER
FIFTY-EIGHT

DUKE COULD HARDLY SLEEP.

He half expected Victor to ambush them here.

Was the man close? Was he watching them now?

Duke had been keeping his eyes open and his senses on alert ever since they set out.

If Victor had people watching them, his hired men were good. Duke hadn't seen or heard them. He'd also looked for tracks and hadn't found any.

Still, he needed to be cautious. Letting his guard down could get them all killed.

He'd chosen a spot nestled on the mountain to stop for the night. There weren't many trees in this area, which would have offered some cover. But they were far enough away from the river that wild animals shouldn't approach them.

They didn't have a tent. That wasn't among Blaze's supplies.

But they did have some water, beef jerky, and granola bars. It would at least give them a little bit of strength and energy.

He started a small fire to keep them warm, and they all sat around it.

The mood was somber—even Duke was feeling down.

They were in over their heads, but it was too late to go back.

He only prayed they weren't all killed while out here.

Part of him wished he had put the kibosh on this idea when Andi had first told him about it months ago. He should have known the situation was impossible. Yet he'd wanted justice. He hadn't wanted evil men to get away with their evil deeds.

But now look where it had left them.

Andi suddenly grabbed his arm and pointed to the sky. "Look!"

He glanced up. Purple and green lights danced in the sky.

The aurora borealis.

"It's beautiful," Mariella murmured. "I don't think I've ever seen it this strong before."

"It reminds me of just how small our place in this universe is," Andi said. "How can you see that and deny that there's a God?"

They sat in silence a moment, watching the lights

dance and explode in different shapes and configurations.

The sight was amazing.

And, for some reason, it seemed almost like a rainbow to Duke—a promise of God's watchful eye and provision.

———

Andi hadn't been able to sleep. At least, she hadn't thought so.

However, she was jostled from slumber just as she dreamed a bear wandered into their makeshift campsite.

She shot up with a start, her lungs so tight she could hardly breathe.

Then she saw Duke's face.

"It's okay," he murmured. "It's just me."

She blinked and glanced around.

A grayish darkness surrounded her.

And she was incredibly cold. The fire had gone out.

The gravity of the situation flooded back to her.

"We need to pack up and get going if we want to get there in time to save Ranger," Duke said. "The sun is just rising."

She nodded and tried to blink away her sleep. Her body was exhausted from everything that was happening.

She woke up Simmy and Mariella, and they stretched, pushing away any grogginess.

Andi glanced at the dark sky one more time.

A faint borealis flickered in the sky.

Something about the way the lights moved made her think of an angel. She wasn't one to normally look for signs like that.

But she couldn't help but think that maybe God had shown her that angel as a way of promising He was watching out for them.

Andi's throat burned at the thought.

Her thoughts on God really had come a long way over the past several months.

And she knew that she needed Him now more than ever.

They packed up their things, and Duke began leading them down the trail again, using a flashlight to guide their steps.

"If I've calculated this correctly, we have about three hours until we reach those coordinates."

"And we find Ranger," Simmy said.

But what if they didn't find Ranger there? Andi thought to herself. What if this was all just a way to ambush them?

She didn't want to think like that. She wanted to stay positive. But she wouldn't put anything past Victor.

However, she did not voice her thoughts out loud.

Instead, they kept walking across the landscape.

No one had much to talk about. There wasn't much to say.

They just needed to get through this.

Needed to find those coordinates.

And if Ranger wasn't there, then they would have to make the six-hour hike back to the airstrip. Blaze should still be waiting there—Andi prayed that was the case and that nothing had happened to him.

She didn't want to think negatively. But anything was a possibility right now. That they would have to continue searching. That valuable time would have been lost.

Then there was Ranger . . . if that photo was real then he needed major medical help.

Andi's gut feeling was that it was real.

She glanced up at the sky again as the sun rose higher.

The angel-inspiring borealis had disappeared.

But she needed now more than ever to know that a higher power was watching out for her.

DUKE GLANCED at his phone again.

They should be reaching these coordinates anytime.

Was this the way the search and rescue crew had come?

He didn't think so. He'd been searching the ground for tracks and hadn't seen any signs that a search party had come this way.

Which way had they gone exactly? Where did rescue crews believe that Glassine's plane had gone down?

And if Ranger really had been left at these coordinates, then how had he gotten there?

Duke had so many questions.

But the only important one was if Ranger was safe or not.

If they did find him and he was in critical condition, then getting him back for medical attention would be another issue altogether.

Duke wasn't sure how they would handle that.

Maybe they should have just called search and rescue from the beginning.

But Duke had a feeling that if Victor found out, he would just move Ranger or do away with him. Victor liked for people to play by his rules and nobody else's.

The women on this trek were being real troupers, and Duke appreciated that. No one had complained.

At a few spots on the trail, Simmy and Mariella had slipped, tripped, or stumbled. But they'd quickly recovered and continued. Duke thought he saw Mariella limping ever so slightly, but she denied it.

For now, he didn't argue.

As he reached the edge of the ridge, he paused and glanced at his screen again.

"What is it?" Andi asked.

He pointed to some trees in the distance. "If these coordinates are correct then Ranger should be right over there."

———

Andi could hardly breathe as she anticipated what they would find.

The best-case scenario was that Ranger was there and injured, but not so injured that they couldn't help him.

The worst-case scenario was that their friend wasn't there, but Victor was instead.

Not knowing caused tension to stretch taut across Andi's chest.

Duke set the pace as they continued toward the area. His eyes remained on his GPS locator.

Finally, they reached the area.

But only trees and some snow greeted them.

"Where is he?" Simmy lunged in front of Duke and scanned the ground. Tears streamed down her face.

Duke put his hand on her shoulder. "The system I have isn't 100 percent accurate. We need to search this whole area to make sure he's not here. But we need to stick together. Okay?"

Simmy nodded, but her eyes looked hollow.

They began to walk the perimeter, yelling out Ranger's name and looking for any signs of him.

An ominous feeling swirled in Duke's gut.

He prayed they hadn't come all this way for nothing. Prayed that Ranger was still alive. Prayed that this wasn't a trap.

They walked twenty feet to the north. Twenty feet west. Then they walked south again.

As they did, Duke glanced around, looking for any signs that anyone had been here. He saw nothing.

Just as Duke determined that Ranger was nowhere around, he spotted two shoes sticking up from the snow.

Was that Ranger?

He rushed forward.

CHAPTER
SIXTY

ANDI SAW the shoes at the same time as Duke.

She rushed forward, her heart lodged in her throat.

As they made it past a few trees, the rest of the body appeared.

Ranger.

It was him!

Simmy darted past them and fell onto her knees beside Ranger. She reached for his face, rubbing his cheeks and pushing his hair back. "Ranger. It's me. Can you hear me?"

Andi's heart continued to pump out of control.

Was he dead?

His legs were partially covered in snow, but his chest was exposed.

Blood had pooled and then dried on his chest.

Andi's hand flew over her heart as the direness of the situation hit her.

Were they too late? If they had kept hiking through the night, would this be a different scenario?

Either way, the situation wasn't good.

"Ranger! It's me. Simmy. Say something." Simmy shook his shoulders.

As she did, Duke knelt on the other side of their friend and put his finger to the man's neck. "He still has a pulse."

Ranger let out a moan.

A joyful but suppressed cry escaped from Simmy. "Ranger, you're alive!"

Andi glanced at Mariella and saw tears glimmering in her eyes as she watched the scene.

Simmy glanced up at the rest of them. "We've got to get Ranger help."

Duke glanced around again as if expecting danger to appear at any time.

Then he turned back to them. "I have my satellite phone. I'm going to call Blaze and see if he can get us a helicopter. It's the only way we're going to get him out of here."

"Please, hurry," Simmy said anxiously, still holding onto Ranger.

The man's eyes had closed again as he started to slip back into unconsciousness.

"Stay with us, Ranger," Duke muttered as he gripped his phone. "We're going to get you the help you need."

As those words left his lips, a stick broke behind Andi.

She turned and saw two people standing there, one of whom held a gun.

———

"Put that phone down," a new voice said.

Without giving an indication of what he was doing, Duke subtly hit Send. Then he lowered the phone onto the ground, his motions stiff. Any quick movements could get them all killed.

He turned to see who was there, and his eyes widened.

Lucy. She held Matthew's arm, a gun pointed at him.

He looked as if he'd been beaten. His eye was bruised. His lip busted. His gaze haggard.

"If you don't listen to everything I say, I'll shoot him." Gone was the smiling Lucy from the trading post. In her place was a cold-hearted, single-minded operative. Even her clothes were different—sleek black pants, boots, and an oversized white down coat with a fur-lined hood.

"Matthew . . ." The word left Mariella's lips in a whisper as she stared at her twin.

"Please don't tell me that you told me so," he murmured.

"Why don't you just let him go?" Duke said. "Haven't you done enough damage?"

Lucy chuckled. "This is only the beginning."

Who *was* this woman? An assassin?

Clearly, she was a professional.

"How did you get here?" Andi asked. "We walked all around this place and didn't see any evidence that anyone else had been here."

"A helicopter, of course." Lucy shrugged nonchalantly. "We've just been waiting for you, waiting to see if you would follow our instructions. Took you long enough to get here. It's cold out here at night. I don't like being cold."

As Lucy talked, Duke's mind raced through the possible scenarios. He knew he could take her down.

But right now, the gun she had aimed at Matthew would make that exceedingly difficult.

ANDI WONDERED how they going to get out of this situation.

They'd been brought here for a reason. But what was it?

Would Lucy shoot them all dead right now and call it a day?

Duke had his gun within reach. Andi's own gun was in her backpack. But it would take too long to get.

If she could just distract Lucy long enough . . .

Andi stepped forward. "Just let everybody else go. I'm the one that Victor has a beef with."

"Andi . . ." Duke murmured.

She glanced at him from the corner of her eye. "It's true. There's no reason all of you need to be hurt."

"But there is a reason," Lucy said. "You all know too much now! There's no scenario where any of you are going to walk away alive. We did our best to warn you off, but none of you would listen."

Andi's heart thumped against her rib cage.

She knew the woman was telling the truth.

"So what are you going to do?" Andi asked. "If you shoot us, the police will find evidence that'll eventually lead back to you. You'll forever be looking over your shoulder. Until you're caught and imprisoned for the rest of your life."

"We have ways around that." Lucy smirked.

"We?" Duke asked.

At his question, someone else stepped out from behind a cluster of nearby trees. A man wearing a heavy, black wool coat, designer jeans, and a sweater that cost more than Andi made in a month.

Victor Goodman. Usually, he sent other people to do his dirty work.

Yet here he was.

"If you want something done right, then you have to do it yourself," Victor grumbled. "So right now I'd like to thank all of you for coming. For playing my game."

Andi shivered. Was that all this had been to him? A game?

She thought she already knew the answer to that question.

But that didn't mean she liked it.

———

Duke feared this wasn't going to end well.

It definitely wouldn't end well for Ranger unless they got him some medical help soon.

His prayer was that someone had answered his call, was listening to their conversation right now. Or that Blaze had gone rogue and called for backup.

"What do you want?" Duke asked. "If you're going to kill us, then just kill us."

Victor chuckled. "Now what fun would that be? I have much better ideas."

Duke's blood turned cold. Part of him didn't want to know what Victor was planning.

"I've always been the smartest one in the room," Victor said. "I've honed my skills for years. It's the only way to get ahead. Now I'm unstoppable."

"By being arrogant?" Andi asked.

He chuckled again. "You have no idea. You were such a formidable match. I've really enjoyed going up against you."

"All this so you can invest in some oil drilling?" Duke asked.

"That's right. I stand to make billions. It's going to propel me into the category of one of the wealthiest men in the world."

"And then what?" Andi asked. "You think you'll be happy then?"

His gaze darkened. "Of course I will be. I'll be unstoppable. Anything I want will be mine. Maybe I'll even make a run for the White House. My mother taught me at a young age that it was a dog-eat-dog world. She was right."

"That's a sad way to live," Andi murmured.

Another emotion flickered in Victor's gaze before he drew in a deep breath. "Anyway, you're going to have to make a choice. Save yourself or save your friend." Victor nodded toward Ranger.

What was this man talking about?

In the next instant, Victor raised his gun in the air and pulled the trigger.

What . . . ?

Then Duke heard the rumble behind him, and everything made sense.

The sound of the gunshot had set off an avalanche.

And they were right in its path of icy destruction.

CHAPTER
SIXTY-TWO

ANDI HEARD the rumble and glanced over her shoulder.

An enormous field of snow toppled down the mountainside.

Toward them.

She gasped.

How much time did they have to get away?

She glanced back at Victor but saw he was already gone.

Lucy had shoved Matthew down and had also taken off.

A helicopter appeared in the distance, swooping low to pick them up and to safety.

"We've got to get out of here." Duke pointed to the east. "Run perpendicular. We'll never outrun it otherwise."

"What about Ranger?" Panic laced Simmy's voice. "I won't leave him."

"Neither will I." Duke ran toward their friend. He quickly grabbed the phone from the ground and shoved it in his pocket before heaving the man over his shoulder. "I've got him. Run!"

His expression looked strained as he began to run with him.

Ranger was likely heavier than Duke. That couldn't be easy.

Andi wanted to say something. To figure out a way to help. But there was little she could do.

"Keep moving!" Duke yelled. "We don't have much time."

As the rumble grew louder and louder, she hurried across the mountain, back the way they'd come.

The ground shook.

If they were buried alive . . . how would they ever get out?

They probably wouldn't.

She couldn't slow down. Her life depended on it.

She glanced behind her. Saw Duke struggling to move forward.

But at least he was moving. He wasn't that far behind her.

Beside them, the helicopter lifted back into the air. She saw Victor peering at them from the safety of his seat.

He might even be smiling.

He had full confidence they were going to die, didn't he? It was the only reason he'd left them alive.

This had all been a part of his game.

Disgust caused bile to rise to the back of her throat.

How far did they need to run? When would the bank of snow reach them?

As she looked up at the mountain, she saw the snow crashing down in waves of destruction . . . less than a half a mile away.

Fear shot through her.

They weren't going to escape, were they?

————

Duke saw the snow coming toward them.

In mere seconds it would reach them.

Bury them.

He had to move faster.

His muscles strained under the weight of carrying Ranger. The man was big and muscular—and injured.

This couldn't feel good for Ranger either.

But they had no other choice right now but to move.

Victor had lured them out here just for the purpose of killing them all. And what a perfect way.

People would speculate that they'd come looking for Ranger and been caught in the avalanche. It would look like a nature-made tragedy.

Slight-of-hand tricks appeared to be Victor's specialty.

The rumble grew louder.

The snow . . . it was closing in.

Duke glanced at the rest of the team again.

They were probably twenty feet ahead of him.

Good.

They might be safe.

That was his last thought before the snow consumed him, sweeping him off his feet and tearing Ranger from his grasp.

Duke tumbled from the jarring impact.

Then he was buried completely.

CHAPTER
SIXTY-THREE

ANDI LOOKED BACK JUST in time to see Duke disappear.

"No!" The word left her throat unfiltered and raw.

She started toward him but saw the snow still coming and paused.

She hated the helpless feeling that consumed her.

Mariella, Simmy, and Matthew appeared beside her. They were just out of the path of the avalanche, but they'd still need to be careful. Things could change at any moment.

Andi continued to stare over the avalanche, waiting for a sign that both Duke and Ranger were okay.

But all she saw was white . . . and several trees and rocks mixed in with the snow.

But . . . where were Duke and Ranger?

"We've got to go look for them." Simmy began to run in the snow.

Andi grabbed her arm to stop her. "You have to wait or you're going to disappear too. Give it a minute. We don't know how deep this snow is."

"She's right," Mariella said. "I watched a documentary about this once. Avalanches are dangerous—before and after the fact."

The four of them stood there a moment, the tension in the air palpable.

"You guys . . . I'm so sorry," Matthew murmured. "This is all my fault."

"Apologize later," Andi said. "Don't beat yourself up too much right now."

They had bigger worries. Like survival.

She glanced around and found a long stick.

Lifting it, Andi shoved it into the snow in front of her. The stick, probably six feet long, was half buried.

She frowned.

"It's going to be tricky getting out to them without getting buried ourselves." Simmy rubbed her arms as if realizing the enormity of the situation.

"You're right," Andi said. "But we need to stay together. And we need to be careful."

As Andi took a step forward, she prayed for the best.

———

White surrounded Duke.

Cold, icy white.

The snow had buried him alive.

Where was Ranger?

He tried to glance around, but it was no use. He could only see the snow.

But his friend couldn't be too far away.

Duke had to find him!

First, he had to make sure he had air.

Using all his strength, Duke reached upward.

At least, he *thought* he was reaching upward.

How could he be sure? Every direction looked the same—white.

Think, Duke. Think.

He'd been through survival training before. Certainly, he could figure this out.

Using his hands, he began to dig out a pocket around him. Then he kept making the pocket larger and larger.

Finally, one part of the snow brightened.

Did that mean the sky was above him?

It seemed like a good option.

He reached forward, but his legs . . . they felt cemented in place.

No . . .

This snow couldn't hold him down.

But it was.

The more he wiggled, the deeper he wedged himself.

Despair tried to burrow itself into his thoughts, but he pushed it away.

It was too early for despair. There had to be other things he could do.

His phone!

He had the satellite phone . . . if it hadn't fallen out of his pocket when the snow barreled into him.

He reached for it, and his fingers touched the hard plastic case.

He still had it!

This might be his and Ranger's only chance of survival.

He prayed they were the only two affected by this, that the women and Matthew had made it to safety.

He turned the phone on and dialed.

Then he waited.

Finally, Gibson picked up. "Duke, what's going on?"

"It's a long story, but Victor triggered an avalanche. Ranger and I are stuck beneath mounds of snow. Ranger was shot. We need help . . . desperately."

"Do you know where you are?"

Duke rattled off the coordinates.

"I'll get someone to you as soon as possible," Gibson said.

"Thank you. Hurry. Please."

"Duke? Stay strong. We'll get there soon."

He ended the call.

As his gaze skimmed the phone, he realized it had an alarm. Maybe if he could sound it . . . someone might hear.

It was worth a shot.

He turned up the volume then hit the alarm. Even though the snow insulated the sound, he prayed it was loud enough.

THE SNOW REACHED Andi's chest.

Cautiously, she kept moving forward.

One wrong step, and the icy precipitation might completely consume her.

Then they'd need another rescue. They couldn't afford any more emergencies. They were already in over their heads—literally.

Andi thought she knew the approximate location where Duke had been taken out. But now, looking at the field of snow, everything looked the same.

She felt as if she'd been dropped into the middle of the ocean with no lifeboat and no clue how to swim.

Avalanches were not her area of expertise. Give her a courtroom over this any day.

But Duke was still out there . . . *her* Duke.

The one who'd become not only her best friend but her soulmate.

She couldn't lose him. She'd fight with everything inside her to make sure he was found in time.

Tears wanted to press in her eyes, but she wouldn't let them. This was no time to cry.

This was a time to fight for the lives of people she cared about.

Andi paused. "Do you hear that?"

Everyone stopped and listened.

There it was. A beeping sound.

It sounded muted . . . like it was coming from under the snow.

Duke. Had Duke set off some kind of beacon so they could find him?

Her pulse quickened.

"That's Duke. It has to be. Maybe Ranger is with him." Simmy paused and then yelled, "Duke! Ranger!"

Panic seized Andi, and she whipped her head around to face Simmy. "You can't yell. It could trigger a second avalanche!"

They all froze.

Listened.

Watched.

Another rumble sounded.

Another avalanche?

No, Lord . . . please.

———

Duke heard a new noise.

Another rumbling.

His heart stuttered.

Was it another avalanche? Had the alarm set it off?

Right before the rumble, he thought he'd heard someone yell his name.

Had he been imagining the sound?

He waited. If more snow buried him, then any hope he had of being found would be gone. He wasn't even sure how much air he had left in his little bubble right here.

And where was Ranger? His friend couldn't be too far away.

Duke closed his eyes and began praying.

A few seconds later, the rumbling stopped.

He listened, trying to ensure he wasn't mistaken.

But he wasn't.

He couldn't hear the noise anymore.

At least that was an answer to prayer.

The sound had come from behind him. Based on what he knew, that could mean that he was facing the river right now.

If his guess was correct and the sky truly was above him, at least that gave him something to work toward.

He began digging the snow from around his legs. If he could just get them free, then maybe he could make it to the surface.

He drew in a rugged breath.

Then he shivered.

It was so cold. He felt the urge to yawn. He knew

exactly what was happening. It was his body's way of trying to get more oxygen into his system.

But the oxygen was running out. Fast.

He needed to work quickly.

Because he didn't have much time left.

CHAPTER
SIXTY-FIVE

THE AIR LEFT Andi's lungs in a whoosh when the rumbling stopped.

But next time they might not be as lucky.

She put her finger over her lips and motioned for everyone to quietly continue following her.

They had no choice but to keep moving if they wanted to survive out here.

They only had each other.

For now, she would keep moving in the general direction where she thought she'd seen Duke go under. From where the beeping sound was coming from.

Logically, she knew Duke had been moved by the force of the snow. She just didn't know how much farther down the mountain he'd been taken.

She resisted the urge to call his name. Wanting to cry out, to see if he could hear her was only natural. But they couldn't chance it again.

They spread out in a line holding hands. That way if one of them went under, the others could pull them up.

A verse hit Andi, one Duke had talked about recently from Ecclesiastes.

Two are better than one, because they have a good return for their labor: If either of them falls down, one can help the other up. But pity anyone who falls and has no one to help them up. Also, if two lie down together, they will keep warm. But how can one keep warm alone? Though one may be over-powered, two can defend themselves. A cord of three strands is not quickly broken.

That verse never seemed more appropriate than now.

They carefully walked across the snow, looking for any signs of the men. The beeping became louder. They had to be getting closer.

Matthew paused, tugging them all to a stop with him. "My foot hit something."

"Does it feel like a rock or a tree?" Andi asked.

"I . . . I'm not sure." He shrugged and shook his head.

"Let's find out." Andi dropped to her knees.

Using their hands as shovels, they all began digging at that spot.

A moment later, Simmy gasped and began to dig faster. "You guys . . . it's Ranger. We found him!"

If Ranger was here, did that mean that Duke was close?

They continued to dig Ranger out until his icy-blue face appeared.

Andi's heart jumped into her throat pressed a finger against his neck. *Please, don't be dead. Please.*

Then she felt it. The soft thumping under her finger.

"He still has a heartbeat," she murmured. "He's alive!"

Simmy let out a cry and began stroking his face with her fingers. "Thank goodness! I was so scared."

So was Andi. But they weren't in the clear yet.

They needed to figure out how to get Ranger out of this barren wilderness now that they'd found him.

But first . . . Duke.

Andi glanced around.

Where was he? The beeps were louder here. They had to be close.

As if to answer that question, a hand suddenly jutted out of the snow probably eight feet away.

Her breath caught. Duke . . . that had to be him.

———

Duke did it. He managed to break the surface of the snow.

Now, if only someone was out there who could see him. Who heard the beeping on his phone.

Please, Lord . . .

He grabbed his phone and shoved his hand higher

through the snow. Maybe someone could hear the beacon better now.

Someone grabbed his hand.

More snow moved above him.

Then the sky appeared.

Then Andi's face peered down at him. Tears pooled in her eyes as her lips parted with surprise.

"Duke . . . you're here." She gripped his hand tighter.

"I can't tell you how happy I am to see you." His relief turned to concern. "But we need to find Ranger."

"We found him," Andi told him. "He's still alive. But he needs help."

Duke let out a breath. *Thank you, Jesus!*

"See if you can get me out of here," he called. "I can help with Ranger."

"Nothing's broken?" Andi stared down at him, worry filling her gaze.

He did another mental check. "I don't think so. I'm just stuck."

She grasped his hand and tugged him.

After several tries, Duke managed to crawl out of the hole. As soon as he was free, he splayed against the snow as he tried to catch his breath.

Andi pulled his head into her lap, tears in her gaze. "I'm so glad you're okay, Duke."

His hand covered hers. "Me too."

"I love you so much." She kissed his forehead. "I don't know why I waited so long to tell you that."

His exertion was suddenly forgotten as her words filled him with warmth. "I love you too, Andi."

She pressed her lips into his forehead and held him tighter.

A sound overhead cut into the moment.

A thumping noise.

A helicopter.

Duke glanced up and recognized the emblem on the side of the aircraft.

It was the Alaska Mountain Rescue Group.

They'd gotten here in time.

He pressed his eyes shut. *Thank You, Lord.*

AN HOUR LATER, the team landed in Coldfoot. Medical personnel were waiting there and rushed to work on Ranger. Their friend was still holding on, though barely.

Simmy remained with him.

Paramedics checked out the rest of them. They were relatively unscathed, everything considered.

Gibson was on the scene also, a pensive expression on his face. Andi wanted to ask him questions, but she knew better than to do so in front of people. Her inquiries would have to wait.

Finally, two hours after they'd arrived in Coldfoot, Gibson approached Duke and Andi. They both sat in the back of the ambulance, drinking some warm water with blankets around the shoulders.

"You guys are very lucky." Gibson paused, his

breath coming out in icy puffs. "That could have turned out a lot differently."

"Believe me, we know that." Duke rubbed his neck and pulled the blanket tighter around his shoulders.

"Were you able to catch Victor in his helicopter?" Andi asked. The question had been pressing on her ever since they'd landed here. She prayed they hadn't gone through all this for nothing.

"We have crews out there looking now. We're hoping to locate him soon. The storm is making everything harder for now, however."

"I can only imagine." Andi set her drink down and rubbed her arms, even though she knew her chill was internal.

She wanted to believe this was over. But until Victor was behind bars, she couldn't relax. The man had weaseled his way out of things one too many times in the past.

As the paramedics attending to Duke and Andie stepped away, Andi's gaze locked with Gibson's. This might be her only chance to talk to him privately.

She lowered her voice and asked, "Listen, are you in trouble? I can tell something's up."

His expression tightened, and he glanced around before answering. "My captain has been watching my every move. I think Victor has been paying him off, and that's why he's let some of our investigations go. I need to bring it up with the commissioner. I'm just waiting for the right time."

"We've already talked to the attorney general," Andi said. "As soon as we have proof, he's willing to press charges against Victor. He might be able to help you out also."

"I hope that's the case," Gibson said. "But we have other worries also. The CID is still looking for Duke, and there's an arrest warrant out for you."

Andi held back a frown.

Yes, there was still a lot at stake.

They weren't out of the woods yet.

Just then, another officer hurried toward Gibson. He paused near them, excitement dancing in his gaze. "Guess what? Crews just found the wreckage from Senator Glassine's flight."

Gibson's eyebrows flew up. "That's good news."

"It gets better." The officer's eyes brightened. "She's still alive. Her chief of staff survived also, but he's in critical condition. The pilot wasn't so lucky, unfortunately."

"What? How . . . ?" Andi glanced at Duke, a silent conversation passing between the two of them.

Glassine was still alive? After all this time?

If that was true, then she could shut down this bill.

Victor's plan would be ruined.

Maybe they still had hope after all.

ANDI STEPPED OUTSIDE onto the deck, holding a mug of hot chocolate in her hands. It was chilly out here, but lately the Alaskan cold hadn't felt so unbearable.

Duke stepped out behind her and planted a quick kiss across her lips as they stood beside each other. The boreal forest stared back, cloaked in the evening darkness. Above them, stars twinkled in the moonless night.

"I can't believe we're back here," Duke murmured, slipping his arm around her.

"Me either," Andi agreed.

They'd come to Craig Rogers's place—Craig, the podcaster who'd set the Arctic Circle Murder Club in motion. They'd later discovered that Craig was Simmy's biological father. When he'd died, this place had been left to her.

Simmy and Ranger had spent the last couple of months fixing it up.

Thankfully, Ranger had recovered from his gunshot wound and was doing well. He'd explained to them what had happened after he'd awoken from his surgery. Apparently, he'd been lured off the trail and away from the search team after he'd heard someone calling for help. As soon as he was out of sight from the rest of the team, one of Victor's guys had knocked him out and dragged him away. By the time the rest of the team realized he was gone and searched for him, it was too late.

They'd found Ranger just in time.

Ranger and Simmy were still getting married . . . tomorrow. Anastasia would be in the wedding.

The only other people who would be there was the murder club gang—including Blaze, Gibson, and Jason —Mariella's boyfriend. Gibson had also mentioned something about the possibility of Morgan coming as his plus one.

Andi was curious to see how that all played out. Gibson still hadn't explained to them who exactly Morgan was, but Andi was anxious to meet her.

Some of them were staying inside Craig's old cabin. But Blaze had driven his RV and offered to let some of them stay there also.

Tomorrow was going to be a glorious day, and Andi couldn't wait to celebrate with her friends.

A lot had happened since that avalanche.

The police had found Victor. His helicopter had

landed near Prudhoe Bay. The police there had almost let him walk away after he explained who he was. But one of the cops had a conscience and had gone against his captain's orders. He had arrested the man.

In the meantime, Andi and Duke had approached Dabney Eldridge again. The attorney general had agreed to press charges against Victor. Andi had strong suspicions that Victor had one of his men set the AG's house on fire a few months ago, knowing that the murder club was staying next door. Which would explain why that matchbook from Andi's past had been left there. However, that might be something she could never prove.

Victor was now in police custody, without hope of bail.

Andi was optimistic that when this went to trial—and it *would* go to trial—that Victor would get the justice he deserved. As more pieces of his past were revealed, Andi felt certain he'd left a string of dead bodies in his wake. More and more people were gaining the courage to come forward.

One of those included an old friend of his named Tito, who claimed Victor—formerly named Hector Jones—had assaulted his sister when they were in high school. There were also suspicions that Victor may have killed C.W. Wells, the man who'd originally started Wells Oil.

There had always been suspicions, but no one had been able to prove anything.

Now maybe they would.

They'd also discovered that Victor's dad was in prison for killing a man in a carjacking. It appeared Victor was a chip off the old block, only Victor had learned to murder with finesse.

Victor, apparently, had been in talks with leaders across the globe about this new oil drilling. That was why he'd called the project Prometheus. He had a much bigger global vision than anyone had anticipated.

Nothing was going to stop him from obtaining everything he wanted—and what he wanted was money and power.

Talise had come forward to share her story. Helena had written an article about it for the newspaper, exposing how vast Victor's corruption was. She'd also documented how the Arctic Circle Murder Club had played a part in bringing Victor down.

Glassine had also revealed how Victor had tried to manipulate her. She'd gone to the village closest to the oil drilling to find out more information from the indigenous people there. That was when she'd realized something suspicious was going on. She began to suspect Victor had paid off the people in the village, though no one would admit it.

Glassine had been rescued in time to cast her vote as a no. The oil drilling might happen one day, but not under these circumstances. Not with so many people playing a game of Risk with Alaska's resources and people.

In another strange twist, Diane Glassine and her chief of staff, Charles Sudan, had gotten married after years of being friends and colleagues. They'd both survived their injuries and had been given a new lease on life.

Meanwhile, other people who worked for Victor had also been arrested, including Lucy. The police believed Devou had killed Skeeter, and that Victor had sent one of his guys to Lockjaw and offered to help pay the reward in order to put more pressure on Andi.

Gibson's police captain was now on leave during an internal affairs investigation. It had been discovered that he was in a significant amount of debt. That had led to him make some poor decisions.

Lockjaw had been arrested for the murder of a woman he'd picked up on the Dalton Highway. He'd hit on her, but she wasn't interested. When she'd rejected him, he'd thrown her out of his truck, and the injuries from her fall had killed her.

He'd be in prison soon.

Andi didn't anticipate their paths crossing again. She hoped she could put that part of her life behind her as she started anew.

With Duke.

Duke had talked to the CID and told his side of the story. It didn't look like the Army would be pursuing the charges against him, especially now since many considered Duke a hero. Bringing down Victor had painted Duke in a new light it seemed.

Andi and Duke had talked about marriage. They weren't officially engaged, but Andi had a feeling it was coming. She knew exactly what she would say when he asked—a resounding yes.

Matthew had done a lot of groveling, and he was still a part of their team. He truly felt bad for what he'd put them through and his role in everything. But he'd also played a pivotal role in discovering Victor's real identity. His heart had tricked him—as the heart was prone to do.

The podcast was as strong, if not stronger, than ever. They had covered the case with Victor extensively. Listeners were flocking to the show to hear more.

The team had done a lot of good work together so far.

They'd found Henrietta Blanco's killer, the Dalton Highway Killer, the Ice Fairy killer.

They'd stopped a madman terrorizing people at a campground in Salmon-by-the-Sea.

The Lights Out Killer was also behind bars.

That was just the start.

The rest of the gang stepped outside with them, each holding their own mugs of hot chocolate—prepared by Simmy, of course. Even though her big day was tomorrow, she still liked to make sure everyone was taken care of.

As they stood on the deck, Andi glanced up at the sky again.

There it was.

The Northern Lights.

She hadn't been able to forget that image of the lights that night at Gates of the Arctic. That night when the burst of light had almost looked like an angel watching over them.

"Would you look at that." Ranger craned his neck upward. "She's a real beauty."

"We've got to be living in one of the most beautiful areas in the world." Simmy smiled as she looked at the sky. "I wouldn't have it any other way."

"I'm grateful to be here." Andi leaned into Duke and grinned.

"You're not thinking about moving away now that this is all settled with Victor, are you?" Mariella stared at her with wide, curious eyes.

Andi straightened, remembering she did have an update to share with the team. She didn't want anything to deflect from Ranger and Simmy's big day. But since Mariella had asked her directly . . .

"As a matter of fact, I do have news," Andi started. "I just found out from the Texas Bar Association that my license has been reinstated."

Everyone around her cheered.

"What does that mean for you?" Simmy stared at her, a touch of hesitation in her gaze as if she anticipated bad news.

Andi let out a breath. "I'm contemplating my options. But I'm not ready to leave Alaska yet. In fact, now that things have been cleared up in Texas, I'm thinking about trying to get my license to practice law here in Alaska."

"Or you could just go full time with the podcast," Mariella suggested with raised eyebrows. Then she glanced at the rest of the group. "We all could."

Andi chewed on that idea. Part of her liked it.

But even if Andi did go full time with the podcast, she still wanted to pursue being licensed to practice law here in Alaska. In the long run, it could only help them.

She had a feeling that Duke might be willing to give up his travel guide services and to turn the business over to someone else also.

Their work together for the podcast had truly made an impact on people's lives.

She'd love to see that continue.

In fact, Andi couldn't wait to find out what the gang's next adventure might be. The possibilities were endless . . . much like the Alaskan sky.

~~~

Thanks so much for reading *Most Likely to Die*. If you enjoyed this book, please consider leaving a review.
~~~

COMPLETE BOOK LIST

Squeaky Clean Mysteries
#1 Hazardous Duty
Half Witted (Squeaky Clean In Between Mysteries Book 1, novella)
#2 Suspicious Minds
#2.5 It Came Upon a Midnight Crime (novella)
Half Truth (Squeaky Clean In Between Mysteries Book 2, novella)
#3 Organized Grime
#4 Dirty Deeds
#5 The Scum of All Fears
#6 To Love, Honor and Perish
#7 Mucky Streak
#8 Foul Play
#9 Broom & Gloom
#10 Dust and Obey

#11 Thrill Squeaker
#11.5 Swept Away (novella)
#12 Cunning Attractions
#13 Cold Case: Clean Getaway
#14 Cold Case: Clean Sweep
#15 Cold Case: Clean Break
#16 Cleans to an End
While You Were Sweeping, A Riley Thomas Spinoff

The Sierra Files
#1 Pounced
#2 Hunted
#3 Pranced
#4 Rattled

Lantern Beach Mysteries
#1 Hidden Currents
#2 Flood Watch
#3 Storm Surge
#4 Dangerous Waters
#5 Perilous Riptide
#6 Deadly Undertow

Lantern Beach Romantic Suspense
#1 Tides of Deception
#2 Shadow of Intrigue
#3 Storm of Doubt
#4 Winds of Danger
#5 Rains of Remorse

#6 Torrents of Fear

Lantern Beach P.D.
#1 On the Lookout
#2 Attempt to Locate
#3 First Degree Murder
#4 Dead on Arrival
#5 Plan of Action

Lantern Beach Escape
Afterglow (a novelette)

Lantern Beach Blackout
#1 Dark Water
#2 Safe Harbor
#3 Ripple Effect
#4 Rising Tide

Lantern Beach Guardians
#1 Hide and Seek
#2 Shock and Awe
#3 Safe and Sound

Lantern Beach Blackout: The New Recruits
#1 Rocco
#2 Axel
#3 Beckett
#4 Gabe

Lantern Beach Mayday

#1 Run Aground
#2 Dead Reckoning
#3 Tipping Point

Lantern Beach Christmas

Silent Night

Lantern Beach Blackout: Danger Rising

#1 Brandon
#2 Dylan
#3 Maddox
#4 Titus

Beach Bound Books and Beans Mysteries

#1 Bound by Murder
#2 Bound by Disaster
#3 Bound by Mystery
#4 Bound by Trouble
#5 Bound by Mayhem

Lantern Beach Exposure

#1 Fractured Lies
#2 Shattered Whispers
#3 Unsteady Ground
#4 Troubled Graves
#5 Deceptive Shallows
#6 Secret Shores

True Crime Junkies
#1 Just the Nicest Person
#2 He Walks Among Us
#3 Never Happen to You
#4 The Dead of Night
#5 Leave the Lights On
#6 The End of the Road
#7 The Secrets She Kept
#8 Most Likely to Die

The Shadow Agency
#1 Shadow Operative
#2 Shadow Chaser
#3 Shadow Assignment

Fog Lake Suspense
#1 Edge of Peril
#2 Margin of Error
#3 Brink of Danger
#4 Line of Duty
#5 Legacy of Lies
#6 Secrets of Shame
#7 Refuge of Redemption

Vanishing Ranch
#1 Forgotten Secrets
#2 Necessary Risk
#3 Risky Ambition

#4 Deadly Intent
#5 Lethal Betrayal
#6 High Stakes Deception
#7 Fatal Vendetta
#8 Troubled Tidings
#9 Narrow Escape
#10 Desperate Rescue

Saltwater Cowboys
#1 Saltwater Cowboy
#2 Breakwater Protector
#3 Cape Corral Keeper
#4 Seagrass Secrets
#5 Driftwood Danger
#6 Unwavering Security

Beach House Mysteries
#1 The Cottage on Ghost Lane
#2 The Inn on Hanging Hill
#3 The House on Dagger Point
#4 The Bungalow on Shadow Road

The Worst Detective Ever
#1 Ready to Fumble
#2 Reign of Error
#3 Safety in Blunders
#4 Join the Flub
#5 Blooper Freak

Raven Remington
Relentless
#6 Flaw Abiding Citizen
#7 Gaffe Out Loud
#8 Joke and Dagger
#9 Wreck the Halls
#10 Glitch and Famous
#11 Not on My Botch
#12 One Hit Blunder

Holly Anna Paladin Mysteries
#1 Random Acts of Murder
#2 Random Acts of Deceit
#2.5 Random Acts of Scrooge
#3 Random Acts of Malice
#4 Random Acts of Greed
#5 Random Acts of Fraud
#6 Random Acts of Outrage
#7 Random Acts of Iniquity

Cape Thomas Series
#1 Dubiosity
#2 Disillusioned
#3 Distorted

Carolina Moon Series
#1 Home Before Dark
#2 Gone By Dark
#3 Wait Until Dark

#4 Light the Dark
#5 Taken By Dark

The Sidekick's Survival Guide
#1 The Art of Eavesdropping
#2 The Perks of Meddling
#3 The Exercise of Interfering
#4 The Practice of Prying
#5 The Skill of Snooping
#6 The Craft of Being Covert

School of Hard Rocks Mysteries
#1 The Treble with Murder
#2 Crime Strikes a Chord
#3 Tone Death

Standalone Romantic Suspense
Keeping Guard
The Last Target
Race Against Time
Ricochet
Key Witness
Lifeline
High-Stakes Holiday Reunion
Desperate Measures
Hidden Agenda
Mountain Hideaway
Dark Harbor
Shadow of Suspicion

The Baby Assignment
The Cradle Conspiracy
Trained to Defend
Mountain Survival
Dangerous Mountain Rescue
Lethal Mountain Pursuit

Crime á la Mode Mysteries
#1 Dead Man's Float
#2 Milkshake Up
#3 Bomb Pop Threat
#4 Banana Split Personalities

Standalone Novels
Death of the Couch Potato's Wife
Imperfect
The Good Girl
The Wrecking

Standalone Sweet Christmas Novellas
Home to Chestnut Grove
How Her Ex Stole Christmas

The Gabby St. Claire Diaries (a Tween Mystery series)
#1 The Curtain Call Caper
#2 The Disappearing Dog Dilemma
#3 The Bungled Bike Burglaries

Nonfiction

Characters in the Kitchen

Changed: True Stories of Finding God through Christian Music (out of print)

The Novel in Me: The Beginner's Guide to Writing and Publishing a Novel (out of print)

ABOUT THE AUTHOR

USA Today has called Christy Barritt's books "scary, funny, passionate, and quirky."

Christy writes both mystery and romantic suspense novels that are clean with underlying messages of faith. Her books have sold more than four million copies and have won the Daphne du Maurier Award for Excellence in Suspense and Mystery, have been twice nominated for the Romantic Times Reviewers' Choice Award, and have finaled for both a Carol Award and Foreword Magazine's Book of the Year.

She is married to her Prince Charming, a man who thinks she's hilarious—but only when she's not trying to be. Christy is a self-proclaimed klutz, an avid music lover who's known for spontaneously bursting into song, and a road trip aficionado.

When she's not working or spending time with her family, she enjoys singing, playing the guitar, and exploring small, unsuspecting towns where people have no idea how accident-prone she is.

Find Christy online at:

www.christybarritt.com

www.facebook.com/christybarritt

www.twitter.com/cbarritt

Sign up for Christy's newsletter to get information on all of her latest releases here: **www.christybarritt.com/news letter-sign-up/**

facebook.com / AuthorChristyBarritt

x.com / christybarritt

instagram.com / cebarritt

www.ingramcontent.com/pod-product-compliance
Lightning Source LLC
Chambersburg PA
CBHW020309160726
47992CB00004B/1453